"What's happened out there?" I asked. "There's so much chaos."

The woman did an eye-roll. "Some war protesters. They set fire to a garbage can or something around the corner."

"Thanks."

As I ran across the street to avoid the smoky air, I saw a slight movement, like the fluttering of a giant bird's wing, in the window alcove of my favorite coffee shop.

I stopped. It wasn't a bird. There was a guy sitting in my usual spot, flipping rapidly through the pages of a book.

The guy in the window seemed completely unaffected by everything going on outside. He was nineteen, twenty at the most, with hurricane-colored eyes, the most incredible I had ever seen. His knife-like cheekbone ridges were even more distinct.

He was a stranger to me, yet I couldn't stop staring at him. I stood paralyzed on the sidewalk. The crossing signal flickered, and I couldn't persuade my feet to move.

He was reading a book with a familiar-looking burgundy cover but must have sensed someone staring and looked up. Saying that our gazes met was an understatement. In one incredible, heart-stopping second, he seemed to commit to memory every aspect of my face. His abundantly large eyes, too wide-set, seemed out of place in his sharp, tawny-colored features.

The sidewalk activity seemed to dull into the background as we stared at each other. Without a smile or any other expression, he returned to his book, as if the exchange had taken place only in my mind.

I felt the ridiculous desire to knock on the window to get his attention. I wanted to see the color of those eyes again.

This was insane. Snapping to my senses, I crossed 45th Street and headed to my car, not daring to look back at the coffee shop. . . .

For my muse: Every line is you.
I love you more now than I did then.

CHAPTER 1

The Window

When they buried my father, they buried an empty casket. That night my mother returned to the grave site. I refused to enter the cemetery and instead watched through the midnight fog as she stood in front of the headstone that read "Mars Alexander." She then fell to her knees and nestled his final medal in the soft earth as a symbol of his life and dedication to our country.

None of this was enough to convince me he was gone. How could someone be dead if there was no body?

"Mars, do you have something to share today?" Stephanie, my therapy group leader, blinked rapidly through her trendy black frames in tune to the heavy hammering on the floor above us. They were adding an "all-ages club" to the top floor of the Kirkland Teen Center in an effort to keep teens out of trouble at night.

No one in high school would be caught dead in an all-ages club. We would continue to do what we always did: buy fake IDs and crash parties at the University of Washington.

My best friend, Erica Esteban, tapped my foot with hers when still I said nothing. The absurd wedge heel she preferred battered my little toe like a gavel. I winced, and Erica smiled in expectation. She'd promised this session of our Military Grief Therapy group would be different: she would make sure I participated today. She said that I needed to deal with my *abandonment reaction* and other psychotherapy buzzwords we'd been learning in AP Psychology that semester.

"I have nothing to share today. Next time," I announced, proud of myself for making the promise sound convincing.

Before Erica could smash my poor toe again, Stephanie tossed back her glossy brown hair and twisted the glinting sapphire earring in her new cartilage piercing. "Erica, your turn."

Erica waited for a pause in the hammering.

"Ricardo's better this week," she said with a deep, tremulous sigh. She said that every week, with the same sigh. Ricardo Esteban was still not talking to anyone, except maybe silently to himself.

"How?"

Erica launched into a story about a morsel of recognition in Ricardo's eyes after their *mami* had made his favorite green corn tamales for dinner the previous night. He'd eaten seven whole bites, according to Erica. More like five bites, I was pretty sure, though Gia Esteban's tamales had ruined me for all other tamales.

I was only up to four bites per meal. I probably should have been ashamed that a legless war veteran was beating me in recovery. At least I was no longer awake all night, afraid of the nightmares that would ensue once I closed my eyes. Now I woke every night clammy and cold at three a.m., to hear only the sound of our grandfather clock ticking endlessly downstairs.

I tilted my wrist and peered at my watch. I needed to make it to the University of Washington campus to register for an SAT preparation class before the Institute closed. I hoped no one else after Erica would choose to share and the therapy session would end on time.

No such luck.

Angel, who had a face like one, started to weep during his turn in the circle. "My mother sees me and thinks I'm *him*. How can I tell her he's gone?" Angel's twin brother had been killed in Afghanistan six months before, leaving Angel to handle the aftermath. He told us once that the grief circle was the only place he felt like he could be selfish and grieve on his own without censoring himself for his large Colombian family.

"Be strong for your mother," people had said to me at my father's wake. I had circulated through the crowd, greeting my father's military friends and my mother's Rotary Club, refilling glasses of rum punch and accepting white-ribboned sympathy cards. Only Bree Nguyen, my father's mentor, had watched me critically, questioning me with that knowing look I hated.

Scattered Ashes

Dona Sarkar

LYRICAL PRESS
Kensington Publishing Corp.
www.kensingtonbooks.com

I'd avoided being alone with her ever since.

"She'll have a breakdown once she realizes he's dead," Angel continued to grieve as if he was the only person in the room. "I know she'll blame me. I was right there; why couldn't I have saved him? Why couldn't it have been someone else?" The rest of us sat in silence, not knowing what to say to that last part.

I watched the second hand on my father's watch, now fitted for me, make its rounds until it edged toward the twelve o'clock mark.

"I need to leave. Sorry." I already had my bag and jacket in hand, so Erica couldn't stop me.

"See you next Tuesday, Mars," Stephanie called behind me.

Yes, she would. And every Tuesday until everyone agreed I was fixed.

Although I made it in record time across the floating bridge to the University of Washington, I was stalled by a river of traffic as I attempted to cross the street. As if I was in one of those not-safe-for-under-eighteen video games, I dodged police cars, traffic cones, and people pushing southward on University Avenue. Probably a half marathon gone awry or something.

An irate group of anti-war activists was ignoring everyone leaving the scene and was still demonstrating on the corner as I continued to my destination, the College Preparatory Institute.

The perky administrator with *Amelie* bangs assured me of a well-spent $270 for the SAT Essay Writing class. "Zayed Anwar can teach an illiterate person to write. He's *amazing*! And really cute too."

I smiled at her, not bothering to mention I was here to score a ten or higher on the SAT section, not fall in love.

"That essay section's been so hard for everyone since it came out."

Including me. I'd never needed professional help on a test before, but my score was too humiliating to disclose to my father's alma mater. I had no plans to attend a community college, so my Monday and Wednesday evenings would have to be sacrificed for the next eight weeks.

"What happened out there?" I asked as I signed the receipt. "There's so much chaos."

The administrator did an eye-roll. "Some war protesters. They set fire to a garbage can or something around the corner. Just go across the street; there's less smoke there."

"Thanks." I took a copy of the receipt, reading the refund policy. *Guaranteed to raise your score by two points!*

I was going to need a lot more help than that.

As I ran across the street to avoid the smoky air, I saw a slight movement, like the fluttering of a giant bird's wing, in the window alcove of my favorite coffee shop.

I stopped. It wasn't a bird. There was a guy sitting in my usual spot, flipping rapidly through the pages of a book.

The boy in the window seemed completely unaffected by everything going on outside. He was nineteen, twenty at the most, with hurricane-colored eyes, the most incredible I had ever seen. His knife-like cheekbones ridges were even more distinct. He was a stranger to me, yet I couldn't stop staring at him. I stood paralyzed on the sidewalk. The crossing signal flickered, and I couldn't persuade my feet to move.

He was reading a book with a familiar-looking burgundy cover but must have sensed someone staring and looked up. Saying that our gazes met was an understatement. In one incredible, heart-stopping second, he seemed to commit to memory every aspect of my face. His abundantly large eyes, too wide-set, seemed out of place in his sharp, tawny-colored features. The sidewalk activity seemed to dull into the background as we stared at each other. Without a smile or any other expression, he returned to his book, as if the exchange had taken place only in my mind.

I felt the ridiculous desire to knock on the window to get his attention. I wanted to see the color of those eyes again.

This was insane. The last time I'd visibly shown any interest in a guy was freshman year, when I'd smiled at Jason Moorehouse and "accidentally" trailed my fingers on his arm. By the end of the day, he was asking me to the spring formal. By the end of the week, we were walking hand in hand to the bus stop. Cut to four years later: we'd posed as "Together Forever Class Couple" for the yearbook and were immortalized in Lakeville High School's history. But only a month ago, Jason had written me off as certifiably crazy, and we were no longer speaking.

Snapping to my senses, I crossed 45th Street and headed to my car, not daring to look back at the coffee shop.

* * *

I had taken over my father's restored Corvette this past year. After all, no one else wanted it, and the beautiful car lay forgotten, buried in the depths of our garage.

"Cars need to be driven, Mars. Otherwise, they die," he always said.

Now, in the quiet solitude of the convertible, I finally had a chance to make my daily check-in phone call. Dad had insisted I make my check-in phone call every day after school my whole life, no matter where in the world he was. He wanted to know where I was and what I was doing.

Keeping an eye on the stalled line of SUVs in front of me on the bridge, I sifted around in my handbag, finding my cell phone under a jumble of keys, lip gloss, and an emergency peanut butter pod. I ignored the line of missed calls from my mother and chose the first number on my speed dial.

"Hey, Dad," I said, no longer surprised by the prompt of his voicemail. "I *finally* registered for that SAT class. I'll get into the U. It's going to happen, don't worry. I'll make it happen."

Despite the fact that Dad hadn't answered my phone calls in over a month, I never stopped believing he was listening to all my messages or would eventually. Most likely he was out in the field and would return my calls upon returning to base camp. I needed him to do that soon. As always, I closed the conversation with telling him that I was sorry for that last morning, and I wished he would come home to us before Christmas.

We'd never been one of those "camcorder" families. My parents were never the ones with an embarrassing tripod in the front row recording school plays or when I was confused by the trick candles on my fifth birthday cake. I used to think those families were cheesy and wondered who was going to spend a Saturday afternoon watching old DVDs.

What I wouldn't give to have a recording of Dad making his famous grilled PB&Js in our kitchen, giving a play-by-play Food Network style. I wanted to hear the raspy intonations of his voice from years of smoking again. According to Stephanie, it was perfectly normal to start to forget. I didn't believe her. How was it possible to forget someone in a few short months?

Traffic finally moved, and ten minutes later, I urged the Corvette to squeal up the boulevard and into Kirkland. The Seattle suburb was almost like a coastal vacation spot, with the lovely Lake Washington beach lining one side and extravagant houses on the other. The downtown vibrated with the energy of out-of-towners with babies and dogs, trendy coffee shops with live music, and restaurants with life spans of six months or less.

I guided the car into the garage of our brick-and-stucco English Tudor house on the waterfront. The historical homes nestled there were all occupied by software and real-estate millionaires who had known each other for years and were practically family. My father, with his unconventional choice of career and sense of humor, had never fit in. However, the house, a wedding gift from my mother's side, was too beautiful not to live in, and so Marsh Commons had been my home for the past seventeen years.

Lana Alexander, my mother, was sitting at the dining room table, her slim laptop open in front of her. Her fingers stopped tapping, and she immediately closed the lid when I slammed the door to the garage behind me. The flat-screen television suspended on the wall of the dining room replayed the commotion from the afternoon at the U. The news made it look far worse than it had been. One interviewee gasped, "It was horrible! I was terrified!"

"I'm okay," I said in response to the relieved look in her eyes. "Nothing happened, just a bunch of traffic."

A waft of warm, buttery chocolate greeted me as I hugged Lana. She held onto me longer than usual. Melted white chocolate-chip cookies, my favorite, were piled neatly on a serving tray, untouched as I took a seat opposite her. I didn't know who'd made them, but I was certain it wasn't my mother.

Lana was a socialite, a real estate agent, CEO of a nonprofit organization, or whatever else she wanted to be that week. No one would ever dare call her a housewife. She and I had always been more like sisters rather than mother-daughter. We both enjoyed spa days, a shared Christian Louboutin shoe collection, and gossip about our friends. It made Dad crazy. He said he always felt like he had two teenage daughters instead of one.

"I *was* worried." She tapped her jeweled fingernails on the closed lid of the pink laptop. "What happened out there?"

"Someone set fire to a garbage can. One of those anti-war groups or something."

"Why didn't you answer your phone? I called five times."

I shrugged. "The phone lines must have been crazy." I didn't tell her that I had been staring at some guy on the street instead of checking my voicemails *or* had been talking to Dad's voicemail rather than calling her. I knew the latter would hurt her feelings since she kept telling me over and over that she wished I would talk with her the way we used to.

I could talk with her about some things: what was happening at school, what was going on with my friends, what she should wear to a benefit. But big topics like that simmering anger at my father that overcame me when I was alone? Not so much. She clearly didn't miss Dad like I did. She never even talked about him anymore. No one did. I was the only one still waiting for him.

Lana pursued her lips and frowned. "Did you register for that class?"

Lana's face reflected my own nowadays, or rather, mine had started to reflect hers in the past year: tapered olive-green eyes and chocolate-colored hair. But my Roman nose and naturally tan skin were inherited from my Greek father. "Sophia Loren's love child," he called me.

"Yup. Starts tomorrow." I teased a single cookie crumb around the tray, and though I usually could have eaten two or three, I had no appetite and could barely look at them.

"What about Wellesley?" Lana wrapped a finger around her Bluetooth earpiece and frowned.

I shrugged.

"You're already a shoo-in. I've been donating to them every year to make sure of that. They're going to name one of the newer dorm halls 'Alexander' after us. And I thought you liked Boston."

I shrugged again.

"An answer would be nice."

"I want options."

"Yes, we know, the U. Not that I wouldn't love to have you around. I just think looking at other places isn't a bad thing. What other schools would you consider?"

"I want to make sure I'm here when Dad comes back." I knew how this was going to end. The same way it had ended every time we'd had this conversation for the past month.

That look on Lana's face. I hated that look so much. That forlorn, my-daughter-is-crazy look.

"This is why I don't talk to you," I muttered. I reached over and pulled her laptop to my side of the table.

Lana didn't hear, or didn't want to show she had. She shook her head, as if shaking all unpleasant thoughts away. "Jason was here looking for you, by the way. He brought the cookies. You should eat at least one. Then call him."

Jason.

I only nodded in response, still too angry with Lana to let her know how much that bit of information surprised me. Jason had broken up with me with the usual promise of "Let's stay friends." We hadn't spoken since, he avoided eye contact with me in the hallways, and all of our old friends followed his lead.

"I still think you let him get away too easily. So he made a mistake. Give him another chance."

Get away? Jason wanted out; I was not going to beg him to stay. I was, however, not going to waste the "in" he'd given me, either.

"I'll have to call Jason's mom to say thank you," I said instead, hoping the promise of a standard social grace would distract her.

Lana crossed her arms and watched me. "Mars. Come on." She sounded just like Erica.

"I don't want to talk about this anymore."

"He wants another chance."

"He brought cookies. For you. A neighborly gesture. Maybe he was reaching out to you." I was, of course, completely joking. As if Lana would let an ounce of sugar pass her lips.

"You should invite him over for dinner."

"Oh really." I looked over the top of the laptop, knowing I was smirking. "For what? Lean Cuisines and mineral water?"

Lana glared at me, not missing the jab. Ever since Dad had left, our kitchen had been used exactly never. He had been the only chef in the house, the heart, everything. Without him around, we lived in a five-thousand-square-foot dollhouse, a professionally decorated shell that everyone admired. Yet no one could see how empty the house had become now that it was just me and Lana. She and I were like two kids who'd been left alone for a weekend.

"You're supposed to be on my side, by the way. Jason was wrong, not me," I retorted.

Lana didn't respond right away. Of course, she didn't think Jason had been in the wrong. What was he *supposed* to do when his girl-friend started to act crazy? Break up with her, of course.

"He made me an outcast, remember? It's his fault I—" I stopped talking. Lana wasn't listening. She didn't want to hear the truth about how I spent my days at school.

"Looks like Jason's finally matured. Besides, your dad really liked him, so you should have no objections." The bitterness in Lana's voice didn't go unnoticed. She'd always been jealous that I'd always tried to seek out Dad's approval, but never hers.

"Likes. Dad really *likes* him," I said sharply. "And I am well aware of that. I'm sure he likes Dad too."

"Mars—"

"Lana." I caught my breath as the internet browser came up to the previously opened page: Matchmaker.com. "Why were you looking at a dating site?"

"Baby, absolutely do not overreact to this."

"To what? To you cheating on my father?"

"Oh, come on! We talked about this last week, and I told you—"

There had been no talking last week; Lana had simply informed me that it was time she moved on with her life. No discussion. And this was what she'd meant. I had refused to listen then, but now there was no denying it.

"You can call it whatever you want, but you are dating while you are still married to someone. You're having an affair! Dad is giving up—" The swelling in my throat cut me off. "He is giving up every-thing for us, our country, and this is what you do behind his back? We need him to come home to us. Don't you want that?"

I was out of the chair before the end of the sentence. I couldn't hear this again, all her reasons for why it was "time to move on." She couldn't be alone forever, I needed a father-figure in my life, her list of "whys" went on and on.

"Let's talk about this, baby."

"I am *not* your baby. It's *your* fault he's gone in the first place. You can at least act like you want him to come back."

I shoved the chair against the dining table and watched it rattle Lana to her core. She turned away from me, a hand covering her mouth, and only then did I notice her bronzed skin and the fresh caramel highlights in her straightened hair. She was wearing a new outfit, a white silky dress with perfectly coordinated jewelry. Lana was a terrible shopper and couldn't put together a decent ensemble without a team of helpers. There was no way she looked this good on her own. She looked absolutely beautiful and available.

So it was over. She was done waiting.

Why was she doing this? We had a life, a system, a plan. It wasn't perfect, but it was all we had left. We were in waiting mode, clinging to each other, hoping for the best, waiting for some certain news.

I ran up the flight of stairs and pressed my back against the wall, hiding. I told myself it was to see if Lana would call one of her friends to complain about her "impossible" teenager, but deep down, I knew that I was waiting to see if she would come after me. I wanted her to follow me upstairs like a real mother would. I wanted her to tell me that she was making a mistake and that she was going to be strong and wait for my father to come home and would hold my hand until he did.

She didn't.

I knew Lana wouldn't come into my room. The number of gossip fests and impromptu fashion shows we'd had up here *before* was immeasurable, but all of that had stopped this past month. In theory, it was lame to be best friends with your mother, but she was different.

My friends were jealous that I could talk to her about anything, and I relished that envy. My snarky barbs with other people, my not-so-good grades, which guys I secretly had crushes on—Lana loved discussing it all. And she always told me about what was going on with *her* friends, their husbands, and secret boyfriends. We always joked that I was seventeen going on forty and she was the other way around.

Now, she was trying to do the parental thing and making big decisions for both of us, something she didn't know anything about and a role she had no right to fill. Ironically, this was the main topic of all my parents' fights, the ones I would stand on the stairs and eavesdrop on.

Dad said Lana didn't set any boundaries for me and was too busy being my friend. He didn't trust her to take care of me while he was gone. Every few years, Dad shipped out as a part of the Army Reserves and returned six months later. Each time, Dad and Lana had become more and more distant from each other. By the time this last trip had rolled around, they had avoided being in the same room and didn't even bother to hide their fights behind closed doors. Lana started to talk to me about whatever was bothering her, and our relationship had grown stronger and closer.

I flung a stack of books off my desk and watched them slam against the wall.

Ugh.

There was no need for me to abuse Dad's books, his most prized possessions. The ancient copies of *The Odyssey* and *Les Misérables* were his favorites, ones he reread every year and would want me to take good care of.

I had my college-level vocabulary thanks to him. We would take turns reading out loud every day after school when he wasn't deployed, and we would look up what each new word meant, no matter how obscure. Thanks to him, I had an almost perfect score on the SAT verbal section.

Lana had tried to give Dad's book collection to the library last month. I'd only realized it when the truck arrived and the pick-up person had asked to be escorted into the study. I'd shoved him out of the house and hidden all the books in my room instead. Now every wall, with the exception of a floor-to-ceiling window facing the lake, was shelf after shelf lined with his favorite pastime: stacks of classics, mysteries, biographies, and his journals.

My cell phone rang. When I saw Jason's number on the screen, I took a deep breath and made my voice extra-husky. The *awesome voice*, he always called it. I wanted him to remember what he was missing and what he had let go of.

"Hello, Jason."

"I came by earlier."

I took a seat on the edge of my bed, setting *Les Misérables* next to me. "I heard." I couldn't think of anything else to say. What did he want, a trophy?

"I heard about what happened at the U. I'm glad you're okay." A door closed at his end. I hadn't realized the incident was such a big deal.

"Yeah, I'm fine. Don't worry about me," I said. "You've pleased Lana to amazing heights with your cookie delivery. She's insisting that you're"—a deliberate pause here—"reaching out to me."

"And what does her daughter think about that?" Jason played along.

"She's a tad confused." I wanted my tone to be coy or light, show him I didn't care. Instead, it just came out sad. I propped myself up on the tuft of pillows fencing my king-size sleigh bed, my mind still on how easy it seemed for everyone to simply move on, forgetting about those they claimed to have loved.

"Mars? Is everything okay?"

I realized I hadn't responded after a minute.

"Yes, I'm fine," I repeated.

"Really?"

"Really," I said in the least convincing tone ever. I did not want to talk about this with Jason. He had proven that he was not capable of handling my family issues.

He was silent, except for light breathing. He knew me well enough to know when I was unconvincingly lying. This was pathetic.

"Lana is dating." As soon as the words left my mouth, I could practically see them, floating in the air in front of me. They seemed to shimmer and dance before dissolving, leaving me blinking back disbelief once again. The words were suddenly very real, and I couldn't take them back.

"I'm sorry," he said instantly in a tone that suggested he more than understood what I was going through. I knew his parents had had some problems a few years ago—counseling, separate vacations, and everything. They were still together, living under one roof at least, happy or otherwise.

"I don't know why she's doing it." I knew full well. The excitement that came with a new relationship. Raising a teenager alone was a downgrade compared to her younger days as one of the most sought-after debutantes in the Pacific Northwest.

Jason said nothing, and I realized I'd gone too far with my honesty. We were "friends," not friends. He couldn't handle this. He'd made that abundantly clear a month ago.

"Do you want to get together tomorrow night?" he asked, sounding unsure. His uncertainty surprised me more than the words.

Now I was the one who was silent. He *did* want me back. And at that moment, I realized how much I wanted to be back. How much I wanted things back the way they used to be.

"I have a class tomorrow night," I finally said. "Maybe later?"

"What?"

"I'm taking an essay writing SAT class at the U. My first session is tomorrow."

Jason was *not* used to hearing "no."

"Oh," he said, sounding doubtful.

"Sorry," I said, wanting to suggest we try for another night, but deciding against it in the end. I was *not* going to chase after him.

"I wish you'd been home when I came by. I miss you."

"Oh," it was my turn to say. He *missed* me? He hadn't spoken to me in a month, and yet he missed me? I felt a flush on the back of my neck. I still remembered the sting of his words when he'd broken up with me.

"Good-night," I said quietly.

"I'll see you tomorrow, Mars."

I twirled my cell phone in my hand for a few minutes more, feeling the heat of the phone start to dissipate. What was happening here?

I lay back on my bed, all kinds of overwhelming thoughts keeping me company, including cynicism and hope at the same time. Maybe Jason was studying me for his Psychology class, analyzing what happened to a fairly normal high school girl after an incident like the one that had taken place in the girl's locker room a month ago.

I used to be "her." The girl who wasn't the class president, or the valedictorian, or any good at sports, but everyone liked her anyway. I was quirky enough with my advanced vocabulary and ornate wardrobe without being weird. I did have my posse: fun, beautiful friends like Candace Littlefoot and Kendall Chang and the boyfriend every girl wanted. I was the girl who wasn't beautiful, but no one realized it because I acted like I was.

After I'd made a fool of myself in a very public and crazy way, people whispered about me in the hallways, like I used to do when I heard rumors about people with reputations like mine.

I wanted the past month to just go away and to have "her" life back. Nothing had changed, and it was time for everyone to realize that, including me.

I curled up on my right side in my favorite position. A book cover caught my eye, the gold lettering glinting in the moonlight. A leather-bound burgundy book, *Sonnets by Theodore Robert Watkins*. I knew I had recognized the book cover the boy in the window was holding.

Watkins was one of Dad's favorite poets, and he had every piece the poet had ever published.

I flipped through the one-page poems till I found one that felt fitting for that moment:

> *Forgetting you was not easier said than done,*
> *I said I would forget you, and you should forget me too,*
> *I never did manage to do my part.*

CHAPTER 2

The Dream

I dreamt I was on a roof. I gazed out over Seattle, coated in a rich darkness. Everyone I knew was there, surrounding me: my friends, Lana and Jason, and him, the boy from the coffee shop with the hurricane-colored eyes. He held out the book he'd been reading. I took it wordlessly from him and tried to read what was written on the front cover. Before I could, Dad appeared by my side. "Mars, what are you doing?"

The alarm rang, interrupting. I was in that state where I couldn't move a muscle. For a few minutes, I lay completely paralyzed, listening to the pulsating beep of the alarm. Usually I was one to shift around in my sleep the whole night, yet that morning I woke up in the same position I'd fallen asleep in, except now I had a dull ache in my heart and a cramp in my shoulder.

I contemplated turning off the alarm and closing my eyes so I could see the end of my dream. It was a cool talent I had, the ability to continue dreams if I fell back asleep in a short amount of time. The flutter of nerves in my stomach regarding my last conversation with Jason won out. I pulled the curtains open and let a glorious fall day spill into my loft.

Early October, the most beautiful time in Seattle. The leaves were in full splendor, drifting gently around and around in the light breeze, the skies a perfect bluish purple with no sign of clouds, a hint of chill in the air begging for the new fall coat to make its first appearance.

The bits of the dream I could recall washed down the drain of the shower. I dried my hair quickly and created a deep side part in my asymmetrical angled bob, really starting to like the way the shorter hair was growing out. I'd hacked my hair off with eyebrow scissors during The Incident. Lana had freaked out and had rushed me to an upscale salon in Seattle for an avant-garde style. Neither one of us thought I would look normal for a very long time, but my fears were slowly being allayed by the rather cute hairdo. The scar on my cheek was also healing nicely. A few weeks more and it would hopefully disappear.

I dressed in a pleated miniskirt, a plum-colored shrunken blazer, and a pair of strappy black sandals from Lana's collection, the opposite of the uniform for girls at Lakeville High School. Unlike my mother, I was a good shopper and enjoyed being trendy at the typically casual public high school, and I was not going to give that up just because I was a pariah. My ex-posse could go back to the way they used to dress, typical Seattle athleisure or geek-gear of logo-tees and socks with sandals if they were so offended by the telltale bright-red soles of my Louboutins.

I stuffed my car keys and wallet into an oversized burgundy handbag and crept down the stairs as quietly as four-inch heels would allow.

No luck. Lana was on the elliptical machine, gleaming with sweat, looking well into her hour-long workout. "Baby, let's talk after school today. I need to . . ."

I slammed the door of the kitchen behind me and waited for a second in the garage to see if she would come after me. The whir of the elliptical machine continued without even a pause.

There was nothing left to be said anyway. She had made up her mind and would do what she wanted. She would sneak around behind my back to go on dates as if she was a teenager, the way she'd always done to my father. If he didn't approve of her spending money on something or going to a certain event, she would just do it anyway and hide it from him. It was just normal for her, and up until recently, I'd really liked that. It made me feel less guilty for doing the same thing.

I parked the Corvette in my usual spot in the school's parking lot, which was already sprinkled with high-end European SUVs, beloved old beaters, and their respective owners.

En route to first period, I made a point to stride past Kendall Chang and Candace Littlefoot, people I had considered my closest friends, but like Jason, they had completely cut me out of their lives after The Incident. Kendall was a beautiful Chinese-American girl who was extraordinarily thin and worked very hard to stay that way. Candace was half Native American and celebrated her heritage with a new tattoo every year. She was showing off her latest, a series of poetic-looking words on her inner wrist, when I passed them. They paused, looked me up and down, and then resumed their conversation about how all makeup remover should be alcohol-free.

I smiled as I took my assigned seat in calculus. Today was a new beginning. I was going to be my old self, and everyone needed to be ready for it. I'd done it before, and I could do it again.

The first day of freshman year, I'd appeared at school in one of Lana's Michael Kors outfits while the other girls in my class were still retiring their Barbies and giggling about sophomore boys. Everyone had been excited to sit with me at lunch, and nothing had changed since until last month.

"...looking almost normal..." I heard Kendall's overly high-pitched voice as she and Candace took their seats behind me.

That was me they were speaking of. I knew the game well. Hell, I'd practically invented it. One day someone was the star of the senior class; the next, they were the primary topic of gossip, a persona non grata. It was classic teen movie fodder.

"Almost. But not yet!" Candace giggled.

I turned around in my seat.

They both smirked at me.

"Ladies," I acknowledged both of them with a nod.

Candace suddenly looked uncertain in the face of my bravado, while Kendall continued to stare at me challengingly.

"You're both looking gorgeous this morning," I said in my most silky voice, earning surprised and then pleased looks from both.

"Kendall, love how you're rocking those eighties jeans. Acid-wash is so . . . you," I tossed behind me as I turned around, laughing at the expressions on their faces.

What had they been expecting me to do? Slink off and hide forever?

"I like your shoes," the arrival of a husky voice behind me took me by surprise. Jason was many things; early to class generally was not one of them. His breath on the back on my neck assured me I wasn't imagining him there.

"You better get in your seat." I barely turned around, my cheeks flushing. I was fully aware that every pair of eyes in the room was trained on me. In my mind, I was fourteen years old again and Jason was asking me to the spring dance.

"Or what?" he whispered back.

I glanced back to see him practically sparkling with his spiky blond hair and cerulean blue eyes. He radiated light, laughter, familiarity. He was my Jason again.

"Ms. Nguyen will mark you absent," I said in my most threatening voice. "She's not kidding about her little rule."

Ms. Bree Nguyen, The Dragon, was not only my father's mentor and oldest friend from the Army Reserves, but also the most fearsome teacher at Lakeville High. She'd been one of the first women in the reserves in the state of Washington, and Dad had enormous respect for her. I always thought this relationship was fairly ironic since my father was a quintessential man's man and thought women needed protection. He'd told me many times that if I needed anything while he was gone, I could call on her, but I never had; it felt too strange, her being my calculus teacher and all. Plus, she kept telling me to call her "Bree", but I couldn't bear to call my calculus teacher something that sounded like French cheese.

"I'll risk The Dragon. So where are we going Friday night?"

"I have plans for Friday."

"What plans?"

"I need to go . . . somewhere." I felt my smile disappear. He wouldn't understand, and I wasn't going to tell him. He hadn't earned that yet.

"Saturday then. Or Sunday. Both. Dinner, then a movie, or a movie, then dinner? There's a bunch of new movies at Lincoln—"

"Mr. Moorehouse!" the tiny, black-haired Dragon of the math department had arrived with her customary mug of green tea in hand. "If you are not in your seat before I finish this sentence, you will be marked absent. Detention, truancy, the full football field. Are those terms you can under—"

Jason bolted into his second-row seat, turning around to wink in my direction, earning yet another glare from Mrs. Nguyen.

I felt myself smile again. He had been horrible to me, but he was predictable. Getting me to go out with him was apparently worthy of utilizing class-clown tactics. I didn't understand why he was doing this, but did understand that at least talking to me again was important to him. Candace also smiled in my direction, which I ignored.

Have you seen Mars today? She looks gorgeous. Jason was flirting with her in calc like crazy. What do you think's going on? Candace would say to everyone she ran into after class.

I hoped anyway.

I headed to the school library during lunch, along with a group of nervous freshmen. I was getting braver, but still, facing the cafeteria tables full of curious or unwelcoming faces wasn't something I was mentally prepared to handle yet. Besides, I enjoyed being the mysterious one, letting them all wonder where I was.

I perused the shelves of the weekly book sale for something new, something old, something long-forgotten. Today's selections were an unread Amy Tan novel, the often-read *One Hundred Years of Solitude*, and my childhood favorite, *Little Women*. My usual pattern was to take three books into the back corner behind the deserted Civil War section and sneak half a breadstick or fruit for lunch. This routine was something I'd started doing only this past month.

"What are you doing here?" I was startled when I saw someone had already claimed my corner. I hadn't meant for it to sound as snappy as it did, but my surprise had gotten the best of me.

Jason was sprawled against the lowermost shelf, head resting on his backpack. "What are *you* doing here?" he asked, crossing his arms above his head and staring up at the brilliant fluorescence of the ceiling lights. "This is my secret spot."

"How did you know where to find me?" I answered the question with a question as I settled in beside him on the floor, kind of wanting him to go away. This was my time to think and reflect. He had no right to stalk me, though it was mildly flattering.

"Are these for class?" he ignored my question in return, sitting up straight and turning his knees so they were facing mine. He picked up my book selections, making me self-conscious as he read the back covers.

"These are missing from my dad's collection. I'm going to buy them for him." I left out the fact that being surrounded by so many of them reminded me of the sanctuary of my own room, a sanctuary I couldn't find anywhere else in the school.

"Oh."

Ask about him, I wanted to say but refrained. I'd learned very quickly over the past month that uttering every single thought out loud wasn't always so well-received.

"You're doing it again."

"What?" I raised my gaze to meet his. He was practically glaring at me.

"Tell me what's going on in your head. Who do you talk to? You're not hanging out with your friends anymore."

"That's a bad thing?" I winced as soon as the words left my mouth. Of course it was a bad thing. Being an outcast was never a *good* thing. "I hang out with Erica and now Chad."

"Mars, we never did talk about what happened."

"Yes, because you didn't want to. You couldn't deal with such 'heavy stuff' in high school, remember?"

"I want to apologize. I'm sorry if I hurt you."

Ah, the conditional apology. He was sorry my feelings were hurt. He was not sorry for his actions. Of course not; why should he apologize for being a coward?

"Why? It's not your problem, remember?" I pulled my knees closer to myself. He'd made the fact that I was alone in this abundantly clear.

"I was stupid. I wasn't there for you. I got scared that I wouldn't be able to help you in your, you know, situation."

I rolled my eyes. *My situation?*

"Just so you know, I did not try to kill myself. I did not need for you to be my psychiatrist. I just needed you to be around. To talk. Or not talk. Nothing more."

"I know, Mars, I heard the rumors, and I just—"

Of course, the rumors. The stories had ricocheted like a possessed boomerang. I'd tried to take my own life with a knife, Lana had me committed, I'd gone to prison for throwing a bourbon bottle at her; none of them were true, of course. We didn't even have bourbon in our house.

Jason sat quietly, and I held my breath as a librarian peeked around the corner and looked satisfied that we weren't up to anything too scandalous. I observed his hands lying flat on the ground, smoothing the ugly beige carpet, and remembered wishing he would engulf me in his arms on that horrible day. I hated being alone and wished he would've just been there by my side.

I could feel myself spiraling into the dark place. The hopeless place. I gripped the carpeting on the floor, grounding myself.

Pull it together. You're fine.

I couldn't let Jason see what I was going through. I was not going to crumple in front of him again, would not give him the opportunity to swoop in with heroics to make up for what he'd done.

"I've been thinking about you this whole month. I knew I was wrong. I haven't been able to sleep at night since we—You have every right to be furious with me," Jason said, bringing me back to the present. "I hope you can forgive me. I'm sorry."

Could I? Maybe.

"I'll earn back your trust, Mars. I'll do whatever it takes. Believe me. We will be together again."

"I don't know," I replied as honestly as I could. "You were pretty harsh."

Jason looked wistful. "Do you remember the night of the blackout?"

I did. We'd been seeing each other for over a month, and nothing other than chaste kisses had happened between us. All of my other friends had boyfriends who sent them love letters and snuck into their rooms at midnight. Jason never did any of those things.

"We were sitting on your porch with the only candle you had in your house slowly disappearing between us," he said. "That was the first night I told you I loved you, and you said, 'I know.'"

I hadn't known that he felt that way, but I had needed to act over-confident so he didn't realize how much he'd thrilled me with those words.

"You didn't say them back." Jason was smiling at me now.

"I did eventually." I remember those days well. I'd held back as much I could, playing it cool, not wanting anyone to know how crazy I was about Jason.

"Yeah, not till that summer almost! It was that day you taught me to make stained-glass windows in my backyard. We were listening to the World Cup soccer match on the radio. You were rooting for France only because you spoke the language."

I laughed. "Yes, and when France won, I said . . ."

"Thanks for sitting through that. No wonder I love you."

Exactly.

"See? I remember everything." He smiled smugly now.

We stared at each other for a second. Did he understand what I was going through? I didn't think so, but at least he pretended to. The bell rang, interrupting anything that was about to happen.

My cheeks burned at Jason's lingering hand on my waist as he helped me to my feet. I closed my eyes, relishing his warm skin, his sweet aftershave, the familiarity. The human contact was so welcome; I didn't want to pull away.

"Mars?"

"Let's go." I reluctantly gathered my belongings, still feeling flushed at where my thoughts had been headed.

"How did you know where to find me? Did you follow me?" I asked as I led Jason out of the Civil War corner.

Jason smiled, holding the library door open for me. "While that's very romantic in a stalker-ish way, I didn't. Erica told me you like to hang here during lunch. She also says you haven't returned her text message. Better get on that."

"I will."

"Sure you have to attend that SAT course thing? I already got my acceptance into the U. I can help you study." The back of Jason's hand touched mine as we wove through the hallways, taking the long route. It looked completely natural to everyone else, I suppose, like things returning to normal. Everyone remembered our romantic "Class Couple" pose in the yearbook, Jason scooping me up into his arms, gazing into my eyes, romance-novel style.

"Thanks," I said, "but I'm already registered. Besides, I'm pretty sure my instructor is more qualified than you." I wanted it to sound teasing, but it came out harsh.

Jason stopped walking as we entered the main corridor and pulled me into him, his shoulder pressing against mine. All around us students opened and closed doors, gossiped, fixed their hair. Every one of them openly stared at us, and Jason stared at no one but me. My breath caught as he gently touched my cheek and brushed away a strand of hair, his nearness distracting and disturbing all at once.

"I'm not giving up."

Then he was gone.

I walked to my next class aware of the looks my classmates were directing my way. Smiling. Jason had made me *accepted* again. No matter what was happening between us, I had to give him that. He knew that by almost kissing me in public, others would realize that the old

Mars was back. I had underestimated him; he knew the game as well as I did, maybe better.

As I entered my favorite class of the day, AP Psychology, my favorite petite, blond energy orb accosted me in the doorway. "You're avoiding me."

"I most certainly am not." I stopped short. The big difference between Erica Esteban and everyone from before The Incident was the fact that there was no drama. I could be in whatever mood I wanted to be in around her—talkative, not talkative. There was never any judgment or questions. She and I had become best friends back in third grade when we had been in the same tap-dancing class together. We used to have sleepovers and ice-skating parties every weekend, but those had dwindled once we went to separate middle schools. Now, back in the same high school, we had rekindled our friendship as if the past eight years had never happened.

"Chad, is she lying?" Erica grinned and curved into her boyfriend, who removed his earphones. "She ran away from me after our therapy session and hasn't called since."

I felt that familiar twinge as I watched Chad catch Erica as she fell backward into his arms. They'd been a couple through all of high school, never apart for more than a weekend. I had never seen two people more in sync with one another's thoughts and actions. They had some kind of crazy pact that they would always be brutally honest with each other and the other person could never get mad at the truth. I'd never had that kind of relationship with anyone, not even Jason. I wondered if it was even possible, given all the messed-up thoughts I always had.

Chad Winters, lanky pseudo-mystic, wrapped his arms around Erica's twenty-four-inch waist while leaning them both forward to gaze deeply into my eyes. "Yes, she is definitely lying."

"Chad is a lie detector, and lie detectors detect, well, lies. What's going on, Mars?" Erica's fast talking and fast topic changing were things I loved about her. Today was no exception. "You look really good today, by the way. Doesn't she, Chad?"

"Yes. Really damn good. But that is not an answer that's going to keep me out of trouble here, so I'm no longer listening." Chad whipped a cell phone out of the pocket of his hooded sweatshirt and became extremely busy fiddling with the many buttons.

"Chad is not a human lie detector." I had to laugh. "And nothing is going on. I've just had a really weird day."

Erica followed me to my usual seat in the back of the classroom and plopped down in front of me.

"Good weird. Or just weird-weird?" She twirled a strand of pink hair peeking out from under her veil of blond curls. Erica was one of those rare personalities who refused a role in any clique or group. She was gorgeous, funky, kind, and smart enough to be in the running for valedictorian. It was odd to have someone like that in our otherwise disconnected high school.

The truth was, I kind of hated her sometimes because she refused to gossip about our peers the way I was used to. She hardly ever told me what people were saying about me. She made me feel petty and small on such occasions.

"Both brands of weird. Guess what Lana's doing?" I filled her in on how I discovered that Lana was dating off of a website.

Erica shook her head. "Lana, I swear. She's like someone's ditzy older sister. No offense."

"None taken. But you have to agree, whatever issues you have with your mom, at least you don't have to worry she's going to start sneaking out of the house in your miniskirts." This actually was a valid concern of mine, given that everyone always said Lana and I looked like sisters.

"Well, at least Lana can pull it off; she's not obese like my mother!"

"Irrelevant!" I gave her a look.

Erica must have felt sorry for me because she divulged a rare bit of gossipy information. "Everyone thinks you've lost weight. And people love your shoes. Also, Kendall wants info about what was going on between you and Jason during calc. She's asking everyone, even me."

"Hmm, she can go ahead and ask me if she cares so much," I replied indifferently. "Honestly, she should probably pursue some interests of her own rather than being so overly interested in my life."

Though I sounded very neutral, I was extremely pleased to hear that my former friends were still fascinated by me. It was as I suspected; they had nothing else to talk about.

"Ugh, I predict you'll be back to hanging with them and ignoring me within a week." Erica rolled her eyes and spun around in her chair.

"Hey!"

She turned and grinned to show she wasn't serious, though I suspected there was some element of truth to what she said. Erica and I hadn't become close again until I'd lost my other friends, including Lana. She'd been a really good shoulder for me the past few weeks, and I wasn't going to cut her out of my life like she was convinced I was doing.

I was sure my evening would be uneventful to even out the day I'd just had. Traffic crossing the bridge to the U was surprisingly relaxed and uneventful. Chatting with my favorite barista at Sureshot as I got my usual White Angel coffee was uneventful.

The barista furrowed his eyebrows, one decorated with a tribal ring, and shared some coffee-shop gossip about some new guy named Zayed as he blended my white chocolate mocha with coconut. The name sounded familiar, but I couldn't place it, and honestly didn't care much.

"He's Mediterranean or Italian or something. Dark hair, striking eyes. He's new around here, and friendly, even talks to the bums. The girls keep asking about him," he said pointedly.

I ignored his remark. "Stop trying to set me up with random guys. My ex wants to go out with me again, and I'm thinking about it, thank you very much."

"The guy that dumped you for being an actual human being?"

I didn't answer.

"Wow, sounds like a great guy. Let me guess: rich, trust fund, drives a BMW, thinks Wallingford is dangerous at night."

I narrowed my eyes, annoyed at him for the stereotype and at myself for being annoyed. He'd hit too close to the truth. Jason was everything he'd said, but much more. Was there anything wrong with wanting to be with a guy who was like me?

Realizing debating with the barista had made me late for my very first class, I sprinted across the street into the glistening white building next to the bank. After taking three flights of stairs two at a time in my stilettos, I paused in the doorway of the classroom to catch my breath.

Normalcy took longer than expected once I saw who was standing in front of the room. It was him, the boy from the window. The one with the eyes. I literally had to hold onto the door frame, watching my knuckles lose color as my heart raced.

Wavy black hair, skin the color of a raw almond, those extraordinary wide-set eyes. He carried himself proudly, the posture of a prince casually swathed in black slacks and a gray V-neck sweater.

"This is Zayed Anwar," my administrator friend was introducing him to the students already in attendance. "He will be teaching this class."

"Hello, everyone." Zayed tilted his head as he made eye contact with his audience. "Please take a few minutes to get acquainted with the items on your desk."

"Please be nice," the administrator added as her parting words to the class. She squeezed my arm in recognition on her way out the door.

I hovered in the doorway, scanning the classroom. The new-paint smell was almost overwhelming in the spacious room with light hardwood floors. There were only twelve desks, most already occupied. A row of windows lined the western wall, overlooking University Avenue below.

I approached, searching Zayed's face for some trace of recognition. His expression remained polite, neutral. It was as if he had never seen me before. Unacceptable. I made a silent resolution to dazzle him as he had me.

"I'm Mars Alexander," I finally said, holding out my hand and giving him the smile that usually got me what I wanted.

Zayed's lips parted as he took my hand. "It's a pleasure," he said. Nothing more.

I claimed the only seat left in the second row. Not too obvious, not too disinterested. I opened the study guide on the corner of the desk and flipped through the first few pages, watching Zayed through my eyelashes. He greeted each student with a smile and a handshake. I noticed several girls doing a double take and whispering with their neighbor about our handsome instructor. I felt a stab of possessiveness. I'd seen him before any of them.

He didn't glance my way once.

He started class with an introduction while perching on the edge of the teacher's desk in the front of the room. A tangerine and a mango were next to a heap of SAT prep books that were neatly lined and stacked. "For the next eight weeks, we are going to get to know each other quite well. I'm going to take excellent care of you, and you will do amazingly well on your exam." He made eye contact with each person in the room as he talked.

I started to warm up on the inside when his eyes met mine again. How could he not recognize me? I could still feel the crazy electric current that had shot through me on the sidewalk.

Zayed continued to outline the objectives of the course. "I'll also need your email addresses before you leave. Don't worry, I won't send any chain letters, unless it's 101 Ways to Torment Your SAT Instructor," he said, earning a laugh, mostly from the girls. "I will be emailing your grades and comments to you once a week, though."

He had a very interesting accent, not quite European, not quite Middle Eastern. It was fairly obvious that English was his second language by the careful way he selected his words.

"Due to our current heavy reliance on computers, students become panic-stricken when asked to write an essay by hand. The essay section is twenty-five minutes long. All essays must be in response to a given prompt; these are often philosophical and are designed to be accessible to students regardless of their educational and social backgrounds."

"Like?" one of the girls who'd been eyeing Zayed asked.

"Discuss whether a big technological change, such as the internet, also carries negative consequences to those who benefit from it." Zayed smiled in her direction. I could see his dimples from across the room. "You'd discuss how information is so easy to access now—but what does that mean for your personal privacy?"

The girl was too busy smiling at Zayed to respond. He smiled back and continued talking. I tried to think of an intelligent-sounding question too, but only came up with "How are these graded?"

I was about to raise my hand, hoping he would turn to me, when he said, "Two trained readers assign each essay a score between one and six, and the scores are summed to produce a final score from two to twelve."

I'd gotten a six. A 50 percent pass rate. I, Mars Alexander the Second, was a failure in the grand scheme of things unless I took action fast. I had to get at least a ten on the next one. I couldn't risk anything lower if I wanted admission into the U.

For the rest of the class, Zayed walked us through the study guide, which consisted of sample essays, some of them done well and some not. He also introduced us to the standard essay structure and common pitfalls, most of which I already knew. More than listening to the lecture, I was mesmerized by his voice, his tone, and the words he chose to thread together into perfect sentences.

I would stay after to talk to him, I decided, to find out about his qualifications for teaching the class. I was putting my future in his hands, after all.

"Miss Alexander?" his voice shattered my daydream. It was the first time he'd looked my way or spoken to me in over an hour and a half.

I knew the ignoring-me act couldn't last. I practically shot to my feet. "Yes?"

"Please sign in before departing." Zayed gestured toward the sign-in sheet on his desk.

The classroom was empty. Where had I been this whole time? I blushed as I approached his desk.

"Your vocabulary is astonishing," I said as I scrawled my name on the sign-in sheet. "Where did you go to school?"

"Paris." Zayed waited till I was done to reach across and collect the sheet of paper. He tucked it into a manila envelope.

"Did you move here fairly recently?"

"I did." He didn't pause as he put the envelope into his messenger bag along with the two pieces of fruit. I saw a flash of a burgundy book I assumed was the same one he'd been reading the day before.

"Do you read a lot?" I probed further, not ready to accept only these indistinct answers.

I forgot everything I was planning to ask as he made eye contact with me. "Miss Alexander, I noticed you were quite distracted today. Please be attentive in class. You've paid a significant amount of money to be here, and I would prefer you get the most possible benefit from it."

"I—"

"Now, if you'll excuse me . . ." Not too subtly, he gestured toward the door.

And there was nothing more for me to say.

CHAPTER 3

The Roof

"We're doing this again." Jason announced. He reached for me after parking his silver BMW on the street at the exact midpoint between our houses. There was, of course, the chance that a neighbor would see us and immediately report the news to one of our parents. I wasn't ready to predict Jason's parents' reaction, but Lana's was fairly predictable.

The Sunday evening date had been good. It was as if the past month had never happened. We'd literally picked up exactly where we'd left off.

I forgot about everything as his lips whispered my name in my ear and then grazed my cheek, avoiding the area where the scar still lingered. He pulled back for a customary gaze into my eyes before touching his lips to mine and holding them for a few seconds, fingers winding up into my hair.

The kiss was expected given the buildup during our date. Tender, gentle, the perfect kiss. Nothing new, nothing different. Something I'd known for years.

Earlier, he'd come inside to chat with Lana, although I was more than willing to leave immediately. We'd dined on fresh-baked ravioli at a fine Italian restaurant in Bellevue and seen a surefire Oscar-contender movie. It had been the perfect date, one we'd had many times before.

"You haven't had enough of me yet?" I murmured, only half-joking.

Jason pulled away again but didn't release me. "I am so far from that. Ride with me to school tomorrow?"

But for the first time in a long time, I felt safe. Protected. I didn't have to think about Lana or Dad or the SAT or anything else. As long as I stayed exactly where I was, nothing else could happen; we could be back together, Mars and Jason, the quintessential Lakeville High School couple.

That thought dissipated as I realized I didn't have that option.

"I'll drive myself tomorrow." I pulled away first. "I have SAT class after."

The mood was broken as I thought of Zayed Anwar again.

"Okay, but you have to make it up to me."

I raised an eyebrow in his direction. There was one person in the car that had making up to do, and it certainly wasn't me.

Jason realized I wasn't amused and quickly leaned over and kissed the scar on my cheek, as if telling me he wanted to heal what had happened between us a month ago. "Will you go to the homecoming dance with me? I'll be perfectly behaved." He raised his hands as if in surrender.

"We'll see." I ducked out of the car before he followed with another kiss and made my way up the driveway under Jason's watchful eye. I waved to him from the doorway, not lingering.

The yellow roses Jason had brought for me were arranged beautifully in a multi-stemmed vase on the kitchen counter, but otherwise the living room was as I'd left it. The rest of the house was dark and quiet. Lana was nowhere to be seen.

We had spoken very little since that night I'd discovered the dating site, mostly about the SAT class and what a jerk I thought the instructor was. She'd been going on dates. I'd been able to tell that by the parade of new Ted Baker dresses she'd left the house in every night for the past week.

I carried the roses up to my room and set them on my nightstand. Yellow for friendship. It was a strange choice for Jason to bring seeing that he was very focused on rekindling our relationship.

I attempted to drift off to sleep, thinking of Jason and hoping I would dream of him that night. He'd asked me to homecoming. We'd gone together to the homecoming dance the past three years. It made sense for us to go together senior year. I could get a dress on short notice.

I could foresee the next few years now that things were back on track. Jason and I strolling across the University of Washington campus, holidays split between each other's families. And at the end of college, he would propose with his great-grandmother's ring. We would move into a beautiful house on the lake and have the perfect family. I would be safe and loved, and my father and Lana would be so very proud of me.

Why, then, did these thoughts not lull me into happy dreams? I finally turned on my nightlight and flipped through that damn Theodore Robert Watkins poetry again.

> *When I breathe you in and out again,*
> *There is no defining line where you end and I begin.*
> *Where have you gone, and how long will this missing piece of me,*
> *This phantom limb, cause me this pain?*

I felt that odd twisting feeling in my stomach again as I closed the book. How could a guy who read such intense poetry be so cold in real life?

A few hours later, I awoke to hear the sound of the front door opening and closing. I didn't want to know if Lana was coming or going. A heavy feeling in my stomach, I burrowed deeper underneath the covers.

Dreading seeing Mr. Zayed Anwar again, I took my time parking the car as far from the College Preparatory Institute building as possible. Even after picking up a chipotle Mexican hot chocolate and walking slowly, I reached the classroom five minutes early. He was already there, looking through the study guide, eyelashes quickly skimming over one page after another. He didn't look up at me once.

Ugh, I hated him for the way he'd spoken to me, like I was some sort of spoiled brat in day care who needed a scolding.

I chose a seat near the door, as far from Zayed as I could manage, and didn't glance his way, except once or twice. I did try to see what he was staring at as he stood by the slanted bay of windows and gazed into the distance.

His band of admiring female students didn't follow my example and instead sat as close to his desk as possible. I pursed my lips and busily read through our study guide for the fourth time.

He welcomed the twelve students and immediately announced a surprise. "Today we'll be having a practice test. Don't be scared, I won't judge. Just think, the lower you score today, the better you'll look at the end!"

I joined the class in groaning, but secretly, I was terrified more than annoyed. This man was going to see my atrocious essay-writing skills. If he didn't already assume I was some kind of airhead, he would know for sure after class.

"Miss Alexander," he said, smiling politely as if nothing had happened as he deposited a sealed booklet on my desk. When he saw me reach for it, he reprimanded me gently, "Please don't open that until the test starts."

I seethed silently. As if I couldn't comprehend the simple instructions, which clearly stated, PLEASE DON'T OPEN UNTIL INSTRUCTED in large block letters. I did not like this man.

The twenty-five-minute test flew by too quickly as I struggled to organize my thoughts around affirmative action's pros and cons. I could feel that I had not improved at all. And now, with the instructor determined to make me self-conscious, I didn't know how I would. I was tempted to withdraw from the class and try again in a few months, with another instructor, like Lana had suggested, but I knew I would be too late to take another two rounds of the SATs before college applications were due. I reluctantly passed my test to Zayed along with everyone else.

That was when the tremor beneath my feet literally shook me out of my chair.

"Earthquake!" someone shouted as I stood up and tossed my pen and cell phone into my purse. Years in Seattle had taught me that the best thing to do with low-level earthquakes was to stay exactly where I was, get under a desk, and not panic.

Then the lights went off in the classroom. Then in the building across the street.

Someone dropped something. Someone yelled for everyone to shut up. Someone started to stand up. I stopped moving and glanced around in the darkness. This didn't feel like an earthquake anymore. I recalled having seen tracks of power lines between the buildings woven in an intricate pattern. All it would take was for one to go down and the whole area would be in darkness.

A minute later, we heard police sirens and ambulances in the distance. I picked my purse up off the desk, wishing something bad didn't happen every time I came to the U. I waited for Zayed to say something reassuring to the class, to give us further instructions, but I didn't hear or see him in the hushed darkness.

The fire-truck sirens outside were enough to spur the classroom into movement. I followed the herd of students to the door and saw that there was a jam in the stairway. Someone was going to get hurt.

"Guys, be careful! We do not want a stampede," I called out.

I pressed my back against the door as the other students ignored me and frantically dashed into the scuffle.

Wonderful.

Only after my eyes adjusted to the darkness did I look up and see that Zayed's shadowy figure hadn't moved from his position in front of the board. He clutched something in his hand and stared out the window, motionless. What was the matter with him? We were looking to him for leadership and guidance, and he was standing there absolutely useless.

"Zayed?" I called from the doorway. "You should get away from the window."

He still didn't move. I had a feeling he was panicking. He was not going to be able to leave this building on his own.

I looked longingly after my classmates, but my instinct held me firmly in place. And there, without warning, I felt the influence of my father as strongly as if he was standing next to me. He had always said that our role on this earth was to protect those who couldn't protect themselves. That was why he'd sacrificed a normal life for himself and his family.

Dad commanded over a hundred men and women in the Reserves and considered it his responsibility to keep not just his people but the innocent people of Afghanistan safe from a recent uprising of locals who wanted the Americans gone. His group had faced hostile sheikhs, land mines, suicide bombers, and other things I didn't want to think about.

The truth was that sometimes I hated him for doing all this for strangers but leaving his family behind. This was going to be one of those moments I would remember to tell him about when he came home: the time I was incredibly brave and saved my SAT instructor from a panic attack. "I don't know what he would have done if I wasn't there," I would say.

The last of the footsteps thundered out of the room. I gingerly made my way to the front, avoiding the dark outlines of desks and chairs.

"Zayed, are you all right?"

"They're here," he whispered.

"Yes, they are." I watched the blazing ambulance lights below. "Don't worry."

We stood in silence for a minute, then the marker he was clutching fell to the ground. The clang was followed by a rolling sound, then silence.

"Zayed, have you ever been in an earthquake before?"

No words from him.

Clearly not.

He was shaking. I could tell being two feet away from him. He quivered as if one wrong step would send him crashing through the slanted windows to the street below. I could tell he wasn't hearing a word I was saying. I wanted to touch him, to assure him that he wasn't alone, but didn't know if that was appropriate.

"Don't worry; this is probably just a small one." I tentatively placed a hand on his shoulder anyway. I was surprised to feel him trembling beneath my fingertips. This was a scary situation, no doubt, but he was overreacting.

A light from an ambulance briefly shone up into the classroom, illuminating Zayed in the spotlight. It rebounded off his irises. He didn't move. Didn't react.

I sighed. Where was my confident teacher now?

"Come with me."

He warily looked at my outstretched hand. I was about to pull it away when he took it into his in a tight grasp, interlacing my fingers with his.

I swallowed. His hands were like ice. I had to get him out of there before he went into shock.

"Zayed, let's go outside. You'll feel better once you get some fresh air."

"The roof," he said faintly.

"What?"

"It's just a staircase up."

"Of course. The roof." I hadn't realized the building even had a roof and was not looking forward to climbing the dark staircase. The backlight from my cell phone guided me up a narrow flight of stairs and to a doorway. Every few steps, I turned to make sure Zayed was okay.

He matched me step for step, holding his messenger bag tightly over one shoulder. I was feeling a lot less afraid by now; the building felt fairly stable, and no other tremors had begun.

"Wow, the entire neighborhood seems to be out." I held the door open. The roof was deserted, an old mossy smell permeating the space. It was obvious no one had been up here in quite a long time. I was surprised that the door was unlocked and that Zayed even knew about it.

I didn't bother asking why since he was in no shape to answer any questions.

"You don't want get too close to the edge," I said unnecessarily, expecting he would release my hand. He didn't loosen his viselike grip for even an instant and instead remained pasted against the exterior stairwell wall as if he would fall off a cliff if he let go.

"Thank you," I thought I heard him say.

We both gazed off into the darkness of the city, dotted with a few blinking lights. I wanted to assume this was an ordinary power outage following a minor earthquake. The way Zayed was acting made me question my theory.

"What happened back there?" I asked hesitantly.

He turned to look at me, really look at me for the first time, his silhouette defined even in the darkness. "I'm sorry." He finally released my hand. "I'm extremely sorry. This was inappropriate. I should have asked you to leave."

And my favorite instructor was back.

"Don't apologize. I'm curious. You seemed, uh . . ."

"You should go, Miss Alexander. I'll be fine. Don't . . . don't worry. Please go. Carefully."

"Uh, sure, let me just make sure some friends of mine are okay." Stung, I pulled my cell phone out of my purse again and started typing on the keypad.

The truth was, I was text messaging gibberish to myself. I glared at him even though he couldn't see me. How dare he pretend to slip into his formal teacher persona? He was so freaked out, I had no doubt he would jump off the roof or something if I left him here. I also had a feeling that if I stayed a few more minutes, Zayed would forget about propriety and start talking, because he was certainly *not* fine.

Another police car arrived. Then three more.

He sighed and leaned his head back against the wall. "We had blackouts back home. Whenever there was an attack."

In Paris?

"So much danger. I never knew if we would survive the night," he said in a voice so low it was clear he was talking to himself.

What was he talking about?

Chills shot through my spine, and suddenly I felt a cold sweat break out on my forehead. My bravado was fading, and my protective feelings for Zayed vanished immediately. I had no idea what I was doing. I was being careless and naïve thinking I could play hero for a man I knew nothing about and was now alone on a roof with.

I turned to leave and willed myself to just go. Get away from here. A text message from Lana had just popped up on my phone, signaling that the blackout had hit the news already. "Baby, where are you? Call me. Worried," the message said.

"There soon," I responded, typing quickly. "Traffic sucks."

Something deep down held me in place. This guy did need my help. This was not an act.

Zayed stared into the blackness of the city unfolding before us. "It's happening again."

He was starting to scare me more with his cryptic talk.

"I've felt this way, the way I think you're feeling now," I said, giving him one last chance to start explaining what was going on in his head. "Like I'm trapped inside my own body. Like no one can hear me."

"Like I can't put my images into words," Zayed said in a voice so low I could barely hear him.

"Yes, like that." He seemed to be doing better. "I'm going to, uh, check on what's going on downstairs—"

His back slid down the wall until he was sitting. He remained silent. I could barely hear him breathe as he rested his forehead on his knees.

The decision was mine. Leave, find my car, call Lana. Or stay. Help this person I didn't know or trust or even like very much.

I would put this story aside as well for Dad: the time I did not leave my SAT instructor alone on the roof when he was in shock. I didn't know what he would want me to do in a situation like this since he was so overprotective, but I knew what the right thing for me to do was.

I knew from my therapy group that in moments of shock or panic, people needed to be reminded of their normal world. "Can I open your bag?"

He didn't answer, didn't even acknowledge the question.

I knelt next to him and rifled through the messenger bag, taking out the book I knew would be there, along with a somewhat-random used book on how to raise kittens. I used my cell phone to shine some light on a page in the middle of the book with the burgundy cover.

"I long for your skin, warmed by sleep. The velvet expanse of your back is dotted with stars that I press my lips upon."

"This is beautiful," I murmured, feeling embarrassed to read something so intimate out loud. Especially to Zayed. Especially sitting face-to-face in the darkness. This was a lot more embarrassing than the one I'd read to myself the other night. "Do you know this one?"

"One by one, I kiss every one. It's not the first for you, to be loved this way, but I am determined to be your last," Zayed recited the rest of the poem, looking into the distance, not at the page. His voice was carnal and raw. This was not the first time he'd read this out loud, that much was obvious. By the end, I was blushing furiously.

"I'll assume that you know it," I said, closing the book. "Why Theodore Robert Watkins?" I asked.

Silence.

"My father introduced me to his work," he said finally.

Mine too.

"I've loved everything I've read by him," Zayed said. "This was the book I was reading when I first saw you."

He finally smiled, and in my direction at that.

I had to laugh as I sat cross-legged next to him. I pressed the back of my hand to my hot cheek. "In that window. Sureshot."

"You stared at me so intently," he said in that same low voice.

"I had a lot on my mind. I didn't think you saw me."

"Your face is unusual. Very hard to forget."

I shivered, both from the night air and the comment. What did this mean? From any other man, it would be a come-on or an insult, but he said it with such matter-of-factness that it sounded . . . okay.

A few nights ago, I saw him for the first time, then I dreamt about him, now we were sitting on a deserted roof, talking in the darkness as if we were friends. This was not something I did or even knew if I should be doing.

"I'm sorry." Zayed backtracked quickly. "I apologize. I didn't mean—I continue to be inappropriate tonight."

"No. I mean, thank you." Embarrassed, I changed the subject yet again. "I look a little like my dad. I'm named after him, that's why I'm Mars Alexander the Second."

I used to hate my name; after all, being named after a planet was hardly a good thing in elementary school. As I'd grown up, I'd learn to appreciate my Greek roots and moreover appreciate a father who wasn't afraid to name me after himself and the Greek god of war.

"You're lucky to have him in your life still," Zayed said softly.

My breath caught. "Yes, I am."

"Did I say something? I'm sorry for being . . . stupid."

"No, nothing like that. He's in the Army Reserves. He's based in Afghanistan right now. I worry about him." The Incident had proved that I was not handling the situation as well as I should be. I was, however, not going to go into details with this person I'd just met.

Zayed stiffened. "Your father is deployed in the Middle East? For how long?"

"Too long," I replied instantly.

I bit my lip, realizing I had over-shared, wondering what had possessed me to talk about this immensely personal information while a crew of police cars were blocking off the block below.

What was going on down there?

Zayed walked to the edge of the roof.

"How often do you think of him? Your father?" he rested his arms on the guardrail and looked back at me.

"How often do I not?" I replied, though I knew I should stop talking. I wasn't prepared for another breakdown. But Zayed was the only one who'd asked about Dad, and I wanted to hear myself answer out loud. "He's been there for over six months already. I just want him to come home now. He's missed so much already. I don't want him to miss anything else."

"I'm sure he is missing you too."

Then why isn't he here?

"I just want . . ." I said slowly. What *did* I want?

"Time to stand still?"

"What?" I almost gasped because this guy was starting to read my mind.

"Are you afraid of the future because there will be even more he'll miss?"

"Yes. Sometimes. I just don't know why he's always overseas. There's so much he is missing here, and he knows that."

"Or do you wish to reverse time? Tell him certain things. Prevent him from leaving?"

I didn't answer.

"Him being deployed is his choice, Miss Alexander. Not your choice, fault, or anything else."

I blinked. Unnerved that he'd figured me out in half an hour, something no one else had managed or dared or attempted to do—ever.

"Tell me about you," I said.

"I've come here to Seattle to start over after losing my connection with my family." The sorrow in Zayed's voice drew me closer to him. "I wish I could relive my last day with them again, for time to stand still."

"What happened to them?" I asked, hoping he would tell me, but fairly sure he wouldn't.

"Please cherish what you have. Your family. They're more sacred than anything else," he said instead, proving me right.

"I try." I swallowed. It was a lie, but it was easier than admitting the truth; honestly, I really didn't have faith in Lana as a parent. I didn't like the decisions she was making that were affecting both of us.

"Only try?" Zayed smiled again, sadder this time around. Even in the darkness, we were close enough that I could see his dimples, his proud chin, and his angled jawline.

"This class is a part of it. My father would want me to get into the University of Washington, which is why I need to score well on the essay portion."

"What do *you* want?"

"To make him proud." I hadn't realized just how much I meant it until I said it out loud. Yes, that was what I wanted. For him to be proud of me when he finally came home.

"You will make him very proud. You and I together will ensure that. I'm with you."

We stood still, gazing out at the glittering lights of Seattle's city center off in the distance as our block continued to be under the cover of the blackout.

The roof, the darkness, the book in Zayed's hands. It was straight out of my dream. The realization left me staggered to my core, wondering what the premonition had meant, and what was still to come.

CHAPTER 4

The Message

Tuesday was ridiculous. I couldn't concentrate on what was going on around me at school and was humbled twice in AP Calculus by Ms. Nguyen for not only answering incorrectly, but answering the wrong question. Kendall Chang giggled, while Jason glanced my way, frowning.

I hadn't returned Jason's call from the night before; I hadn't wanted to describe what had happened over the phone, and had even wondered how much to share with him. The news channels all said the incident at the U was a freak power outage, caused by wind.

There had been no wind that night.

I woke up worried about Zayed, hoping he'd gotten home safe. All my hostility toward him had vanished overnight.

I had drifted in and out of sleep, disoriented, ready for the morning to arrive after I had a brief but *very* intimate dream about Zayed. I dreamt I led him up the staircase to the roof again, but this time a hundred flickering candles guided the way. I dreamt he backed me into the wall and suddenly we were in my bedroom. He asked me a question I didn't remember. Then he whispered, "I can't believe this is real." And then other things happened that I struggled to remember but couldn't.

I woke up, my heart racing. It *wasn't* real, but unfortunately it was one of those things where I knew I wouldn't be able to look at him the same way when I saw him again. I wanted the next twenty-four hours to fly by so I could see him, and yet I dreaded meeting him again because I knew I would be horribly awkward.

Did Zayed and I really spend two hours on the roof, holding hands for the majority of the time? Talking, then not talking. At the end of it, we'd descended the stairs of the Institute into a dissipating crowd of police cars and curious onlookers. Neither of us said a word as he walked me to my car. He waited until I was safely inside, mouthed a "thanks" with a hand on the driver's side window. Then he disappeared into the obscurity of the night before I could say a word.

I opened and closed my hand, which was still a bit sore from his firm grip. No one had ever held my hand that way before, like my grasp was the only thing keeping them standing.

I wanted to call him that morning to make sure he was all right but didn't have his number. I didn't even know where he lived. So I put on last year's designer boots and a short sweater dress I had never dared to wear before and headed to school feeling restless, jumpy, like I wanted *something* to happen. I couldn't go on today like nothing had changed, when something had. I didn't quite know what it was, and I couldn't even point a finger in the general vicinity, but something had changed for me.

Ms. Nguyen seemed to agree and asked me to stay after. I slumped in my seat, feeling the stares of the students around me as they left the classroom. I didn't want to talk to her; she would ask me how I was doing and if there was something she could do to help. She would want to talk about Dad. My phone buzzed, and a quick glance told me it was a text message from Erica. "Media Center. Meet me."

"Are you attending your therapy sessions, Mars?" Ms. Nguyen asked, referring to the support group meetings. She had surprisingly taken the seat in front of me after the room had emptied out, rather than ruling from behind her desk. I'd never seen her out from behind her desk before, and that in itself was jarring.

"Yes." I tapped my heel impatiently against the tiled floor. That was not a lie; I attended Military Grief Therapy group every Tuesday evening without fail. I'd sat in the circle of six every week and listened to stories about sacrifices, loss, and fear: things I knew too much about. I didn't share stories about Dad. I didn't want to, not with teenagers who had put their fathers and mothers and brothers and sisters into the ground.

"Good." She nodded her approval, saying less than I thought she would.

"Sorry I missed some questions today. I'll study up on chapter six tonight. I should go." I wanted catch up with Erica and also see if I could dig up some contact information for Zayed.

"Tell me about therapy. What have you shared so far?"

Silence.

"I like to listen, for the most part. I'll ... I'll start to participate vocally in a few weeks."

"Mars."

"Ms. Nguyen, I know what you're going to say." I was prepared for the "you need to achieve closure" speech I'd already gotten from Stephanie.

"No, you don't. Please call me Bree outside of class. Your father always did." This was like the eighth time she'd asked me to do so.

"Uh-huh." I was *not* going to call her Bree.

"I was going to say that it's fine to be an observer. Sometimes you learn the most through the pain and sorrow and actions of others."

"Oh." Okay, this conversation was not going as I'd anticipated. I had no idea where she was heading. Or why it mattered to her. My grades weren't as fantastic as they could be, but they were hardly suffering. It wasn't like I'd been a math genius in the past.

Ms. Nguyen, Bree, watched me with her bright-blue eyes, suddenly more intense than I'd ever seen them. "I've been in this kind of situation before. I thought I was doing the right thing by being there for the people around me. Always ready to listen."

I was curious about what had happened, but didn't want to encourage any further discussion.

"It's very common for teens to start risky behaviors such as drug and alcohol abuse, getting into fights and sexual experimentation."

I almost had to laugh at that one. I was apparently dealing with some different kind of thing because in the last month I'd stopped seeing my boyfriend, stopped going to college parties, and had avoided all confrontation.

"Another common way to deny pain is to act overly strong or mature."

Again, no one was accusing me of that. In Lana's words, I was acting like an immature brat.

"I think I should have a conversation with Lana about how she's doing. Is she attending a support group?" Bree seemed to hear the sigh that I had thought was silent.

I didn't answer. Lana was not attending any support group. She was handling this whole incident in her special way of pretending it didn't exist.

"When I lost my husband, I watched. And listened. Maybe Lana would—"

Now I knew where she was going.

"I have not 'lost' anyone. And neither has Lana. I'm sorry, Ms. Nguyen, but you guys really"—I felt my defenses flare up—"need to leave me alone. I'm fine. You don't have to worry about me."

I left the classroom, knowing I was in trouble with her and would be in even more trouble with Lana, but not caring. I had enough going on without having to explain to everyone around me that I was dealing with everything just fine. That, really, the best thing everyone could do was just go back to normal and stop worrying about me.

Erica eyed my legs, clad in red knee-high boots, as I flopped into the workstation next to her in the Media Center. "Nice."

I smiled in response. I loved these boots; I should wear them more often.

"Where were you last night? Jason said you were trapped in some blackout at the U and you didn't call him. Or me. He's worried about you. Me too."

"I was in the College Prep Institute building for a while during the blackout." I logged into the workstation I was sitting at, observing that my nails were chipped and in dire need of a manicure. I had half a mind to skip therapy that evening and spend the time with a pampering session at the Luxe Salon on the Kirkland waterfront.

"Alone?"

"With my instructor. He's new, and he was scared and I didn't want to leave him."

Innocent enough, I thought.

Erica twirled a strand of pink hair, her signature move for not buying it. "Tell me more."

I glanced over her shoulder toward a very curious-looking Candace, who wasn't even pretending not to eavesdrop, and lowered my voice. "You're going to think I'm crazy. He needed me to stay. He has these eyes that are amazing. Tormented almost. Heathcliff eyes."

Recalling the night out loud, I realized how intoxicated I'd been. How drunk on being anonymous, sharing thoughts with another person that I certainly would never imagined sharing in the light of day.

Erica touched a hand to her heart and pretended to swoon.

"Like he has so much he's keeping inside. We wound up talking up on the roof, and I just wanted to, I don't know, protect him. Be there for him."

I recalled his catlike eyes watching me closely and reacting with edgy movements. Perhaps he was a runaway, escaping an abusive home situation. Or maybe he'd committed a crime, robbed a bank or a store. Of course, it could be that he was an illegal alien who had snuck across the Canadian border.

All of those possibilities suggested that he would be hiding from the law. None of them explained how he had such exquisite vocabulary and how he was able to secure a teaching position at the Institute.

"There's something about him that's . . . different. I feel so weird with him. Like good-weird."

"You're blushing! Did something else happen?" Erica smiled, looking wicked.

"Well, I had this dream . . ."

"Was I in it?" A voice too close to my ear for comfort startled me.

"Jason." I whirled around, wondering how much he'd heard. His brilliant smile suggested not enough to raise suspicion. I chided myself for wanting to hide such an innocuous thing from him.

"I am going to leave you two alone now." Erica took her headphones off her workstation. "Call me later, Mars. I mean it."

"What's going on with you?" Jason didn't mince words as he perched on the edge of my table.

"Nothing." I searched his face. Could I trust him with what I was thinking? Would he get the wrong idea about my protectiveness toward Zayed? Men were jealous for silly reasons, and I didn't want to give him anything to obsess over.

Jason had no reason to be threatened. I was pretty sure Zayed thought I was an absolute moron. Maybe he would be civil toward me for a few days, but I could bet that he'd go back to his professional, cold demeanor fairly quickly. All of the dreaming and intimate thoughts about us were surely just on my part.

"You and Erica looked like there's something more than nothing," he prompted again. "And you weren't in the cafeteria at lunch. Were you in the library again? What's going on? You can talk to me, Mars."

I had already decided not to. No, there was nothing worth sharing about the previous night. It was a fluke. Something that would be forgotten by the end of that week. Whatever it was didn't affect Jason at all.

"I'm sorry I've been flaky about this. The blackout was pretty scary. I just needed some downtime. And sleep. I'll talk about it in therapy today." The words came bubbling out before I could stop them. I started to feel ambushed with all of these questions.

"I understand. But we're good?"

"Sure." I smiled.

"Perfect." He flicked my bangs off my forehead in a way that always made me feel like a five-year-old. "I need to head to gym. You remember we have Friday off, right? Can I claim you for the whole day? Maybe we can look at homecoming dresses and tuxes?"

I sighed, smoothing my bangs back onto my forehead. The invitation was in "boyfriend" territory. Just what I wanted.

"Okay, maybe," I found myself wanting to stay noncommittal. "And I will need to be done by four or so."

Jason raised an eyebrow.

"Lana needs me to do something that evening." I cut off the question before he asked.

"I'll take that as a yes for Friday then." Jason laughed and squeezed my hand before leaving.

It was not a *yes*.

Candace smiled in my direction once Jason was out of sight. "We heard you're going to homecoming with him. We should go jewelry shopping or do manicures," she said, gesturing toward my hands. I assumed this was her way of advancing a friendship.

I nodded politely and said, "Yeah, definitely." I knew she'd overheard every piece of that conversation and would quickly send out a message to her whole crew. The rumor mill surrounding my resurgence was going to drive that group crazy.

My smile quickly became disbelief as I clicked on the only new email message from the College Prep Institute.

Mars:
The light you shone for me led me not just out of darkness, but also to the promise of community in the city.
I was forced to lean on another person last night. Though you were a stranger to me, I felt as if you were able to see me beyond what anyone else has in the light. Like your father, you too are capable of heroism.
Thank you,
Zayed

But then maybe the blackout *wouldn't* be forgotten by the end of that week. I was suddenly very anxious for the next twenty-four hours to pass so I could see Zayed again.

"Mars, you should share something today." The flag was thrust into my hands by Ken, the thirteen-year-old kid next to me whose mother had died in the service years ago. He didn't talk much about her, focusing rather on his new stepmother and how much he loved her, as well as how he felt like he was betraying his mother's memory.

I had a hollow feeling in my throat every time he shared, a vague understanding resonating inside me that it was possible I was experiencing the same thing. Appreciating the good things in my life didn't mean I didn't miss my father or love him any less. This was one of those rare moments when I felt like I was actually connected with the five other people in the group. I liked the innocence and honestly Ken displayed and wished I could share such personal thoughts as well, but I didn't know how to start.

"What's something different that's happened to you lately?" Stephanie asked in her usual overbearing way. "Anything. You need to share something today." She was a skinny hipster type with voluminous brown hair and giant, fake eyelashes. I found her to be very "academic" about the meetings. She was collecting course credit for her psychology degree and acted like it. She certainly didn't act interested in making a real difference to any of us.

"Different? Good or bad different?" I asked, buying time.

Krish, the older, dark-haired girl across from me, the one with a face so beautiful it broke my heart, smiled sorrowfully at me as if saying she understood. She had lost her sister and father in the service, and the aftereffects had shattered her family. She cried often in these sessions.

Octavio, the quiet boy on her right who was the sole caretaker for his veteran father, glanced at me as well for a second, before shifting his glance back to his usual spot—Krish's face. He was clearly into her, but she was still too shrouded in grief to notice.

Erica gave me a little encouraging nudge.

Today I felt like I had something to say. I'd spent the entire afternoon even more restless than before.

I'd responded to Zayed's email with a casual:

> You're most welcome. Looking forward to seeing you tomorrow.
> —M

And then I hit REFRESH on my email six times in case he responded. He didn't, but that didn't stop me from rushing to the Media Center between all of my classes for the remainder of the day to recheck my email. No response had arrived.

By the end of the day, I was cursing myself for responding in such a stupid way. Why hadn't I thought of something profound? No wonder I was failing the SAT.

"Someone called me a hero," I finally said, glancing to my left and right. It felt strange to say it out loud. It felt a little conceited yet unbelievable all at once. "That's never happened before. It made me think of my father and how people call him that all the time. It made me start to realize why he serves."

I felt Erica predictably nudge me—hard. "More details please," she whispered. I was going to get it later for not telling her this in private.

I twirled the flag between my fingers. "I helped someone during a blackout. And he thought I was heroic," I said. I felt the rush of pride again, the same one I'd felt after I'd reread Zayed's email for the third time. For once, I wasn't the one who'd needed saving.

"That's awesome." Ken smiled in my direction, flicking the lighter he always seemed to carry with him. I was afraid he would set his spiky hair on fire. "Cool."

"It feels good to take care of someone else for once if you're not used to it." Octavio, the quiet Caretaker Guy acknowledged in his hushed way.

Angel, the guy who usually wept, and Krish both gave me encouraging smiles as if asking me to continue.

"I felt good." The words didn't do my current set of feelings justice, but I wasn't ready to share any more. I didn't understand why I glanced at the clock on the wall every thirty seconds, watching the hands move slower each time I looked.

I wanted to talk to Zayed again. Discover if I might actually have the opportunity to help him further to maintain my hero status a bit longer.

I passed the flag to Erica. Her older brother, Ricardo, had lost his legs in Iraq while trying to save local kids from a field of land mines. He was trying to adjust to life in a wheelchair. She always talked about how painful it was, watching him struggle when he'd always been the brave one in their house, the one she had always looked up to, and she was having a hard time letting go of that idea.

I waited for her usual gushing story of how well Ricardo was doing.

"Sometimes I'm so angry with him—" Erica practically spat out, surprising me with her vehemence today. "Why did he have to let himself get hurt like this? He just sits in his room all day. He has nightmares. Our family needed him; he was the first one of us to actually be smart and capable. And now." She paused, her voice wobbling. I grabbed her hand, shocked to see Erica like this.

"And now, it's all up to me. To figure out what I'll be doing in college. It won't be art anymore. That's too impractical. I need to figure out what I should be so my little sister has someone else to look up to. That's all." She practically threw the flag to Octavio.

No more art for Erica? I frowned. That was an extreme measure. Chad and I had no idea what we wanted to do in college, but Erica had always known. She'd known since third grade that she was going to be the next Mondrian.

I resisted the urge to tell her I would do anything to have my dad home, wheelchair or otherwise. At least she could see Ricardo. Talk to him. Hear his voice. When events and decisions in her life became overwhelming, he would be able to come through for her. Eventually, he would be able to get a job, support their aging parents, and be her brother again.

That was not what she wanted to hear right then, though. She wanted someone to say, "Poor Erica, you don't have to be strong for your family now. You have the right to be angry. Be angry, we're here to listen."

I would say all of those things to her. I would try to be a good friend to her, like she had been to me. I kept coming to therapy week after week because I would be accountable to her and her questions if I missed a single session.

"Erica, I understand your anger," Stephanie rested her chin in her right hand and tilted her head. The overly practiced move annoyed me. It was clear this woman had absolutely no idea what anyone else in the room was going through. "But you have to understand, Ricardo didn't want this injury for himself. He wanted to do the right thing. He never wanted to be a burden on your family."

I wanted to roll my eyes but didn't. Who *wanted* to be a burden on someone else, especially someone they loved?

In my case, it was almost the reverse. Because of the amount of time Dad had been gone, it felt like he didn't even want to come home anymore, like he felt we didn't need him. I knew it was because of his relationship with my mother, and maybe even because of the last conversation we'd had. I hoped he checked his voicemails sometime soon to see everything he'd missed out on and realized there was a lot going on at home that he really needed to be a part of.

I hadn't called Dad's cell phone for my daily check-in. I'd had so much else on my mind I hadn't even thought about it. The realization startled me. It was already happening. I was starting to forget not just his voice, but also to include him in my life. I couldn't let myself become one of them. Everyone else—my mother, people who pretended just because he wasn't here in town, in front of their eyes, he didn't exist anymore.

"The key to dealing with grief is closure," Stephanie said once the circle was complete. "You must get it before you can move on with your lives. You need to identify your MER."

MER. Damn her and her MER. The Minimal Effectiveness Response was the least a person needed to do to get closure. Like confronting someone who had caused them pain. Or burning a box of the ex-boyfriend's pictures. As if doing some sort of arbitrary, clichéd gesture would suddenly make everything okay again. As if that was going to be enough for the kids in the room to be able to let go of the experiences they had gone through.

This was why I hated therapy.

Ignoring my contemptuous look in her direction, Stephanie stood up. "Whatever your MER is, you need to do it. You need to keep doing it every day until your emotional situation is dealt with and you are the person you are meant to be."

Closure was supposed to be a finalization, to tie up all the loose ends in a nice lovely package, make some kind of sense out of what had happened. It seemed that whenever something bad happened, a clock started ticking. When will so-and-so have closure? When will they be done grieving?

The kids in therapy needed to take the time to journey through the five stages of grief to acceptance, no matter how long that time was. I wished the group leader would respect and encourage that, rather than trying to prove what an effective "teen grief therapist" she was by pushing six teenagers to a quick resolution and a check mark on her performance evaluation under "Has your therapy leader helped you deal with your grief?"

I knew I could do something about it, report her to the committee and ask for another therapist, someone who actually understood what we were going through. I also knew that would be hypocritical since I hardly ever paid attention. It was something I was doing to appease people, and I didn't need to get overly involved.

I was the first to leave the teen center, as usual. I knew Erica would be fine, I'd seen the "MINIPAX" license plate of Chad Winters's Mini Cooper under the glimmer of my headlights as I veered out of the parking lot. She wouldn't be alone tonight, but I would, just like every other night lately.

I went home and sat at the kitchen island without turning on the overhead lights, wanting to talk to someone. Despite her flaws, I missed having Lana at home waiting for me. We would giggle over funny things that had happened while we analyzed every word.

Instead, she was out with God-knew-who.

I eyed my cell phone, considering calling her, but given our last few conversations, or lack thereof, I didn't know how to start or even if she'd answer.

I could sit and feel sorry for myself, but my stomach growled, reminding me I'd had nothing but a cup of coffee during lunch. My lack of appetite seemed to be getting worse, and all of my pants were now starting to hang loosely on my hips.

I heated up a skillet and let a pat of butter melt on it. I spread almond butter on one slice of leftover brioche and raspberry preserves on another and created Dad's gourmet PB&J. I neatly cut the corners off and toasted both sides in a hot buttered pan for a few minutes, topping them with a sprinkle of sea salt. I sliced the sandwich in half before eating a few bites, sitting alone in the darkened kitchen.

The taste of the creamy almonds and sweet relish of raspberry bits surrounded by hot flaky bread transformed the kitchen into a warmer, lighter place, something it had been years ago when I used to eat PB&Js with my father and Lana.

Those days were gone. Things were never going to be as they had been. When Dad came home, he and Lana would divorce, and I would be at college. The three of us would never be a family again. Even thinking that far ahead was too tender a thing for me at that very lonely moment.

I knew it would be one of those nights when I would wish morning would just come so thoughts wouldn't keep swirling around and around in my head while I tried to sleep. The pride at my heroics, the realization that I was starting to understand why Dad was away in another country, and then the devastating, crippling sadness that came with thinking of him.

I reached for Lana's pink laptop, giving myself permission to check email one last time, expecting no response from Zayed, but just in case. As soon as I saw the new message, I knew a night of strange dreams awaited me.

> Mars:
> Will you care to join me for tea after class tomorrow? I'd like to talk further about your practice essay. Please do not change existing plans if you have them; we will talk another time in that case.
> Zayed

CHAPTER 5

The Tea

I was nervous about seeing Zayed again. It was silly. I had no idea why I should be nervous. After all, *I* was the hero. He was the one who'd taken the first step and sent me a "thank you" note and set up our tea appointment. I resisted calling it a date. It was not a date. He was going to talk to me about my essay. I was going to listen and take notes and hope to improve. This was business.

I changed my outfit before going to the U. Three times. What did one wear to "tea"? And especially in the evening. Finally, I settled on a taupe-colored skirt, black riding boots, a white sweater, and a burgundy scarf with a floral motif.

Conservative, professional, but still pretty, I told myself as I pinned the scarf in place around my neck, trying to make it look as casually draped as possible.

I watched Zayed all through class on Wednesday evening. He gave me a friendly smile and wave when I came in, but as usual, he was busy talking to students. He looked relaxed. Normal. Freshly showered with his hair still damp. No signs of the distress from Monday.

I folded and refolded my hands awkwardly at my desk, not knowing where to look as Zayed lectured about making an essay argument that was based on personal experiences. I didn't want it to seem like I was staring at him. Every time I glanced his way, he was certainly staring at me. I blushed every time, remembering my dream about kissing him in my bedroom. Finally I resorted to staring at the blank whiteboard behind him.

I wondered who else he was meeting for "tea" to discuss essay writing with. I'd been surprised when I received my practice exam back, scored with a seven out of twelve. It was actually higher than I'd expected, so that gave me some hope that our tea appointment wasn't going to be all about my failings at essay writing. Maybe we'd even get a chance to chat, and under the most extreme circumstances, we could finish some of the conversations we'd started during the blackout.

Once class ended, I took five minutes packing my two items, a study guide and a pen. I then stood admiring the metallic art hanging in the back of the classroom while waiting for the last student to leave. A girl, one who always sat in the front and asked lots of questions, was standing at Zayed's desk, showing him something in a catalog.

I was secretly glad for the delay. I was starting to experience a mild fear that conversation today with Zayed would be awkward. In my mind, we were the people from the roof. In his mind, we might just be teacher-student again. The night on the roof had been extraordinary due to extraordinary circumstances. I had no right to expect the same sparkle again.

I would lower my expectations, I vowed. If I was able to get some help with my essay, I would consider the evening a success. He was, after all, my teacher and nothing more.

The active fluttering in my chest told me otherwise.

The blond girl was starting to annoy me more with every passing mile-a-minute word. "I, like, really need to do well. I really, like, want to go to this one college, and I need kind of a high score. Do you think we could maybe, like, get together sometime . . ."

No, you cannot get together with him.

I frowned. There was that possessiveness toward Zayed again, something I had felt since the first time I saw him. I didn't like it, but it was there.

Every time I turned back, Zayed was smiling patiently at the girl and nodding. It was his polite smile, not the one showing his dimples I'd seen for an instant that night on the roof. After five minutes of this, I decided I was going to rescue him from his persistent admirer.

I strode to the front of the room and slid into place behind Zayed's chair. "Excuse me. Hi."

The girl tucked a lock of her thin blond hair behind her ear and stared at me with a "who the hell are you" look.

"Mr. Anwar has a conflict right now, so if you could please schedule an appointment with the receptionist downstairs, that would work wonderfully. Is there anything else I can help you with?"

She glanced at Zayed, who glanced at me, as if asking me to continue.

"Uh, no. I was almost done here anyway. Thanks." She retreated from the room, still looking baffled by the whole conversation.

"Very effective, Miss Alexander." Zayed was laughing even before we heard her heels clattering down the stairs. "I see you're someone who does not appreciate being kept waiting. You look lovely in white," he said, lightly touching my shoulder. "If you don't mind me saying."

Oh boy.

I blushed, not minding anything he was saying. It was quite amazing how different and expressive his face was when he wasn't trying to maintain his frosty, professional façade. The mesmerizing gray of his eyes continued to draw me in, time and again.

"Do you frequent the tea house in Wallingford?" he asked as he swung his seemingly heavy messenger bag easily over his head.

"I've never even heard of it." Nor had I ever actually heard anyone use the word "frequent" as a verb before in real life.

"Will you allow me to introduce you to it then? We're taking the bus." He started to lead the way toward the staircase. I eyed the flight going up. First the roof and now a bus. I had enjoyed the first adventure I'd experienced with Zayed, but public transportation was a bit of a stretch.

"I have my car. I can drive us." I jangled my keys.

"You'll like the bus. Please?" He held out his hand for mine.

Without thinking, I took it.

The west end of the University District whirred by outside bus number thirty-one as we made the ten-minute commute into Wallingford. The lights from the various Thai restaurants, independent coffee shops, and kitschy boutiques seemed inviting and mysterious all at once.

"Now tell me, why the bus?" I asked as we passed a donut house, a lamp store, and a movie theater. We sat facing each other, both openly staring at each other. I almost felt as if we were in a scene from a movie.

"Being around people who are different than me. To get to know the culture. It's interesting, don't you think?" He gestured toward the rear of the bus with a tangerine that had magically appeared in his hands.

A few students dozing. A couple anxiously expressing their loving feelings toward each other. A blind man and his seeing-eye dog. This was a Seattle I didn't experience every day, I had to admit.

"This is a topic I'm doing a paper on for my cultural anthropology class. Public transportation through the cultures and how it affects society." He peeled the skin of the tangerine off in one easy piece and broke off a slice of fruit, which he passed to me.

"You're a student at the U?" I asked in surprise, taking the orange sliver. He hadn't mentioned it even once, and I'd automatically assumed he taught SAT prep full-time. "What's your major? How long have you attended?"

"Near Eastern Languages and Civilization. This is my first year, though I already realize I would like to teach full-time and am thinking of pursuing a master's degree."

That meant he was only a year older than me. He seemed so much *worldlier* than me, so much more knowledgeable.

"What kind of course work do you have? Are you finding it challenging to study and teach at once?" I accepted another piece of tangerine, enjoying the eruption of sweetness.

"Islamic studies, which I know a lot about. But also history and anthropology classes that are completely new for me. I enjoy learning, though. Always." Zayed produced another tangerine from his messenger bag and began to peel that one open as well.

"Me too," I said automatically, although that was not completely true. "Why do you have a book on kittens?" I asked without thinking too much about it.

He looked taken aback.

"It was in your bag. I saw it that night . . . on the roof."

"Oh." He smiled, his face relaxing into that expression I loved seeing. "I have attracted a stray kitten. She followed me to my flat one afternoon, and I brought her inside to give her a dish of milk. She won't leave now."

I laughed at the perplexed expression on his face. "That's so sweet; she's adopted you. Have you named her?"

"Do you think Coconut is a silly name? She's brown and white."

"No, I think that's cute. You can call her Coco for short."

"Coco. Oh, this is our stop." He pulled on the signal cord and reached out for my hand.

It felt completely natural to take his hand and follow him off the bus. A week ago, I wouldn't have been able to imagine holding anyone's hand but Jason's, yet this felt . . . fine. Normal. *Fitting.*

I watched him as he looked right, then left, and set off left. He was one of the few guys I'd ever known who was able to wear a fringed scarf over his black military jacket and make it look effortless.

"I've driven through here to go to Fremont, but never really walked around," I said. Even at the late hour, the neighborhood was still alive with students and locals alike, leaving restaurants in groups and carrying bags of groceries. Several people strolled by with elaborate ice cream cones.

"It's a nice area. I walk over from the U sometimes. But I noticed your shoes have a high heel, and also, it's rather dark out."

I glanced down at my feet. I hadn't realized he was observing me so closely, but then again, I clearly remembered that first day he and I had seen each other. How quickly he'd seemed to memorize my whole face. It was a talent. I touched my cheek, self-conscious about the scar. I wondered if he'd noticed that as well.

"Here we are." Zayed touched my elbow outside a relatively nondescript storefront with a sign above the door that read TEA HOUSE KUAN YIN on a board shaped like a teapot. A NO CELL PHONES ALLOWED sign was featured prominently in the window. The inside of the shop was painted a well-worn yellow but was also brightly lit and welcoming. Clusters of tables and armchairs were arranged as if to encourage conversation. Tables populated with laptops and books created the perfect environment for homework or Web browsing. The scent in the air was something I'd never experienced before. Spicy, sweet, but also nutty.

"It's lovely, isn't it? The aroma?" Zayed asked as we made our way to the rear of the store to place our orders.

"What is it?"

"It's qahwa, pink chai from Kashmir in India."

"Really?"

"No, I made that up, actually. It might be from Iran. But it is pink."

I smiled. "Wherever it's from, it smells amazing."

I took note of the bins full of—I assumed—tea leaves. The selection was unlike any Starbucks I'd ever seen.

"Would you care to share a pot of it?"

I was too busy sorting through the merchandise on the sale rack to answer. Teapots from all over the world. Heavy-looking cast-iron ones with matching warmers. Tiny bone china sets of cups and saucers. The colors and textures were dizzying. I had no idea there was such a culture of tea drinking in Seattle.

Zayed led me to a group of two comfortable-looking tattered armchairs and a low-slung table between them. "Why don't you get settled and I'll arrange for the tea?"

Arrange for the tea. It sounded fancy. And it was. He returned with a large white pot and two delicate teacups and saucers. A square sandwich and a plate of cookies accompanied the tea.

The rolled-up sleeves of his fitted white cotton shirt revealed defined forearms and a beautiful silver watch on his left wrist. He managed to look both elegant and boyish as he set the tray down in front of me.

There was a sparkle in his brilliant gray eyes as he knelt in front of me and the coffee table. I forgot what I'd been thinking as his shoulder purposefully brushed up against my knee. He stared at me, and I felt that stare even more intensely than his physical touch.

I didn't understand why being near him affected me this way. Or why being near me seemed to be having quite the same effect on him. I could tell by the slight flush in his cheeks and his quickened breathing. It hadn't been this way on the roof. Suddenly we both seemed to be incredibly aware of each other's physical presence.

Who knew, maybe he'd had a suggestive dream about me as well.

I could wish, anyway.

I watched him pour the tea ceremoniously into my cup. Not a single drop of the creamy pink liquid spilt. I loved watching his curly eyelashes net over his eyes as he focused on the task. I loved those eyelashes; they were like tiny, silk bird wings when contrasted with the creaminess of his golden skin.

These observances and the reactions I was having to them were disturbing at best and, most likely, inappropriate. This was my instructor. It was probably against the rules for him to fraternize with a student. And then there was Jason, who I was sure would not approve of this evening.

Zayed seemed to be in no hurry to put distance between us as he pulled his chair right up to mine, our knees touching.

"There are some talented poets on the shelf. I come here to read sometimes." Zayed gestured toward the bookshelf on my right as he rested his hand on my wrist.

Wow.

I couldn't help it. "You're quite the poet yourself, Zayed. I liked your email. The 'thank you' one."

He looked embarrassed, but pleased. I loved when he looked so happy.

"My strong feelings toward what you did for me made the words form more easily than usual. I'm an amateur poet at best," he admitted as he added a spoonful of sugar to his tea.

His feelings toward me?

I swallowed, not knowing how to inquire more about these feelings. "Do you have a collection? Of poetry I mean?"

Zayed laughed. "Only in my head."

"You should write them down. Like Watkins."

"As I should do many things." He suddenly stopped smiling. Before I could ask about it, he took a sip of his tea and, seeming satisfied, set the cup down and removed his hand from my wrist. "Will you try yours and tell me what you think?"

I let the milky taste linger on my tongue. "This is very good. What's in it? Black tea and milk?"

"Green tea, actually."

"Really?" I tilted the cup, watching the thick pink liquid swish around and lace the sides of the porcelain. "It's so creamy. So good."

"Yes. Green tea leaves are boiled with baking soda, pistachios and star anise for over an hour. That's what the internet said anyway."

I smiled. Hearing him say "internet" with that accent was funny.

"How does it become pink?" I was staring into the cup when I felt Zayed's hands cover mine and lower the cup to the tray.

"A chemical reaction."

A chemical reaction. Yes, we definitely had that. No matter how I tried to convince myself of it, we were not just two people who happened to be at the same place at the same time enjoying each other's company. Whenever we touched there was a spark. And then there was the velvety texture of his skin and how I wanted to feel it again, in many places, after he released my hands. There was something happening here, something out of stories and movies that I had never experienced before.

Usually I would be very conscious of people around us observing our hand touches and gazes at each other. At that moment, I didn't give a damn if the entire Lakeville High senior class was in the tea shop with us.

I felt as if I was melting into the leather armchair as I savored the hot tea. When I opened my eyes again, I wanted Zayed to still be sitting across from me, watching me in a way no one else had ever watched me. Like I was the most fascinating creature in the world and he couldn't get enough.

"Tell me what Paris is like this time of year," I asked, playing the part of instructor, letting my eyes fall closed again. The previous night had been restless. I couldn't stop thinking about this date and had barely been able to close my eyes out of excitement and nerves. The warmth of the air in the tea house combined with the monotonous din of the atmosphere lured me to a warm, safe place where I could finally close my eyes.

"What would you like to know?" Hearing a snap, I pried open an eye and saw him breaking a shortbread cookie, leaving half for me. He was still watching me.

"Anything. Your favorite thing."

"The architecture is magical." He rested his cheek in his palm, gazing at me, yet through me. "Every building was created as if it may have been the last building that would ever be built again. Each one special, pulsating with a personality of its own. In autumn, the streets are like photographs. The gargoyles watch the residents go about their lives, guarding them. It's lovely and thrilling at once, the city. Have you been there?"

"I have, but I didn't see it like you have. Not with your *vie en rose*. How long did you live there?"

"Not long enough."

I waited for more, but I didn't get it.

"I think we should talk about your essay," he finally said. "Or I might keep you here all night."

A tingle at the base of my neck assured me that I would enjoy that.

"Your essay had quite a heart. I wish the follow-through had a body. I think the primary issue you're having is lack of conviction."

I made a show of chewing my half cookie, a burst of lavender exploding in my mouth. I had no idea what he was talking about.

"The question was 'Do memories hinder or help people in their effort to learn from the past and succeed in the present?' You were to plan and write an essay in which you develop your point of view on this issue."

"People have to keep their memories in mind so they don't make the same mistakes again." I recalled having written that sentence, which I repeated.

"Which is a fine point of view, but your examples weren't supporting your argument. For example, you talk about beating cancer and how if someone can overcome cancer once, they can do it again if they keep the memory of how strong they were the first time."

I nodded. "So?"

"This example felt impersonal. You didn't have any personal anecdotes in the essay. Is cancer or cancer survivors something you have experience with?"

"Not really."

"Why did you choose it?"

"Because," I replied indignantly; the writing hadn't been *that* bad.

Zayed seemed to sense my mood changing. He picked up his teacup again and stopped talking. Watching me again.

"What?"

"You're a fighter."

"I am not!"

"You're fighting right now! I don't mean in a bad way. I mean you are a survivor. You don't back down easily."

I set my lips. "I guess not."

"I like that."

"Oh." I shifted back into my chair. "Thanks."

"You should write about something that has personal meaning to you, Mars. Not only will the writing feel more genuine, but you will more easily be able to understand the arguments on the opposing side and use preemptive rebuttals to support your argument."

I stared at Zayed. The truth was, I didn't understand his thought process or what I was supposed to be getting from this discussion, and that scared me. As a senior at one of the best high schools in Washington state, I was expected to be able to carry on conversations with anyone from anywhere in the world about topics ranging from pop culture to philosophy. Yet, here I sat, distractedly watching a woman trying to squeeze herself behind my armchair, holding a power cord for a laptop.

"What would an example of what you're saying be?" I tried my standard question for when I didn't know the answer in class.

"In the second paragraph, you talk about how countries that have been ravaged in war need to move forward and appreciate what is being done for them. *This* is much more personal. But did you see how the point of view changed and how you no longer support your premise? Now you're saying they shouldn't remember the past."

"What I meant was that people in these countries need to keep the memories of what happened to them in mind, but they should also re-member the people who helped them."

"People like your father, you mean."

"Yes," I answered quickly. I had already talked more about Dad to Zayed than I'd planned to, but somehow every conversation came back to him.

"This is why this argument is more genuine, because this is some-thing that's more real to you. What are other examples from real life where you believe past experiences play a key role?"

"My therapy group," I finally blurted out.

"Will you tell me about that?" Zayed poured more tea into his cup and refilled mine, touching my hand for much longer than needed. It was as if he knew what had been going through my head and also how unwilling I was to let him know what it was. I was reluctant to talk about therapy with Zayed; I didn't want him to think there was something wrong with me.

"Please go on, Mars," he asked gently as I continued to hesitate. "I won't make fun anymore. I'm very sorry if I've offended you."

I smiled at him as he squeezed my hand. This time we left our fin-gers intertwined.

"The leader of our therapy group isn't someone who's had a

tragedy to deal with, at least recently," I said, willing to let him in a little bit. "She isn't someone who can understand what the rest of the people in the group are experiencing, so she's not as efficient. She doesn't know what to say and sometimes she can come off as very insensitive."

"And the lesson to be learned?"

"We need a leader who can relate to these experiences of sadness, loss, and grief. It has to be someone who has memories of those emotions and can understand that people take different amounts of time to heal." I took a deep breath. These were all concepts I'd learned about in psychology and had found fascinating. "The leader who has been through something similar is going to be able to give people the time they need. They are going to be able to understand that even if someone knows they need to move on, it doesn't mean they can just do it. Acceptance isn't one step."

"It sounds like you'd make quite a fine therapy leader. Have you considered volunteering for the position?"

"What? No."

"You seem to have the experience. You definitely have the desire."

"That's crazy. I don't have the experience. Why do you say that?"

"Because you understand what those other teenagers are going through. Because you feel a deep empathy for them. Because you seem to passionately care about this subject," he said. "Have you enquired about filling the role in your group? This might be a good way for you to get hands-on experience with psychology and therapy in case you're considering pursuing it as a career in college."

Zayed was reading way too much into my desire to make our therapy sessions more productive and useful. It did not mean I was about to make a commitment to studying something as terrible as grief for a career.

"Mars?"

I didn't like the way he was looking at me anymore. Like he was not going to back down. And I didn't like the way he seemed to know exactly what my thoughts had been at the last therapy session. Those gray eyes knew entirely too much about me already.

"Can we get back to the essay?" I asked.

"You're not comfortable talking to me about this. I understand. I apologize for overstepping."

"No, it's not that." I couldn't help but protest, even though I knew I sounded incredibly immature. "I do need your help with the essay though."

Zayed must have sensed me shutting down and paused to cut the tomato, basil, and olive focaccia sandwich in half. "I'm enjoying this night. This is the most fun I've had in months."

I blushed again.

We chewed for a few minutes.

"When will he come home to you? Your father," Zayed asked finally.

"I don't know. He was supposed to be back a month or so ago." I almost snapped. I hadn't meant for my tone to be so harsh, but I asked myself that same question every day and came up with the exact same answer. I was more than ready for a definitive answer and was sick of no one being able to give me one.

"Do you have an idea of why he isn't back?"

That was the question of the year, wasn't it? Where was he, and why wasn't he back?

"He always said that he would stay there until his infantry had completed their mission. He wasn't going to leave the civilians with no protection." I recalled one of our controversial dinnertime conversations. Lana had insisted that going above and beyond for the Afghanis was not part of his job. Dad had insisted that it was the heart of his job. I had just wanted the fight to end.

"That could be a long time. Until the civilians are safe, I mean. The country is very unstable, and insurgents rise all the time. It's very hard to quiet every insurgent group, or even to know who or where they are."

"How would you know?" I asked, knowing I sounded snarky. It wasn't as if Zayed had been in the line of war while living cozily in Paris.

"Have you tried to contact him? Or has he contacted you?" Zayed pressed on, ignoring my question.

I shrugged, hating the look Zayed was giving me. A *you're-keeping-something-from-me* look. As if he was one to judge, with all of his cryptic rooftop talk of blackouts.

"This sandwich is pretty good. Not as good as my PB&J, though," I changed the subject on my own, ready to drop the topic.

"What is a Pee-Bee and Jay?" Zayed asked, having a final bite of his sandwich.

"You've never had a peanut-butter and jelly sandwich?" I set my half sandwich down and dusted off my hands.

"What an odd combination. I don't believe I've had peanut butter in anything."

"You're missing out." I smiled, realizing what I was about to do. "How about I bring you one on our next date?"

"Does that mean this one has to end?" His face broke into a smile. Those dimples. They would be my undoing.

I felt that familiar fire from my dreams start to spread through my belly again.

I had a thought. "Do you have plans for Friday?"

I felt a little giddy as I drove home that night and parked in the darkened garage. The evening had been very different than I'd expected. I didn't understand why I felt so comfortable around Zayed. On one hand, I was not someone who opened up to new people quickly, and yet with him, I was talking about my most personal thoughts. My father, my therapy, Lana, the uncertainty around it all. We'd argued, we'd debated, and we'd laughed. I loved every moment of it and wanted to see him again. I wanted to see him tomorrow. I could tell he wanted the same by the way he'd lingered next to my car instead of saying good-bye right away. At one point, he touched my chin, and I thought he was about to kiss me.

He didn't, but in my mind we were past that point already.

I wanted to make him laugh with my stories. I loved hearing him laugh. I didn't understand what was happening or why. I barely knew this guy, but I was already planning what I would bring other than PB&Js for the plans we'd made to spend more time together on Friday. I hadn't realized I was smiling, but when I entered the house and saw someone kissing Lana in the kitchen, that smile disappeared.

CHAPTER 6

The Choice

"His name is Vivek. Vivek Joseph. What kind of name is that? I think Lana's a little old to date a 'Vivek.'"

Erica didn't answer as she brushed at her canvas with another stroke of paint. I still had no idea what she was painting. Distinct giant red brushstrokes covered the black canvas in straight diagonal lines. I assumed she knew what she was doing as she was an artist by profession. Several of her paintings hung in galleries in Kirkland downtown as a way to earn extra money for her family.

I'd skipped school. Convinced Erica to do the same. We were holed up in her bedroom, me venting, her painting. At some point, we'd both called the attendance office at school pretending to be the other's mother and pledging "the time of month" as the reason for our respective absences. Usually we did this at my place and had Lana call in for both of us, but given my fight with her last night, I had a feeling she wouldn't be feeling too generous today.

"Are you angry about his age, or that he exists in Lana's life?"

"Both. Can't I be angry about both?"

"You can be angry about anything you want to. At least you're actually showing it for once. The therapy group will be impressed."

"Don't share this with them, please," I warned her. I was not ready to discuss this with anyone but my closest friend.

"Here. You finish." She shoved the paintbrush in my hand.

"What do you mean? I don't want to ruin the painting."

"Mars. It's a bunch of lines. Do what you want!"

"What the hell is she thinking? Doesn't she know this makes her look ridiculous?" I practically stabbed an angry red line onto the canvas. I watched the thick paint form raised ridges as it dried within seconds. This *was* actually somewhat therapeutic.

"It makes our family look stupid. My dad's off fighting in some never-ending war. He doesn't call. He doesn't come home. And now Lana's dating some twenty-five-year-old!"

"He's really twenty-five?" Erica asked from her dressing table, where she sat arranging her hair into an elaborate updo, her pink highlights effervescent and glittering under the dim black light that rained down the walls of the bedroom.

I nodded. "And he's rich. Like, owns-his-own-plane rich."

"Trust-fund brat?"

."Ugh, that's the problem. No. He created a start-up in college, which got bought out for almost a billion dollars by some company. He just consults with local companies now. That's only when he's not traveling or having fun!"

"So his name is Vivek, he's hardworking, seems to like Lana—"

"I have no idea why. She's like twice his age." I created a swirl of red in the center of the canvas. It almost looked like an exploding rose at that point. The Briar Rose unleashed.

"More like fifteen years older. And she's gorgeous, may I remind you."

I glared at Erica as I took another swipe at the canvas.

"This isn't funny."

"Do you even know anything about him? Or do you hate him on principle?"

"On principle, and if you loved me, you would hate him too."

"I'll hate anyone for you, Mars." Erica grinned.

"Thank you. Now stop smiling like that!" I snarled. I knew I was acting like a brat, and this whole thing had been fairly predictable. As soon as Lana started looking for eligible bachelors, I knew she would end up with someone almost immediately.

Men fell in love with her vulnerability, charm, and incredibly beautiful eyes, just like the first time she had met my father at a war rally. He'd asked her to marry him within a week.

That was supposed to be forever. I didn't understand how she could have someone at the house she shared with my father so quickly.

"How long have they been going out?"

"They met on that Matchmaker site, and last night was their fifth date! Can you imagine? Five dates in like two weeks!"

The fact that neither of them had real jobs and could spend days and nights together didn't hurt things, I supposed. I could only hope that the free time would expedite their relationship and they could move onto the fighting and breakup stage quicker.

"Did he come over just to meet you last night?"

I'd stood frozen in the kitchen for almost a minute before Vivek saw me and pulled away from Lana to greet me. He was good-looking in a somewhat classic, soap-commercial way. He looked ridiculously young in a graphic t-shirt and slim jeans with a hole in the knee. He looked like he could easily still be in college.

He was polite even as I gave him the icy treatment, responding to my questions with an easygoing smile. He promised to come by and make breakfast for us soon, suggesting he was a good cook and that our kitchen could use some "breaking in." It was my father's kitchen; it didn't need anything from him, I'd wanted to say but had turned on my heel and retreated upstairs instead.

"Apparently, Lana told him I would 'love' him, and he had to meet me. I talked to him for maybe five minutes."

"Is she going to keep seeing him?"

"Of course she is," I said, rolling my eyes. "I think she loves that I disapprove of him. Now, it really can be just like the first time, when my grandparents hated my dad."

"You think she just wants to relive her youth?"

"Yes! Except, he's a child. *And.* And get this: his family is from India. He's one of those first-generation success stories. I wonder how excited his parents are going to be when they hear about his forty-year-old girlfriend who isn't divorced from her husband *and* who has a teenage kid!"

I huffed a breath. Lana had tried to talk to me after Vivek had left about how they were taking things slowly. Apparently, the only reason he was at our house was to meet me. She said I should try and get to know him rather than immediately despise the idea of him. She assured me things were not serious between them and I had no reason to overreact.

I gave her a week until he proposed to her and she accepted. I wondered how she would send divorce papers to Afghanistan. I doubted there was a fax machine ready at my father's campsite.

The argument had totally ruined the wonderful evening I'd had with Zayed. Something bad always happened after I saw Zayed. Every. Single. Time. I was not a believer in signs, like my father was, but even I had to admit something wasn't right. I couldn't quite zone in on what it was, but I knew it was there. Last night, I'd half been hoping Lana would be home so I could talk to her about Zayed. I had a feeling those days really were gone.

I sighed angrily.

"It's good you're handling this in a typical way with a hissy fit. Not keeping everything bottled up." Erica swung back out of her chair and joined me at the canvas to look at my handiwork. "This looks pretty good. Very abstract."

With the exception of a jagged black border, the entire canvas was a zigzag of sharp red lines and the blooming rose.

"It looks crazy."

"It reflects your emotions. And has really good texture. I want you to take it with you."

I handed her the brush and flopped down on her bed. "You sure your mom won't be furious when she finds out we're here?"

"Nah." Erica deposited all the paintbrushes into a jar with some sort of solution. "She's been so busy working her two jobs and worrying about Ricardo, she doesn't care what I do."

At least Erica's mother was worried about her family, rather than herself, I wanted to say, but refrained. With Erica, I knew I could vent and be as self-centered as I wanted, and she seemed to enjoy it, but I was slowly starting to realize that she was keeping a lot in. I wanted to give her the opportunity to share some of her angst as well.

"At least tomorrow will make you feel better," Erica said.

"Yes." I didn't let any expression show on my face. I had no idea how Erica knew about my plans with Zayed. Had I told her? I didn't recall having done so, but I'd arrived at her doorstep ranting and raving that morning, and who knew what I'd said.

"What are you and Jason going to do? Leave town or stick around?"

Jason. I'd completely forgotten about our conversation in the Media Center.

"Wow, I don't even know."

"Can we assume you guys are officially 'back together'?"

"You know, I, again, don't know," I finally said. "We haven't talked about it." Actually we had talked about it, and I had given him all the signs that that was what I wanted.

After last night though, I wasn't sure where we stood anymore. Where *I* stood.

"He told me you guys are going to homecoming together. Do you have a dress yet?"

I shook my head. I hadn't really accepted his invitation and found it presumptuous of him to be talking about it with my friends.

"You're so lucky. I'll never get to go to homecoming or prom or anything. Chad hates doing anything mainstream. No fancy gown or cool hairdo for me. Ever." She sighed, touching her hair, still in a formal-looking updo, sounding truly envious.

I wanted to tell her it wasn't all fairy-tale castles and magic, that school dances were usually just a reason for the so-called princesses to gather and gossip about who was wearing a recycled gown and who had disappeared behind the bleachers of the gym with the most popular prince in school.

"You could go alone. Or you can just come with me and Jason if you want to see it for yourself," I offered half-heartedly. I didn't feel much excitement about going at all and knew she would be disappointed after experiencing it for herself.

"Yes, that's just what I want. To be the third wheel on your rekindled relationship!"

Rekindled relationship, I wasn't so sure of that. As much as everyone thought Jason and I were perfect together, I wanted the option to make that choice on my own. And right now, I was too torn about my feelings for Zayed to make that choice.

I spent the rest of the afternoon watching Erica paint a smaller canvas and then start on a mural of a forest on her bedroom wall. Each scene she painted was more beautiful and abstract than the last. I watched her create something that she would have forever and wondered what I was doing with *my* time.

Erica had always had a plan, despite her latest announcement that she was giving up art to pursue something more "practical." She'd always said she would go to art school and also study history so she could support herself and her family by working at a museum or gallery while she tried to make a name for herself in the art world.

I had no such plan. I couldn't see beyond scoring high on the SAT and getting into the U. What I would major in or what a potential career would look like was something only Zayed had ever mentioned.

It was funny; he was the only one to actually treat me like a real person. Ever. He seemed to actually respect my wishes and what *I* wanted.

It was becoming increasingly hard to keep reminding myself that yes, he was smart, funny, and ridiculously good-looking, but he was also a stranger. I didn't know anything about him, really.

I almost started to tell Erica about Zayed several times but, for some reason, felt like his and my conversations were sacred. Like I would be betraying him by talking about the way he saw Paris or his views on learning from the past. It was just between us. The whole thing sounded ridiculous to try to recollect anyway.

As I was leaving Erica's house, I spotted someone sitting in the living room just staring out the window. I peeked outside to see what Ricardo was looking at. A mail truck. Someone mowing a lawn.

"How's it going?" I asked, knowing I wouldn't get a response.

He didn't even blink, just continued staring blankly outside.

I used to have an intense crush on him before he'd gone off to the Middle East. I'd never told Erica that because I knew she'd insist on telling him.

I sat next to Ricardo for another few minutes, saying inane things to him, hoping maybe he'd respond to my presence. I wondered if somewhere my father was in a similar state. Wondering if this was the reason for his long absence without any communication.

"Bye, Ricardo," I finally said, glancing back at him once. He was almost unrecognizable from the guy who'd left home a year ago. I wondered if that guy who used to wink at me as he whizzed by on his motorcycle was still in there somewhere.

A feeling of déjà vu overcame me when I walked into my house that evening, carrying a bag of groceries from the Natural Market. Vivek Joseph was again standing in my kitchen. This time, he was eating a piña colada yogurt. He paused in mid-scoop when he saw the look of surprise on my face.

What, did he live here now?

I stepped around him and yanked open the refrigerator door.

"Lana's getting ready," he preempted before I could open my mouth. "I'm just waiting for her."

I gave him a look that said *does it look like I asked* as I started to unload groceries.

"We're going to dinner at Columbia Tower. Do you want to join us? I can change the reservation."

"No," I said shortly as I pulled out a freshly baked loaf of French bread from my reusable grocery bag and placed it on the counter. A jar of raspberry preserves and organic peanut butter went into the refrigerator.

"What are you planning to make?"

"Leg of lamb. What does it look like?" I gave him another Look. For being a genius, he wasn't very smart.

"How was school?"

I ignored him.

"Hey, do you guys have a computer science class? You should try to take that next semester if you can."

I continued to ignore him.

"No, seriously. Just friendly advice that'll help you in whatever field you choose to go into."

"Nerd," I muttered under my breath.

"Hell, yeah, I am." He'd heard me. "So, what's your favorite class?"

"Auto shop." I couldn't stay quiet anymore.

He smiled.

"Hey, listen, Mars. Why don't we go out sometime and talk. Just the two of us."

That was enough.

"Why? It's not like you're going to be around after next week. You know Lana's dating like five other guys right now, huh? One of them is a neurosurgeon."

I didn't know any of that to be true, but he didn't need to know that.

I thought I would see some anger, at least some indignation on his face. Instead he laughed. "You remind me of me."

"That's because we're like the same age," I practically snarled.

He laughed harder, infuriating me more.

"Mars, you should absolutely join us. I really want to get to know you better. Your mother said you're brilliant, unquestionably so."

I hated, hated, hated that he thought he knew me. I felt my cheeks start to burn angrily.

"While I'm sure you appreciate the 'perfect family' picture Lana's trying to sell you, you should probably ask her about her husband. You know, the one who's off in Afghanistan? The one who could come home any given Friday?"

He stopped laughing. "Your mom told me you were having a hard time with what's happened."

What's happened?

"Do not talk about me behind my back. Listen, you ass—" I started to use some choice words.

"Mars, good you're here." Lana clattered down the stairs in her favorite silver heels, her dark hair bouncy and full. "You'll join us for dinner, right? The view from the tower is amazing. Especially on a night like tonight. And you'll love the chocolate soufflé."

"I have plans with Jason," I lied haughtily, turning my back to them as I headed back to the garage. "I'm late."

"Let's talk tonight," Lana called after me.

Or not.

I'd had been half hoping Jason wouldn't be home, but his father waved me toward his room after their housekeeper let me in.

I sat at the edge of his bed and watched him scroll through his music collection on his computer.

"I need to cancel for tomorrow," I said finally.

"Really, why?" Jason frowned, looking confused and even a little annoyed. His cornflower-blue eyes were almost midnight-colored in the evening light, exactly matching the ratted hoodie he always wore at home.

I don't need to explain myself to you, I wanted to say.

"I have a bunch of essay work to do. My instructor is willing to spend some time with me tomorrow. How often do we get a day off, right?" I laughed nervously. *Technically*, it was true. Zayed and I would talk about my writing at least at some point.

"I was hoping to do a road trip, maybe Chuckanut Drive, up to Bellingham? We could pick apples and eat pie at Rosabella's Garden."

"Oh, that does sound nice." I suddenly felt a twinge of guilt. I wasn't lying to Jason, but not telling him the whole truth. I was leading him on, but I still didn't understand my relationship with Zayed and was not willing to let go of everything I'd built with Jason. Yet. It was cowardly of me; I wasn't in denial about that.

I also knew that meeting Zayed had very little to do with my essay anymore. And I believed that he knew that too. Why we were meeting and why I was so excited for it was something I looked forward to finding out. And I hoped he did as well. All I knew is that I had that same fluttery feeling in my stomach thinking of meeting him on the corner of 45th and University Avenue tomorrow morning. I had no idea what I would wear. Something white definitely.

"How about I meet with Zayed and try to get done quickly. I'll come to your place and we can head out around maybe noon or so?" I attempted a compromise and surprised myself with another twinge, this time of disappointment that I had already restricted the amount of time I would be able to spend with Zayed.

"That sounds better, but I still don't like it. Finish up with *Zayed* soon, okay?"

And I didn't like his tone. I didn't like the way he said Zayed's name. He wasn't my dad; he had no right to talk to me like that.

I was about to say something mean when Jason abandoned his computer and pulled the chair up to me so that our knees were touching. "What's going on with your essay? How is this Zayed guy teaching you this stuff?"

Over poetry.

I didn't say that out loud, though I really wanted to.

"Well, my ideas have heart, but no body."

"What does that mean?"

I wanted to explain it poetically like Zayed had, but it sounded silly when coming from me.

"I have no impact in the body of my essay. Or something." I was slowly starting to understand what Zayed had been saying. If I thought about it truthfully, I hadn't given examples in the essay that really meant something to me. I needed to take that big step he'd been talking about if I was going to succeed at getting a higher score.

"Oh, your body has plenty of impact. We can prove that tomorrow," Jason said in that teasing tone I used to love. He rested his hands on my knees and leaned forward to kiss me. I softened slightly. Jason was Jason; this was how our relationship had always been. How could I expect him to be something else?

I let his lips catch me on my forehead and forced a laugh. "We don't want your father to find us like this." As if his father would really care enough to check on us. Jason had less parental supervision than the kids on teenage soap operas.

"Okay." His expression bordered between hurt and doubt.

I belonged with Jason. Everyone apparently knew that except for me. Erica, Lana, even Candace Littlefoot. Because of him, things were starting to be back to normal for me. Yet I was having a hard time convincing myself that being "safe" was the thing I wanted when the unknown was just so much more fun.

Zayed didn't come.

I waited at the corner of 45th and University Avenue for half an hour, the early-morning fog circling around and around me like a pack of gray wolves. I felt ridiculous standing on a street corner holding a paper bag with a PB&J for each of us. I peeked into Sureshot and the Institute—several times—but he was nowhere to be found. I tried the phone number he had given me, and it rang and rang. No voicemail, no response.

When I heard the thunder, I knew it was time to go.

As I drove home, I wondered if there had been a miscommunication or if I should've waited longer, but in my heart, I knew that he was not coming. Had never intended to.

I sent him a simple one line email:

I waited for you.

There went my flirtation with the unknown. Whatever it had been, it was over.

CHAPTER 7

The Confrontation

I didn't spend the day with Jason, either. I couldn't. I couldn't pretend everything was fine and I'd just happened to finish early with my essay work. I sent him a text that I was feeling sick and had turned my phone off.

It wasn't a lie that I felt sick. I'd crawled back into bed, peeled off the black over-the-knee boots and white sweater dress I'd worn for the occasion and had immediately fallen asleep, the first time in weeks. I woke up hours later realizing it was after four. Friday. I needed to get to the airport in case . . .

I could barely open my eyes and fell asleep again. I dreamt of shapes and figures, nothing concrete. I hated what was happening to me. I hated the gentle pulsating pain of disappointment in my chest every time I thought about the way Zayed looked at me when he served me tea. The brush of his shoulder against my knee. The certainty in his eyes when he'd promised me, "I'll be there."

I hated what I was becoming. Pathetic and clingy and desperate for something I didn't even fully understand. This was not me. This would not be me. I swore to myself that when I rose from the bed I would be changed. Zayed Anwar was out of my life, and under no circumstances would I let him back in.

The next morning, I was awoken by a clanging noise downstairs. I thought it was the thunder from the storm brewing outside. Or maybe a burglar. I drifted off to sleep again. Five minutes later the noise started again. Ten o'clock on a Saturday morning. This was a most inconsiderate burglar. I threw on a terrycloth robe over my leopard-printed pajama bottoms and tank top and crept down the stairs.

The refrigerator was no longer in the cubby it belonged in; rather it was in the center of the kitchen. A very guilty-looking Vivek Joseph peeked out from behind it.

"Hi, Mars," he whispered.

"What are you doing?" I said in a normal tone.

"I wanted to make Lana breakfast, but your refrigerator just made a weird noise and refuses to turn on."

"Did you break it?" I asked.

"I was trying to fix it."

"Do you know how to fix refrigerators?"

"No."

"Okay, then please call a repair guy," I said.

"I'm an engineer. I can figure this out. Do you have the manual?"

"No! No one keeps that." I glanced up at the staircase to where my parents' bedroom was. Vivek was spending the night already. There went promises of not "moving too fast."

"Fine, I'll just look online."

Clearly, he was not going to go away. I ran upstairs, brushed my teeth, and washed my face. I was not making the effort to actually get presentable in the hopes that Vivek would give up and leave soon.

I noticed Lana's bedroom door was still closed. She slept with earplugs in, so I was not surprised the noise hadn't woken her.

When I returned, Vivek was navigating Lana's laptop expertly and had brought up a page with a diagram of refrigerator parts. "Hmm, this looks simple enough."

I pulled up a stool and watched him fiddle around inside the freezer, doing more damage than anything else with every piece of machinery that he took out and discarded as "not important."

I dug around in the bag of PB&Js that sat on the counter, uneaten from the previous day. I couldn't believe it was less than twenty-four hours ago that I'd been standing on a sidewalk like a fool waiting for a guy who I barely knew to show up for a "not" date.

It sounded ridiculous, but the disappointment still stung, prickled at my skin, just as much as it had the first moment. Why had I looked forward to it so much? Why had I let my guard down with him so quickly?

But what if something bad had happened to him and he wasn't able to contact me?

Or what if he didn't think of me "that way" and had figured out I was starting to develop feelings for him and realized he needed to end it quickly?

I didn't want to think about this anymore, but I kept hearing his words over and over again. "I'll be there." I knew I would be spending the day hiding and thinking. And rethinking.

I barely knew Zayed. He was undoubtedly made of something very different than me, so why did I feel such a connection with him? Like there was so much more to our relationship than just teacher-student or even friends?

It didn't matter. Like it had been yesterday, it continued to be over. He had decided that for us. There was no point in even spending time thinking of it.

"Lana asked you to spend the night already?" I couldn't help but ask Vivek as I unwrapped one of the sandwiches.

He eyed the bag longingly until I passed it to him. "I stayed in the guest room. Had too much wine last night."

"Yeah, sure."

"I did." He gestured behind him to where the guest room was. Sure enough, the door was open, the bed unmade. "I thought it would be nice to make breakfast for Lana."

Normally, I would yell at him, but I felt too horrible after sleeping for over twenty-four hours. I wasn't in the mood for a confrontation with Lana or anyone else and just wanted to put some food in my stomach and go back to burying myself in my bed.

"Lana doesn't eat," I mumbled from around a bite of peanut butter. "She definitely doesn't eat breakfast."

"She eats my cooking. I made a green lasagna, and she had almost half."

Green lasagna? I knew she wouldn't eat that.

Lana used to love to eat; she used to be quite the foodie. One of the few things she and my father had loved to do was try new restaurants every weekend. Those had been their date nights: three-course meals at the most unusual restaurants, from Tom Douglas's Pacific Northwest classics to eclectic holes-in-the-wall. Ever since my father had started to deploy more often, her interest in food had dwindled to the point where I couldn't remember the last time I'd seen her eat anything. Her waistline had also declined to the point of where she was thinner than me or any of my friends.

"Why do you call her Lana?" Vivek asked me, having devoured his sandwich in under a minute. He had a trace of jelly on his chin, which I was tempted to point out but didn't. I was still annoyed with him for waking me from my first good night of sleep in weeks and for wandering around in my house as if he lived here. I was too preoccupied with my own issues to waste energy being angry with him and would sit back and hope he was one of Lana's phases.

"I don't know. Just habit. I don't think she likes being called 'Mom' anyway." The truth was, I had never thought of Lana as a mother. Not even once.

"These are some good PB&Js, by the way."

"My father's recipe. Did Lana tell you about him?" I couldn't help but slip that in.

Vivek stopped fiddling with the ice maker. "Yes, she did. I'm sorry to hear about him. She still loves him very much, you know."

"It's you who will be sorry when he comes home." I swallowed.

"Uh-huh. Anyway, I know what's wrong with the refrigerator."

"What?" I crumpled up the paper bag.

"You guys need a new one."

I rolled my eyes. That seemed to be everyone's solution. Throw out the old if it was inconvenient and get something new and shiny.

"One with a digital reading on the outside. I saw some cool ones at that appliance store in Bellevue."

"Fine, but right now you need to finish all the ice cream in there. And all the other stuff. You don't want it to go to waste." I tried not to smirk as he gauged my face to see how serious I was being.

"For real?"

"Yeah. Lana hates it when people waste food. Big pet peeve of hers. She's on the board of three food-drive charities, you know."

I couldn't believe how gullible the guy was as he scrambled around the kitchen looking for spoons. It was the least I could do to mess with him. He deposited one in front of me as well. "You're helping."

He and I each dug into cartons of cake batter with sprinkles, salted caramel, and blueberry cheesecake ice cream. After a few minutes of silent chewing, I spoke up. "Why are you dating her?"

"She's amazing. Strong. Proud. So sure of what she wants."

"Uh-huh."

That was an act. I knew her better than anyone, and I'd never seen her be strong for anyone.

The doorbell rang.

"Are you kidding me?" I glanced down at myself and back at Vivek. "You get it. It's going to be evangelists wanting to convert us to Scientology." I hated the religious evangelists who stopped by every few days to tell us to not believe in wizards or vampires or whatever. I decided to let Vivek deal with getting rid of them today. I dipped my spoon into the cake batter, then the salted caramel, then the cheesecake ice cream.

"Are you mixing those?" Vivek asked as he walked into the living room and toward the door.

"Why not?" I grumbled as I licked the spoon.

"Teenagers. Thank God I'm not one anymore."

"Just barely," I muttered.

I would allow him to make breakfast with the remnants of the refrigerator contents since I was starving, but then he had to leave. I didn't want him in my house, didn't like the fact that he'd taken out three plates from the cupboard. Didn't like that he knew where to find the plates.

I almost choked when Vivek came back in with a very surprised-looking Zayed Anwar in tow.

"Delivery for you," Vivek said.

"Why are you here?" I gasped, realized I looked ridiculous holding a giant serving spoon heaped with ice cream in mid-bite.

"I got your address from the registration file."

"Uh-huh, great. But *why* are you here?" I waved the spoon around, not knowing what to do with it. Vivek took a step toward me as if to say or do something to relieve the tension that had suddenly materialized in the kitchen.

The doorbell rang again.

"*That* must be the evangelists. I shouldn't keep them waiting." Vivek looked grateful as he retreated out of the room once again.

"I'm sorry for yesterday. I broke a promise to you." Zayed whispered, looking very sorry indeed. "I had to apologize in person. I'm sorry if I'm intruding. Is there something I can do?"

"You can *not* surprise me at the break of dawn!" At this point, I'd dropped the spoonful of ice cream on the counter, leaving a sticky mess.

"It's ten-thirty actually."

I was still in pajamas. Zayed, dressed beautifully, in dark denim jeans, an incredibly soft-looking V-neck shirt, and a striped scarf, was seeing me in *pajamas*. Oh God, my hair. I wanted to melt away like the puddle of ice cream.

Zayed grabbed the roll of paper towel before I could and dabbed at the rapidly melting pile of sprinkles and cheesecake.

"I waited for you. If you didn't want to come, you could have just said so," I said in a tone I was hoping wouldn't be accusatory but certainly was.

"It's not that I didn't want to come. I wanted to very much. There's just something I have to tell you—" He reached out and touched my cheek, surprising me. I felt a stab of disappointment as I realized he was only wiping a dab of ice cream off.

"This one's for you too, Mars," Vivek said quietly, as he gestured toward the newest arrival in the kitchen.

Jason stood in the doorway. "You look like you're feeling a lot better."

Zayed and Jason stared at each other.

"The refrigerator broke," was all I could think of to blurt out, and I took a step back from Zayed.

"Mars, do you want to introduce me to your friends?" Jason glanced at Vivek, back at Zayed, then finally at me. The stare was hard and questioning.

"Vivek Joseph. I'm a friend of Lana's. You must be Jason, the neighbor. Lana has told me a lot about you."

She had?

"She has?"

"Absolutely." Vivek took Jason's hand in both of his and gave it a solid shake. "I hear you make a mean chocolate-chip cookie."

"Uh, no, that's my mother." Jason almost smiled.

I took a deep breath. Vivek was doing a fine job of saving me from this unfortunate situation, but I was not going to rely on him.

"Jason, this is Zayed Anwar. He was just here to—"

"Drop these off." Zayed had reached into his messenger bag and pulled out a stack of what looked to be college applications.

Jason reached across and took the applications from him. "Michigan? Harvard? I thought you were going to the U, Mars. Wasn't that the whole point of this essay class thing?"

"Keeping my options open." I had no idea what these applications were about. It was a possibility that Zayed had them for someone else and this was just an excuse.

"Really? Why?"

I was starting to get annoyed with Jason. He had no right to question me like a child in front of other people. I was about to respond with something vocal and inappropriate when Vivek chimed in. "Lana insists that Mars at least think about other places. Speaking of Lana, we'd better clean up some of this mess before she wakes up."

The doorbell rang yet again.

"Let me get that." I watched Vivek leave the room, feeling desperate to follow him and run far away from here. Something bad was about to happen—as it always did after I saw Zayed. I closed my eyes for a second, trying to pull myself together and bracing myself for the inevitable.

Zayed and Jason were facing off when I turned back around, the college applications Jason clutched the only thing keeping them separated.

"The Institute has pretty good customer focus. Door-to-door delivery service of applications and all," Jason said in the arrogant tone I knew well. This was his *who-do-you-think-you-are* tone. The one that had won final rounds of debate tournaments the past three years.

Suddenly, I hated that tone. How dare he stand in my house and talk down to my guests? And how did it affect him where and how I applied to college?

"I am very invested in my students' success." Zayed's tone was completely cool, his stance rigid. I hadn't seen him this way. Commanding and unafraid. I liked this Zayed, one who was not willing to back down to someone who was clearly trying to intimidate him.

"Yes, he is." In two steps, I was standing between them. I wasn't in my usual stilettos and realized I was a good foot shorter than both guys. Also, my hair was pointing in every direction by then. I hardly stood a chance of intimidating either one of them at this point, but I was certainly going to try.

"Mars has been very preoccupied lately with this class of yours. I hope it has a payoff." Jason ignored me and continued to glare at Zayed.

"She's going to the U, you know. It's a great school. Lots of her friends will be going there as well. Her father was an alum."

"'Was'?" I felt my cheeks starting to burn. "No 'was,' Jason. He *is* an alum of the U."

Jason finally looked straight at me. The look in his eyes was disdainful, condescending, and almost hateful. I was taken aback. This was supposed to be the person I'd been planning to build a life with and around. I was suddenly scared of his expression and wondered where the Jason who'd apologized so profusely had disappeared to.

"Mars will be accepted into any college she chooses," Zayed said quietly, observing the looks exchanged between Jason and me. "She is an intelligent woman. The choice is entirely up to her. I am here only as a guide. And I will help her in any way she wants."

"Yeah, I bet," Jason muttered through gritted teeth.

"She is very talented," Zayed said, not sounding upset at all. "I would hate to see that talent *wasted* on things that aren't worth it. Or any preconceived notions of what she is not capable of doing holding her back. I'm sure you as a friend would agree."

Jason said nothing and stood his ground, crossing his arms as if waiting for Zayed to leave.

"Anyway." I felt Zayed's warm touch on my shoulder. "I feel we're upsetting Mars with all of this talk so early in the day."

"Why don't you take your applications and leave now?" Jason stepped closer to Zayed. They were almost nose to nose. Jason's golden hair and complexion were a contrast to Zayed's fiery eyes and dark features. One of these men I'd known my whole life, and the other was a stranger. Yet I felt closer to that stranger than I'd ever felt with Jason.

"I, of course, will do that or anything else Mars would like me to do," Zayed glanced at me, a little half smile on his face. He laid his hand on my shoulder. The gesture was one of friendship and support—not intimacy, but I knew Jason wouldn't see it that way.

I wanted Zayed to stay. I put my hand on top of his and silently thanked him for believing in me and for not letting me be overridden by someone who was *supposed* to care about me.

"Zayed is staying." For as long as he wanted to. I was surprised at how firm my tone was. I smiled at him, hoping he understood that I really did mean it.

"They won't come back." Vivek came back in, apparently having exorcised the house of evangelists. "They now think we are the House of Satan."

I took a deep breath, glad the discussion was over. I didn't think I would ever be grateful for Vivek or even accept him, but he had helped me manage this situation several times that morning. I had to give Lana credit for choosing someone with some common sense.

"I'm leaving." Jason starting walking toward the door, glancing back at me.

I couldn't let him leave angry, despite the circumstances. We had been in the middle of some kind of relationship, and I owed him something resembling an explanation. I followed him into the front foyer.

"Are you okay, Jason? I'm sorry about this morning."

He didn't answer even as he reached the front door.

"Jason?" I put a hand out as if to touch his arm, but something told me to pull back at the last second.

"What the hell was that bullshit?" He whirled around so quickly I thought he was going to hit me. "I thought you were sick. I thought I'd come over and cheer you up. And here I find your SAT instructor sitting in your kitchen like he's been here all night. What is going on between you and Zayed?"

I needed to deny everything. After all, technically, there was nothing going on with me and Zayed. Or was there? He had disappointed me, but then had gone beyond anything I'd expected in coming by in person to apologize. I didn't understand it at all.

I finally said, "I don't know." Because I really and honestly didn't.

"I'm worried about you, Mars. Looking at schools that are far away from here? What are you running from now? You seem to be falling into that pattern again." Jason leaned against the banister leading upstairs and crossed his arms.

"What pattern?"

"Crazy."

I felt like I'd been slapped. I'd known it. I knew people said it behind my back, but this was the first time I was hearing it said to my face. And from my so-called boyfriend at that. He had never defended me to anyone, I'd known that, but I hadn't realized how much he agreed with them and most likely joined them in bashing me.

"Well, if I'm so crazy, we really don't need to be seeing each other anymore, do we?" I said quietly.

I knew Zayed and Vivek were in the other room. Our insulation wasn't so wonderful that they wouldn't be able to hear every word of this conversation. I didn't give a damn. This needed to be said.

"Mars, don't throw these stupid fits. We were fine. Everything was fine between us until you started acting like a freaking psychopath and hanging out with that guy—"

"How am I a psychopath? Actually standing up for myself? By being with someone who will defend me instead of letting people say what they want about me, like you did all this time?"

"Here we go again."

"Here we go, what? Here we go with me actually expressing how I feel as opposed to what I'm supposed to feel?"

"*You are in denial.* When are you going to understand that?" Jason's voice was getting louder and louder. "You belong in an institution. I wish Lana had actually put you there the first time."

I hadn't cried, not once over the course of the past month, and I was certainly not going to start now. Not in front of this hateful person who'd betrayed me yet again. I wouldn't give him that satisfaction.

"Your father is *not* coming back. He's dead. Gone. Dust. Over. If your mother sleeping with some other guy doesn't show you that, I don't know what will!"

"Shut up, Jason," I whispered, staring up at the ceiling. Sixteen. Seventeen. Seventeen marble tiles. One for every year of my life. One for every year I'd known Jason and apparently had never known him at all.

"He's not. Coming back. Deal with it." Jason sneered. "Maybe your new boyfriend can help you understand it because I am done."

Jason slammed the door behind him.

I could have chased after him. Told him he was right. Pretended. Like I had been doing this whole time.

I could have done many things.

But I didn't. Because I didn't want to.

Because I hated him for possibly being right.

When I turned around, Lana was standing at the top of the stairs, the tears I struggled to hold back streaming down her face.

CHAPTER 8

The Breakfast

Lana held me while I cried for the first time since The Incident. "It's okay, baby. It's going to be fine."

"How could he say those things?" I whispered more to myself than anything else. "Maybe I am crazy for believing he'll come home to us, but what else can I do? Give up like all of you have?"

We sat in the darkened living room, the room with the white leather couches that were never used, the fireplace that still cradled ashes from the last time we were in here, the night after Dad had left. We'd lit a fire and stared at it for half the night, me pretending to do homework and Lana pretending to read a magazine.

That had been the first night I'd had a bad feeling, which had lasted since. The outburst from Jason was almost a relief. There had been so many whispered rumors about me, the delicate way he'd broken up with me the first time, the way people tiptoed around the topic of Dad. Finally, someone had said what they really felt.

"It doesn't matter," Lana whispered. "All that matters is that you're okay. I'm okay. We're fine. Both of us."

I wiped away the last of my tears on my shoulder. "No, we're not."

"We will be."

"No, we won't," I said bitterly.

"We will be." Lana pressed my knuckles against her lips and kissed them. "I got a very angry phone call from Ms. Nguyen. She suggested that I start seeing a therapist or join a support group rather than being selfish and just sweeping these issues out of sight. She's worried that by you and I not talking about what happened, I'm actually hurting you more than helping you."

"I don't want to talk about it." I was furious at Ms. Nguyen for interfering. She had no right to treat me like a four-year-old.

"But we have to. Don't you see that? We need to grieve about what's happening. You need to know that this feeling will not last forever and you are not alone in this."

"You're ready to just let him go. Why are you just assuming he's dead? Why is everyone acting like he's gone?"

Tears appeared in Lana's eyes again.

Take care of your mother.

"I get this terrible feeling that you're just pretending that he's gone on one of his long overseas trips," she said, the quiver apparent in her voice. "Mars, he's not going to come back this time."

"You don't know that," I whispered into her shoulder. "You don't have proof."

She held me tightly, and I just sat there inhaling the safety of her Chanel No. 5, neither of us talking.

Lana sniffed the air, the scent of cinnamon permeating the room. "I wonder what is going on in the kitchen."

For the past few hours, every once in a while we'd hear a noise or a clang, along with the front door opening and closing. Now there was just silence from the other part of the house.

"Just to get one thing clear, Jason is not allowed in this house or near you." Lana stood up and reached out her hand for mine. "I can't imagine such hideous behavior from that kid. It's absolutely unacceptable."

"They're our neighbors and your friends. What are you going to do, slam the door in their faces?"

"Absolutely. No one is allowed to talk to you that way."

I was secretly thrilled but knew that this would be harder for her than it would for me. She cared a lot about what her friends and neighbors thought, and she could hardly avoid the Moorehouses.

I heard the whispering die down in the kitchen.

"You ready to go in and see what Vivek and your friend have been up to?" she asked, dabbing underneath her eyes to erase the mascara smudges.

"His name is Zayed, and he's my SAT teacher."

"I see."

I was grateful that she didn't ask and I didn't have to answer the big question. Why was he here? He still hadn't given me a straight answer, and I was not buying "to apologize in person," which could have waited till Monday. Or "to bring college applications," which was just ridiculous.

I was afraid to face Zayed but knew it was unavoidable. I'd practically confessed my feelings for him, not having any idea if he shared any of them. I'd never done anything like that before and had no idea what to expect after.

The kitchen had been transformed. The center island was populated with dishes loaded with omelets, toast, bacon, waffles, some sort of sandwich, and an assortment of pastries.

Zayed and Vivek relaxed at the dining room table, holding mugs of coffee, a French cruller cut in half between them. Both stood when they saw us enter. I waited for one of them to make the first move toward us, but neither did.

"This is amazing, you two. How did you do all this?" Lana gave me a gentle nudge when she saw me hanging back in the doorway. I wasn't ready to go in and face Zayed. He knew how I felt about him now; he knew what I thought our relationship was. With my luck, he was just a concerned instructor and thought I was an overly dramatic teenage girl with a silly crush. I suspected I wouldn't be able to live down the humiliation of the morning for a very long time.

"Zayed managed to fix the refrigerator. We also got a few things delivered." Vivek was immediately by Lana's side. Again, that acting like he lived here annoyed me, but I had bigger things on my mind as Zayed also approached.

Zayed avoided eye contact with me and glanced in Vivek's direction. "Can I pour you a glass of juice? We squeezed the oranges ourselves."

I watched out of the corner of my eye as Lana led Vivek into the alcove and whispered something to him. They were both smiling, so I assumed nothing terrible had happened. I was hoping they would return quickly, but they looked to be taking their time. I couldn't avoid Zayed any longer.

"Hi," I couldn't think of anything else to say. "Please ignore my hair. I wasn't expecting company."

I had absolutely no makeup on, my eyes were red from crying, and I was in leopard pajamas and slippers. I could barely look him in the eye.

"You look loveliest right now. Free."

That was a nice way of putting it. Free, like a cavewoman. I'd always prided myself on looking put together at all times. Unlike my friends at school, I never arrived in sweatpants or old jeans. I was horrified that Zayed was seeing me this way, naked of my armor.

I blushed and tilted my head in Lana and Vivek's direction. "They're talking about you," I informed him, anxious to change the subject.

He glanced over and shrugged as he poured me a glass of juice. "They ought to be. My appearance today was random at best, somewhat sinister at worst."

I laughed, surprised to hear him think that. "It was surprising. But definitely not sinister. I'm glad you stayed."

"I am too."

"Thank you." I let my hand cover Zayed's as I took the glass of orange juice, not letting go, yet still not able to look him in the eye. "Thanks for everything."

He faced me squarely, still holding onto the glass of juice. His eyes were clear and sparkling. "I'm sorry about what happened. I was rude to your friend. It was not my intention to cause you issues, but I was not going to listen to him talk about you as if you were ordinary. You are exceptional. He wasn't able to see that, and it infuriated me."

I was exceptional all right. Exceptionally crazy in Jason's eyes, and I apparently belonged in an asylum. He would tell everyone about this morning before the weekend was up. I didn't know how I would face him or my classmates again.

"It was just a matter of time before he and I had that discussion," I tried to smile but felt the dread starting to rise inside me again. Bad things really did happen whenever Zayed showed up. I had to deal with that reality. But not now, not when he looked so concerned and beautiful and stood *in my kitchen*. "It really had nothing to do with you. I'm glad you're here for breakfast."

"It's an honor for me. And Mars, I know there is something in our relationship that's special. This is new for me, but I am enjoying the adventure we are on. I'm enjoying you very much. I would like to continue to enjoy you in a non-instructor kind of way, if you'll have me."

I stared at him. Was this his way of asking me to be his girlfriend? Because the answer was a complete yes.

"Mars, guess what the most exciting thing is." Vivek was back in the kitchen, Lana following him before I could wonder more. Zayed quickly dropped his hand, leaving me holding the glass.

"What?"

"The refrigerator already made thirteen ice cubes. It's really fixed. Come check it out."

I joined him at the freezer, and sure enough, there were thirteen little ice cubes clinking around in the ice maker. The frosty air from the freezer cooled my cheeks and gave me a chance to think about what I was going to say to Zayed next. Dating had never been a problem for me, but this was something much more than that. If I would *have him*? I would definitely have him!

"Wow, that's cool, Vivek. Pardon the pun." I tried not to sound sarcastic. I'd never seen anyone so excited by appliances before. It was a little odd, but not bad, I had to admit grudgingly.

"Now it's time to eat," Lana said as she started to fix herself a plate. "I'm dying to try some of these waffles!"

This was a phrase I never thought I'd hear her say again. This was bizarroland. Upside-down reality. I wasn't going to question it but rather enjoyed this rare moment of closeness between me, Lana, and these strangers who had pulled us both back from the edge of madness that morning.

"I made that." Zayed gestured toward the dish of scalloped potatoes on the island.

"I'll have to have extra then." I took a second spoonful just to see his tender smile flash in my direction once again.

We all sat at the dining room table with full plates, glasses, and silverware clinking. Lana was the first to taste her food, spearing a piece of bacon. I noticed Vivek watching her as she took a bite. My words to him about her eating habits had apparently made an impression. After watching her devour a good portion of bacon and eggs, he seemed satisfied and dug into his blueberry waffles.

"What is this? This is really good." I had a nibble of a sandwich, a baguette cut in half stuffed with vegetable coleslaw of some sort and grilled meat.

"That's a Vietnamese sandwich, one of my favorite things in the world," Vivek pointed out. "It's more of a lunch street food, but we had time, so . . ."

"It's delicious." Zayed echoed me bite for bite. "Vivek knows how to make some very interesting foods. He calls them 'food on the move.'"

"Hot dog stands, crêpe stands, taco trucks, you know the drill. Zayed has never seen a taco truck before. You should take him to that famous one in Greenlake, Mars."

Lana frowned. "Taco trucks?"

I had to laugh at the look on her face. "Exactly how it sounds, Lana!"

Zayed laughed too. "Mrs. Alexander, I was as surprised as you."

"Food on the move. I never would have taken you as a fast-food man, Vivek. Another surprise," Lana agreed.

"That's my goal." Vivek shrugged, sipping his glass of milk. "That's what the software I created did, surprised people. I love to make people smile."

"What was your software?" I asked around a mouthful of pancake. I hadn't eaten this much in months. I was way past the four-bite plateau I'd been stuck at. Each dish was more delicious than the last. I could feel myself bordering on fullness already but couldn't help tasting everything.

"It was an add-on to people's computers. It dropped in little personalized messages at funny times while people were online."

"Like?" I swallowed.

"Like you would check your email, and you would get a little pop-up thought bubble that said, 'You have another message from Zayed, Mars. I think he really likes you!'"

I nearly choked. Zayed blushed. Lana raised an eyebrow, not looking terribly thrilled.

"Wow, and a company paid you lots of money for this?"

Vivek nodded. "It made people smile. I love that."

I glanced around the table. He had certainly accomplished that in my house that morning, despite the earlier circumstances.

"Do you follow Islam, Zayed?" Lana asked, observing Zayed's plate.

I tensed, also having noticed that he had taken a little of everything except for the bacon and sausages. I'd assumed he was Muslim from his choice of major. I hoped that wasn't going to be a big deal since we didn't follow a religion. I didn't want any religious stigma to enter the discussion during such a nice meal.

"My family are progressive Muslims. I was raised quite liberal, but don't follow the faith as much as I should anymore," Zayed answered easily. "I do miss the community aspect of it very much. And the peace and ritual of prayer."

"I miss going to church on Sundays the way my family used to when we were young." My mother scooped up a bit of salsa with the remainder of her scrambled eggs. "A house of worship feels like a bond that brings people together and holds them together through hard times. I don't feel like I've had that since I left the church."

I glanced at her with mild surprise. I hadn't known that was something she missed. My father was the one who didn't believe in religion or displaying religious symbols, but I'd never thought about how it affected her. I started to wonder what her life had been like before she married my father and what else she'd given up.

I could see Vivek trying to be discreet as he squeezed her arm under the table, and I swallowed. I wanted to say something but didn't know how to without seeming really immature in front of Zayed.

"It's not too late, Mrs. Alexander." Zayed refilled Lana's glass of juice from the pitcher he'd carried to the table. "I'm sure God would welcome you back if that's what you wanted."

Lana glanced in my direction. "Maybe."

"How did you learn to cook so well, Zayed?" I changed the subject, not comfortable with how personal the conversation was getting. I had just tasted the infamous scalloped potatoes, and they had practically melted in my mouth, the best potatoes I'd ever had.

"My mother was ill once, and my father insisted we give her a break. Luckily she'd been collecting recipes for over ten years and had an entire collection of them in the kitchen. For me, it's a matter of following directions exactly rather than attempting any sort of creativity."

"You're from Paris, you said?" Vivek asked. "Are your parents still there?"

Zayed shifted. "In the Latin Quarter."

"Oh yeah, around where? I was in Les Gobelins near Le Grand Hotel for almost a month. I love that city."

"Around there, near the Sorbonne. I love the city as well."

"And you lived there your whole life?" Lana asked.

"Yes," Zayed nodded, focusing on cutting a piece of toast into small pieces.

"Your English is really good for having lived in France for so long," Vivek commented.

Lana nodded in agreement. "And your vocabulary. It's very charming and literary."

"Thank you." Zayed blushed again, his golden skin flushing beautifully. "I read as if I were possessed when I was younger. My parents said I kept our neighborhood bookstores in business. I read every English book for children I could find before I was ten years old, then graduated to Shakespeare."

"*The Secret Garden* and *Little Women* too?" I asked, mostly teasing.

"Absolutely. There are more books written for little girls than boys. I was teased mercilessly, of course, by my friends, but I didn't mind so much. I loved *Little Women*. I didn't have any sisters, so the story was especially fascinating to me."

"That's one of my favorites. I wanted to be Jo March when I was younger. I even slept in our attic for a whole year writing a book on parchment like she did," Lana laughed.

Vivek and I exchanged a glance; this news was new to both of us . . . my mother wanting to be the world's most famous fictional tomboy. Such a bizarre and revealing morning this was turning into.

"My parents wished I was like you two," Vivek sighed. "I was practically illiterate because I spent all my time playing outside rather than reading. I was put into a special class."

"And now look at how far you've come," Lana squeezed his hand.

Ugh.

"Do your folks live in town?" I asked quickly.

"No, I'm trying to convince them to visit, but they refuse. They're in India, in Mumbai. They say I work way too much to spend time with them when they're here."

"Is that true?" Zayed asked.

"Absolutely. But now maybe they have a reason to come." He smiled affectionately at Lana.

I nearly gagged. There was no way they were already serious enough to be at the meet-the-parents phase. Lana echoed my sentiment by frowning in his direction with a sharp shake of her head. As if they had already had this conversation and the plan had been negated. Even she was aware enough to know how it looked for him to be seeing a married woman who had a teenage daughter.

She was all smiles as soon as Vivek broke eye contact. He'd backed down this time, but I didn't expect that would last too long. He didn't seem like the type to give up easily.

"This was a great way to spend the morning," he said, gesturing toward the French windows in the dining room. The storm that had started earlier that morning hadn't let up. Cascades of rain showers swirled and endlessly lashed the windows outside. "Did you guys see the weather report today? Cats and dogs and horses outside. There's snow in the mountains already. Can you believe that?"

"There are cats and dogs and horses outside?"

I smiled while Vivek tried to explain the figure of speech to Zayed, while Lana observed the whole exchange with interest. All three were soon laughing at something else.

I'd watched Lana actually take more than two bites of a meal. I'd watched Vivek graze her hand without making a show of it. I'd watched Zayed watching me during our strange yet completely normal "family" breakfast. The house was different today. Warm and full, just like I felt on the inside. I hadn't felt this way in so long, and the sensation was unfamiliar, extraordinary, but so welcome.

CHAPTER 9

The Status

My mind was active as I loaded the dishwasher. Usually I would wait for the housekeeper to handle chores, but I needed to do something to stop analyzing the morning and what it meant.

I'd wanted to drive Zayed back to the U District to give us some time to talk, but he'd said good-bye at the front door and insisted on taking the bus back. I'd stood in the doorway of the house until he disappeared from view onto Lake Washington Boulevard. Usually this would have discouraged me, but he'd promised to make up for standing me up. I'd wanted to tell him that he already had and much more, but I'd refrained. I wanted to see him again. Soon.

I rinsed off the four plates before putting them into the lower rack of the dishwasher. We had never used four plates for breakfast in our house, always three and recently only two. People used to ask if I liked being an only child, and my honest answer had always been "yes." I'd loved having my parents' undivided attention and never having to wear cutesy matching outfits or having to share my toys.

But now the house suddenly felt very empty with everyone gone. I wished I had someone to talk to about what I was feeling. I eyed my cell phone. The daily check-in phone call hadn't happened in over a week. Before I could feel too guilty, I grabbed the phone and hit the first number on my speed dial.

"Hey, Dad," I said to the voicemail as I finished the last of the dishes. "We had a really weird breakfast today. Zayed, remember him? He came over, which was a surprise. Jason and I had a huge fight. He and I are over for good this time. I know you really like him, but he said some pretty horrible things. Even Lana doesn't want me to see him again. Sorry."

I took a deep breath. "I need you to call me soon, okay? There's something going on with Zayed, and I don't know what it is. Every time I'm around him, I feel like I'm losing my mind. Something bad always happens, though. Every time. I need to talk to you about it. That's the dishwasher you hear in the background. I'm doing house-work. I know, weird, right? Well, it's been weird lately."

The voicemail beeped, signaling my time was up.

I hung up the phone. "I miss you and love you. Come home soon," I whispered to the empty house.

I waited nervously by the door, listening to the doorbell ring over and over. Talking to Dad's voicemail hadn't been enough for me, and I had decided to do something I hadn't planned on.

The doorbell rang again.

Open the door. Do it now. I willed myself. *It's what Dad would want.*

The doorbell stopped ringing, and I immediately grabbed the handle.

"Hey, Bree." I forced a smile at my calculus teacher.

"I'm glad you called."

"Um, me too." I just stood there like a moron, not knowing what to do next. I really had no plan or good reason for asking her to talk.

"May I come in?"

It was weird having Bree sitting in my living room. She and Dad had always met on the Army Reserves base, never in our house, so this was a first.

"Can I bring you some tea?" I offered after I'd stared at the floor and the ceiling for a few minutes.

"No, thank you, Mars."

"Waffles?"

She laughed. "How was your morning?"

I relaxed a bit. "Good. We had some guests."

"That's new, right? You and your mom really haven't had too many visitors lately."

"Mom's new boyfriend."

Bree watched me closely. "That bad, huh."

"He's kind of stupid."

"Really?" Bree got a flicker of a smile on her lips. It wasn't like I didn't know how dumb I sounded.

"Yeah, he's way more into her and into us than he should be."

"Could it be he's just trying to be a friend?"

I shrugged.

"Who else?"

Who else. How to explain the other guest?

"A friend of mine from my SAT class."

"I see. What's his name?"

"Zayed." I realized she'd tricked me into admitting my guest was a guy. "He's just a friend."

"You said that already."

I blushed.

"So, how long have you known him?"

"Just a few weeks, but he's a really nice guy. Very caring. He's helping me with some of the college application stuff."

It was a relief to actually talk about Zayed out loud with someone. I rocked back and forth.

"That's very good." Bree smiled. "I'm glad to hear you talk about that. Where do you plan to apply?"

"The U."

"Where else?"

I shrugged.

"Mars Alexander the First's alma mater, huh? You know your parents met there, right?"

I nodded. I knew the whole story. He and I used to regularly take walks through the campus during the first days of fall, him pointing out various buildings and favorite hangouts, including the ballroom where he met my mother at a pre-war rally. That had been one of my favorite ways to spend Sunday afternoons.

"Bree, where's my dad?" I came out with it before I could change my mind.

She swung her foot in a circle. "Where do you think he is?"

"Off base somewhere."

"Are you wondering why he hasn't contacted you?"

I nodded. "Have you heard anything at all? Some confidential mission or secret military stuff or anything? I promise I won't say anything to Lana."

Bree glanced up at me. "I would have told you if I knew anything, Mars."

"Do they make you say that?"

She laughed. "No. I really would have told you."

"Oh."

"Is that why you asked me here?"

I sighed and didn't answer.

"I feel like we're just making things up. Like we're always just . . . waiting."

The grandfather clocked ticked for almost a minute. I looked over at Bree, hoping she'd have something profound to say.

"You mean everything to your father. You know that, right? If there was anything he could do to make your life easier . . ."

Then why wasn't he here?

I walked into the cafeteria for lunch on Monday after almost a two-month-long absence from the giant hot tub of gossip. I knew people were talking about me and whatever rumor Jason had started following our fight, but I was done hiding. I ignored pointed stares at I stood in line for my pot roast and fries.

"Mars, oh my God, you look amazing." Kendall looked shocked when she turned around and saw me, right behind her in line. Candace flanked her closely; the two were dressed in almost identical velour hoodies and acid-washed jeans tucked into furry ankle boots. Clearly, they'd been reading that month's fashion magazines and hadn't realized that just because something was in fashion didn't mean it needed to be worn.

"Hey, guys."

"You look like a French model. Everyone thought you were crazy when you cut off that amazing hair, but I really think the bob is cute!" Candace piped up. "You look really good despite, you know, the breakup."

I contemplated going back and hiding in the library again just to avoid this kind of discussion. True, Candace and Kendall had been more friendly recently, but I really wasn't in the mood to talk to them. I'd been thinking of this for months, the moment when they realized they needed me and came crawling back, but now I felt nothing. I just wanted them to go away and leave me alone.

Where the hell was Erica? I squinted around the cafeteria, but she was nowhere to be found.

I peeked to the front of the line to see what the holdup was. Some freshman was enquiring about the calorie count of French fries. This could take a while.

"We heard Jason caught you with some other guy and broke up with you!"

"Uh." News generally traveled fast at Lakeville High, but this was ridiculous. What was Jason telling people about Zayed? Had he sent a group text to our entire senior class? I felt a flare of anger. Zayed didn't concern him at all; Jason had no right to talk about him in any way.

"We can console you through the breakup." Candace attempted to link her elbow through mine. "We need to go to the mall. Do you want to skip third period and go?"

"Uh, I better not. My mom's gotten really strict lately about skipping and stuff." This was not true. Lana wouldn't notice if I didn't go to school for a month.

"We should get you a makeover at Neiman's. That way Jason will totally *die* when he sees you and your new man at homecoming." This was their subtle way of asking about when I would be unveiling "my new man."

"Yeah, sure. Later, though." I had no desire for Jason to die or anything else. And I was not asking Zayed to go to homecoming with me. It sounded juvenile and silly just thinking about it. I had a feeling he'd never been to a school dance, and I wasn't going to be the one to induct him into that aspect of American culture. "What's going on with you guys? Did you find dresses for the dance yet?"

I stood through ten minutes of pleasantries about what they each had been doing while the line moved up one student at a time, everyone seemingly asking about the calorie count of French fries.

Kendall was getting tired of sneaking in an outfit to school every day and changing in the girls' locker room. Her parents were strict first-generation Chinese immigrants and insisted that Kendall didn't show her knees or elbows. Kendall's fashionista status couldn't be challenged, and she had two wardrobes to deal with—one in her closet, and one in a cardboard box marked "Christmas decorations."

She couldn't wait to graduate and go to college so she could wear whatever she wanted.

Candace struggled with the eternal question only Kirkland teenagers dealt with: to tan or not to tan. She insisted that having a tan made her look thinner yet was terrified of getting wrinkles. She'd finally succumbed to getting a spray tan once a week, but couldn't ever wear white due to the clothing stains from her skin.

"But that's okay, right? It's after Labor Day, so I really shouldn't be wearing white anyway."

I made a sympathetic noise at Candace. I couldn't believe I used to be a part of these discussions and actually enjoyed them. That day I could think of nothing but what Zayed had asked me about "having him" and what I would say to him when I saw him next.

"I'm sorry for not talking to you for a while. Are you really mad at us?" Candace took the lull in the conversation to drop that in.

Kendall glanced sideways at me to see my reaction.

I exhaled a breath, surprised they'd brought it up. "Why did you do it?" I knew the answer. I just had to hear it again.

They looked at each other, neither wanting to admit the truth.

"You can tell me, you guys, I'm not mad. Promise." I smiled to show I really wasn't.

"We were afraid people would talk about us the way they were talking about you. You really went crazy that day in the locker room, Mars. People thought you were going to kill someone. I mean, literally." Kendall knew how shallow she sounded. I could tell by the look on her face. "You understand, right?"

I'd been waiting for that, an apology, some kind of explanation. I thought it would make me feel better, but it didn't. It meant nothing to hear it. I realized I didn't care anymore. I hadn't cared in a long time what anyone thought of me, or if I would ever be considered "normal" again.

"Besides, everything's okay now, right?" Candace asked hopefully. "I mean you're dating some hot older guy and . . ."

I laughed. "I am not dating anyone."

"But Jason said—" she started to protest.

"Don't believe everything you hear, Candy."

"You have to sit with us and tell us the whole thing." Kendall waited for me as I paid for my lunch. "Come to our table."

I glanced over at the table and our old gang—lots of girls dressed exactly like Kendall and Candace and their boyfriends, discussing the same things we had for the past four years.

"Thanks, guys," I smiled politely and picked up my tray. "But I'm really behind in my homework and have to get something done before English."

I didn't give them a chance to answer as I strutted to the only open table in the middle of the cafeteria, the one under the giant starburst skylight. No one ever sat there because of its unobstructed view from anywhere in the cafeteria. This table was not for the shy, and I was done feeling like I needed to hide.

Zayed had sent me a short but effective email that morning that I had actually printed out and carried around in my wallet. I had pulled it out several times during the day until I memorized the words. I pulled it out again as I took a bite of pot roast.

Breakfast with you was the first time that felt like home and family to me here in Seattle. It was especially hard for me to leave when I turned back and saw you standing in your doorway, staring at me with that look on your face. You have no idea how that look affects me, and I pray you don't use it to your advantage too often. I find you devastating and beautiful at once. I count the hours until I will see you again.

I felt his presence beside me every time I read it. He had a way with his words, and I couldn't imagine anyone else saying those things and not sounding ridiculous. Just reading his words again made me feel powerful and in control. It was a feeling that was completely new to me.

I opened my notebook to a blank page and thought about what I would write back.

Dearest Zayed,

I don't know how you manage, but you are able to enrage me and then astound me in mere seconds. No one has ever stood up for me the way you did with Jason. The most amazing thing is that I truly do believe you mean it when you say that I can do anything, that I am capable of greatness.

*You're the only one who's ever believed that, and because
of you I am starting to believe it myself.*

*Thank you for what you did, but you are still not forgiven
for standing me up on Friday. I will think of an appropriate
punishment by the time you receive this.*

Yours,

Mars Alexander II

"So the rumors are true." Erica materialized at my lonesome table
just as I finished signing my name on the letter with a flourish. "You
are here. I heard about it in the art studio and had to come and see for
myself."

"Hey." I smiled at her as I closed my notebook. "Yes, I am here.
And I'm not going anywhere."

"You seem happy," Erica sat down opposite me and picked up a
French fry off my plate. "Really happy. What's going on?"

I contemplated answering, but I was enjoying keeping Zayed to
myself.

"So it is true. There is someone else. Jason is telling everyone you
cheated on him."

I raised an eyebrow, an artful arch I used to practice in front of the
mirror when I was younger, channeling Vivien Leigh in *Gone with
the Wind*. "Cheating? Really? To cheat, we actually should have
been seeing each other, I think."

"I thought you were." Erica gave me a look. I knew I hadn't told
her the full truth about my interest in going out with Jason again. I
had led her to believe that everything was okay and I was extremely
happy that he and I were back together.

"We went on exactly one date. I don't think Jason should get so
attached."

Erica folded her arms. "Okay, I want to know what's going on
with you. You know I won't tell anyone."

I wasn't worried about Erica spreading news. The truth was that I
barely understood what was going on between Zayed and me and
had no idea how to put it into words for someone else to understand.

"Let me figure it out first," I finally said. "I'll tell you, I promise."

"Is it the guy from the roof?"

I couldn't hide my smile.

"Wow. It's really bad when you don't even try to cover it up. Who is he? When do I get to meet him?"

"Um . . ."

"Mars? What's going on?"

Yeah, what was going on? My face was tingling, my stomach twisting; all the other voices were dimming into the background. All I wanted to do was close out the world and just think of him, his scent, and his presence.

"Nothing's happened," I managed to say. Yet.

"Oh really. Nothing? That's not what Jason's saying."

I was getting annoyed with Erica for listening to Jason. It wasn't like they traveled in the same circles or were great friends. I wondered why she was listening to him rather than me, someone she had known forever.

"Absolutely nothing. We're just friends." For now.

"But you do like him."

I contemplated trying to explain and finally showed her Zayed's note as a response. She read it in record time, eyes widening. "Oh. My. God."

"We're just friends." I started to laugh at the look on her face.

"Oh. My. God."

"Seriously, there's nothing going on."

I no longer believed this at all. There was definitely something going on. Zayed knew it, and I knew it, too. And I couldn't wait to find out more.

CHAPTER 10

The Absence

Zayed wasn't in class that night. I was convinced he would show up until the very last minute. I'd even arrived early with a marshmallow mocha in hand and the letter I'd written him in my purse. I sat by the door and peeked into the stairwell every few minutes, but I didn't hear his buoyant footsteps once. We ended up having a British substitute who had probably graduated from college before the SAT had been invented. It took him five minutes to read the instructions for the writing exercise we were to do that day.

"So, ahem. The goal of the exercise is . . . Let's see here. What does this say? Ah yes, the goal is to look at the phrases—one at a time—I presume, then decide what emotion you feel. Yes, that's right."

He looked expectantly at us.

"Hmm, let's read that again, shall we?"

Annoyed with Zayed, I stopped listening. Where was he? He'd *just* sent me an email that morning saying he was looking forward to seeing me. Where could he have disappeared to in a few short hours?

I flipped to the section in my booklet and decided to interpret the exercise as I chose.

"On the mountaintop" was the first phase. What emotion did I feel?

I was a bit scared of heights, so probably I felt sick. I doubted this was what the exercise was supposed to be.

"In a crowd," was the second phrase.

"Alone," I wrote down.

"In front of the Christmas tree," was the third phrase.

"Sad," I wrote down. "Nostalgic."

"In the driver's seat," was the fourth one.

"Free," I wrote.

I sighed and scribbled half-hearted answers to the rest of the prompts. I didn't understand the point of this exercise, and without Zayed to help relate it to what we were trying to improve on in our essays, the class quickly lost interest, and everyone left early.

I felt sorry for the substitute, but I was starting to actually get concerned about Zayed. He had disappeared—again—and was not answering his cell phone.

Where was he?

Without thinking too much about it, I wrote an email to Zayed when I got home:

Where were you? Class was terrible without you. Answer your phone!

I didn't get a response back that night or the next. I was so mad I skipped the group therapy session the following night and instead camped out at the University Bookstore. I told everyone it was to do some more research on an essay-writing topic, but Erica claimed it was obviously because I was hoping to run into Zayed. To prove her wrong, I made it a point to pore through all of the SAT practice books—in between glancing out the window to see if Zayed might have appeared at Sureshot.

He didn't show, but I did read everything I could find on good versus bad essays. I noticed one thing all the good ones had in common: they were deeply personal and almost sounded like diary entries. Whenever I read one, I felt real emotion and even found myself gritting my teeth or laughing out loud at some of them. They didn't feel mechanical or canned or textbook at all. My goal was to invoke *that* kind of emotion in my reader for my next essay.

By the end of the week, people were back to ignoring me in the cafeteria, and I spent the hour doing homework at my sun-washed table. Sometimes Erica would join and ask prying questions about Zayed, but most times she left me alone. She'd realized she wasn't going to get any more information other than that I was seriously mad at him.

Finally after a week's absence, I got a reply to my email.

Mars,
I sincerely apologize for disappearing without notice.
I was called away on an important project by my acade-
mic adviser. I will be gone another week but look
forward to seeing you soon.
Yours, Zayed

"What the hell kind of project are you working on?" were the first words out of my mouth after the classroom had emptied out after class. I hadn't seen him in two weeks, and it was hard to believe, but he looked even more gorgeous and mysterious than ever. He had a scruffy, unshaven look that was just . . . amazing.

I wanted to throw myself into his arms, but refrained.

"My adviser wanted me to speak to some other people about my experience with Islamic studies."

"What people?" I asked suspiciously. He was being purposely vague, and I didn't like it one bit.

"Oh, other students. Graduate mostly." He twirled in his teacher's chair in front of the room casually.

"Where?" I was not having any of it. He did not have the right to disappear without notice for two weeks after turning my life upside-down.

"Different universities around here."

I perched on his desk with my legs crossed. "Like Washington State and Portland?" I wondered what he knew about Islamic studies that was so special that he was brought in as a special guest lecturer for various universities. He was an undergrad. How much experience could he possibly have?

He nodded before I could ask more detailed questions. "We're going to write a paper on the topic. Please don't ask me more, Mars, because he's asked me to not talk about it. He's very possessive over the topic."

I frowned. What was wrong with this adviser that he pulled a student out of school for two weeks to discuss some topic all over the state?

"Is everything else okay?" I asked, softening slightly as Zayed pulled his chair close to the desk, close enough to rest his elbows on my folded knees and gaze into my eyes. Zayed was too nice to say no and must have gotten dragged into some professor's pet project. "How are your classes? You must have missed a lot."

"Well, I'm having the most difficult time with all the dates in my history of Europe class. I can't seem to keep track of all the numbers."

"Oh, I know what you can do. My friend Erica is a history whiz. She can help you for sure."

He looked pained at the thought of sharing his learning woes with someone else.

I also realized I wasn't really willing to share Zayed with anyone yet.

"Or," I hurried on, "you can use mnemonic devices."

"What's that?"

"You know, like little phrases to remember things by. One I remember is 'In fourteen hundred and ninety-two, Columbus sailed the ocean blue.'"

Zayed started to laugh.

"Don't laugh. It works! See, I remember that, and I haven't had history in three years!"

"What else?" Zayed continued to laugh, pulling his chair even closer to me. I was starting to get all breathless again, like always when I was around him.

"Flash cards! Make them with the date on one side and the event on the other. I can help you go through them."

Zayed had stopped laughing and was now smiling at me.

"What? You think flash cards are stupid, too? How did you ever learn anything in high school without flash cards?"

He shook his head and stood up. "Flash cards are a good idea. Thank you, Mars. It's nice to have an adviser who can give me long-term ideas on what to focus on, but it's really very nice to have a friend to talk to about these small things."

Friend. And although he took my hand in his and led me downstairs for a cup of coffee at Sureshot, my heart sank a little at the use of that word.

"Mars has something to share," Erica announced at our Tuesday therapy group session, passing the flag to me. "It's about her feelings."

I glared at her. I did not need to be outed in front of a bunch of people I barely knew. And I was hardly sure of my feelings, much less ready to verbalize them. I knew Erica was tired of waiting to hear more about Zayed. Frankly, I was getting tired of waiting for something to happen. After the "friend" remark, I'd dialed down my interactions with Zayed to only the teacher-student ones. No more emails. No more letters. He'd come to me once he was ready. I hoped.

Everyone stared at me expectantly.

I picked at an overgrown fingernail and stared at the floor. "I feel good. Normal." Despite everything, I was feeling like things were starting to be less tumultuous. There had been a lot less drama lately, and I was enjoying the lull.

"Tell us about that!" Stephanie jumped on that statement. "What's changed? What's normal?"

I glanced around the circle. Did I really want to share all this news with this random group of strangers?

"Well, I think I'm starting to accept some things for what they are. Some people will never change, and some people might, given enough time . . ."

"Is it that guy?" Ken interrupted, clearly not in the mood for a philosophical talk.

"What guy?"

"That guy you played hero for." He grinned. "That elevator guy or whatever."

I had to smile. "The roof guy. Yeah."

"Have you seen him lately?" Stephanie pressed.

I nodded.

"And?" Krish, the heartbreakingly pretty girl, leaned forward, more animated than I'd ever seen her. "What has he said? What has he done?"

I shrugged. "Nothing. We're just friends. He said so himself."

Erica sniffed. "I doubt that. You should see the letters these two write each other."

Krish's eyes widened. "Ooo, let's see one."

"You should read one to us," Octavio said.

"Maybe he's waiting for you to say something?" she persisted.

"He's the guy; he should make the first move." I retorted. "Anyway, I'm not in a rush to push him into anything. And I'm not reading any of his letters!"

"Maybe he's shy," Angel offered up. This was the first session he hadn't cried.

Yeah, right. He'd had no problem ripping apart my essay from that week with very direct comments. "Bit clichéd" and "Lacking emotional or tangible support here." Shy, my stiletto-clad foot.

"Okay, let's get back on topic, everyone." Stephanie seemed to tire of our regular-people talk. "Let's discuss insomnia. Who has it?"

I rolled my eyes. I sat there silently for the rest of the session, watching the others. Whenever one of us needed help or seemed to be having a hard time talking about something, the others would jump in, animated and helpful. That's when we felt like a real circle, working on something together. Listening to each other. *Helping* each other, rather than each person talking, one at a time, and Stephanie taking notes.

If I was in charge, I would treat this like a project. We were all in it together, with the common goal of helping each other heal—whatever that meant. Healing was different for different people. For some, it was letting go of guilt. For others, it was something more practical, like finding ways to support their family.

Maybe I actually could take charge of this group and do something great with it.

I almost laughed at the thought. I could barely manage my own life, much less help others with their issues. No, Stephanie wasn't very good, but she was probably doing a better job than I would.

As the group was ending, the others hung back after Stephanie left to chat some more about Zayed.

"I think you 'like him' like him, Mars. I think you should tell him so. I bet he likes you, too." Ken got in the final word.

I had to smile. How simple it sounded from a thirteen-year-old. I did indeed " 'like him' like him," but I certainly was not going to tell Zayed that bit of news—not yet anyway.

I vowed that I would be able to write an "emotion-invoking" piece for the practice essay Zayed announced we would do in class the day before Halloween. I was determined to not give him another chance to comment on the lack of feeling in my essay.

"A little inaccuracy saves a world of explanation." Is it always essential to tell the truth, or are there circumstances in which it is better to lie?

I reread the prompt. This was going to be interesting. I grabbed my pencil, and as soon as Zayed gave the cue to start, I started scribbling. *A lie is never the best answer to any question. How genuine can any relationship be if the truth can't be shared? Lying to protect children from the realities of the real world is a common practice among all parents, including my own, but what they don't understand is that they are teaching us that deception is more important than setting a good example...*

I wrote about how my parents had always put up a big show of happiness and togetherness throughout the past few years, but I knew they had been drifting apart. Their lies were more painful than the reality that they might be separating. I wrote about how I felt that the only reason they stayed together was because of me, and now that Dad wasn't around much, it was my responsibility to keep them together.

I wrote about how when I looked for a partner for myself, the one thing I expected from him was full and complete honesty.

The twenty-five minutes passed in seconds, and I was practically breathless when I was finished.

The following class session, Zayed gave me a rueful smile when I came in. "Miss Alexander," he said cordially, as he always did in front of other people.

Uh-oh. Had he hated my essay? Was it that bad? Was I really not improving?

I was too scared to look at the result for a full thirty seconds but finally peeked. An eight. I was getting there. Definitely making progress. I was more excited to see the note at the bottom of the page from Zayed, "Congrats, Mars . . . lovely writing on this one. I would like to celebrate this occasion. Can I claim you for next Sunday?"

CHAPTER 11

The Storm

"I'll give you anything you want today." Zayed called from across the street. "But only if you reach me safely. Please be careful!"

I kept an eye on the speeding cars and raced across Roosevelt Street, splashing through puddles, staining my over-the-knee suede boots and not caring. "I lived. I'm here to collect."

Almost a week had passed since Zayed had sent me the note about meeting on the weekend, and I had literally counted down the hours. By hour forty-seven, I was ready to have myself sedated to pass the time. He and I had exchanged half a dozen emails during that time, each one growing more daring than the last. We said things to each other we would never think to say in real life. These were definitely not the communications of people who were just friends.

> Zayed: We are definitely on for Saturday. Looking forward to it. Be prepared to be mine for the whole day. I have plans.
> Mars

I'd gotten one back from him almost instantly:

> Mars: I'm prepared to be with you the whole day, as always. (You looked beautiful in class tonight. I almost said something, but thought it would be inappropriate, given the other people.)
> Zayed

I was happy he'd noticed since I'd spent over an hour trying on outfits before finally settling on a red sheath dress with asymmetrical, diagonally placed zippers all over the front. I responded without thinking:

> I wouldn't have minded if you had said something. I think everyone knows anyway what's going on.

Damn! I realized as soon as I hit SEND. I'd just come right out with my assumption that we were in a relationship. I could always claim I'd meant our out-of-class *friendship*, I reasoned with myself. Mortified, I hit REFRESH constantly on my email waiting for a response.

It came an hour later.

> I make my feelings fairly obvious, I suppose. I can't stop looking at you. Can you blame me? (What do you want to do with me on Saturday?)

I replied with a lot more bravado than I felt:

> I can't say in email what I plan to do with you, unfortunately. All I will say is that we will need some privacy.

My heart pounded loudly as I waited for a response, which came moments later. I still couldn't believe I was really going out with Zayed Anwar. The gorgeous, untouchable SAT teacher. I kept feeling like I was dreaming the whole thing. I wished more than anything that I'd taken a picture of him so I didn't need to keep visualizing every detail. Those shoulders, wonderfully broad shoulders, perfectly filling out his shirts. I could fit my whole body between his neck and shoulder.

> I won't sleep tonight if I think about that much more. (I'm even more excited now to see you again.) Goodnight, sweet Mars. Yours, Zayed.

I was acting crazy and not giving a damn about it. This was a completely different feeling for me—like every time I saw him, I could barely contain myself in my skin. He surprised me constantly by being extremely shy one minute and then outlandishly daring the next.

When I spotted Zayed waiting for me, hands in his pockets, inhaling the fall air, my breath slowed down, my footsteps stopped, and I just wanted to stare at him. I wanted time to stop so I could remember that moment, that first glimpse, for days to come.

What was happening to me?

Both of us stared at the sidewalk as I approached him. I felt suddenly shy. We'd said so much in our email love letters. Suggestive, passionate words. I didn't know how to greet him now, in the light of day, with him knowing how I felt about him.

"You look beautiful," Zayed said finally, gently touching my shoulder, both of us avoiding eye contact. He shoved his hands into his pockets again. "Where would my lady like to go first?"

His lady. A few weeks ago, I would have laughed if someone had called me that. Who did they think they were, Sir Galahad? Coming from him, it didn't sound ridiculous at all.

"We're here." I gestured to the structure I'd asked him to meet me in front of, just a few blocks north of the central University District. The Seven Gables Theatre, named after its gabled roof and handsome with its dark-shingled exterior. Dad and I had loved spending rainy Sunday afternoons here watching foreign and independent movies. It was one of the few movie theaters I'd never been to with anyone else.

"This place was built in 1925 as a dance hall. Also, it's supposed to be haunted," I said with a gleam in my eye. The history of the place was one of the things I loved about it.

Zayed's eyes widened. "I'm terrified of ghosts."

"I'm just kidding." I assured him, though I was not. "I'll hold your hand, don't worry."

He looked visibly relieved, but I grabbed his hand anyway.

"That's the other theater in Capital Hill that's haunted. That one has a ghost who lives there permanently."

"Please don't take me there." He actually looked frightened this time, which amused me even more.

"Only if you do everything I say. Come on now." I touched the corner of his elbow and led him up the steps into the theater.

"Paris, je t'aime?" Zayed saw the name of the movie I had bought tickets for. "Mars, you are not paying for anything."

"Try and stop me." I waved the tickets in his face. "I assumed you might be homesick. This movie is one of my favorites. Did they not release it in Paris?"

Zayed didn't answer as he took in the movie poster. *Paris, je t'aime* was a collection of love stories set in Paris. They ranged from casual encounters to extraordinary paranormal events. I loved each one and knew Zayed would too. I had been so excited that they were having a special showing at my favorite theater.

I led him into the parlor in the theater where we were to wait for the movie to start. The comfortably decorated room hosted constellations of sofas around coffee tables piled with newspapers and catalogs of local events.

"This is charming." Zayed was contemplating the series of historical photographs of the Seattle area cascading along the walls of the parlor. I'd read them all many times, so instead I sat back on a couch and watched him. The smooth line of his back, his long lean legs. Just staring at him made my pulse start pounding. Just a few weeks ago we'd been strangers. Now when we were apart, I silently accumulated stories that I would tell him when we were together. He was a part of my life now, a very big part.

I swallowed, asking him silently if I was letting him in too quickly. I didn't know what our relationship was, and I wasn't in a hurry to define it. It wasn't just dating. And not just friends. All those terms I'd always used seemed so small compared to what I felt for him and the way he looked at me when we were alone.

"Why did you bring me those applications?" I asked finally. I'd been wondering about it since it had happened, and no explanation I had come up with explained it.

"You spoke about Stephanie, your therapy group leader," Zayed said, finally sitting next to me, easily reaching for my hand and clasping it to his heart. I felt my heart rate start to race because of how close he was and because I could see the rise and fall of his chest under his jacket. I knew he felt it too from the tremor in his hand around mine.

This was the most intimate relationship I had ever had with another person, and yet we had barely even touched each other.

"I did?"

"At the tea house. About how she wasn't effective. Or empathetic. It was obvious to you she had never undergone a tragedy of her own and failed to understand how to handle one."

"Oh." I felt my cheeks flush. I hadn't realized I'd disclosed so much in my fit of anger.

"And you expressed much passion around helping those kids, as you said, and how they needed to understand that they were not just grieving the person they had lost or who had changed, but also the activities and the relationship that bonded them together."

"I said all that?"

"You did. And I realized that, Mars," he placed a finger under my chin and raised my face to look at him, "even though you claim you have absolutely no idea about your major in college yet, child psychology might be a viable path."

I stupidly stared at him. He'd extracted all of that information about me from a simple rant, and here I'd been thinking for years about "what will Mars be when she grows up?"

I would have based the decision around who my boyfriend was, what my father would want, or what my friends would do, but never around what I was passionate about or interested in.

Child psychology. I'd never even thought about it.

"The reason for the applications is that both the University of Michigan and Harvard have excellent undergraduate psychology programs. You will certainly have the SAT scores to qualify if your high school grades are high enough."

No one had ever taken this kind of interest in my future before, thinking not of how it would benefit them, but only what would be good for me. No one had ever believed that I would be able to get into the university of my choice on merit alone rather than alumni status or donations.

"Thank you for thinking of me, Zayed, but attending a university out of state isn't an option."

Zayed looked confused. A little hurt even. "Will you share why? Financial concerns?"

If only the explanation was that simple. I almost laughed; that was the only reason that *wasn't* an issue.

"Too far from my family."

"Oh. But weren't you planning to attend Wellesley on the East Coast?"

"How did you know that?" I frowned.

Now it was his turn to blush. "Your mother mentioned it at breakfast to Vivek while you were away from the table."

"I'm not going; that's just her wishful thinking. I need to be here for my father."

"Oh. Is that what he would want? For you to put your future on hold, only to wait for him to return home?"

And that's where it became not his business. This was a private decision I was making, and no one had a right to force their opinion on me.

I stood up. "The movie is going to start."

The silence between us was rare and uncomfortable as we sat waiting for the previews to begin. We both raised our legs and shifted to the right, allowing the last few patrons to fill in the theater. My knee grazed his, and they stayed touching even after our feet were safely back on the ground.

Finally, Zayed glanced at me and whispered. "I am here to support you with anything you want, Mars, as long as you're happy. I am not here to make your decisions for you."

I felt a warm sensation spread through my core. It was strange to be with someone who wasn't telling me anything except "be happy." I hooked my fingers around his arm and squeezed. He didn't pull away, nor did I as the movie began. Eventually, his hand found its way to my knee, where it stayed for the next hour.

The movie was a series of eighteen short films, each set in a different area of Paris. The story was a tribute to love, and especially a tribute to the city of love. I glanced over at Zayed during the "Quais de Seine" segment about the blooming friendship between a Muslim girl and a Caucasian boy in the fifth arrondissement and found him watching me with a smile.

I leaned my shoulder against him around the midpoint of the movie, savoring the citrusy scent and warmth of his skin. He turned to me, the stubble on his chin grazing my cheek. We stayed there, still, cheek to cheek, perfectly balanced until the movie ended.

"So?" I was dreading the moment when the lights would come back on and sat there still while the credits rolled by.

"I did love it," Zayed said as we stood up and exited the theater.

"I knew you would. Which one was your favorite?"

"The woman who lost her son."

"The cowboy one?"

"No. The man with the horse. No cows."

"He's a cowboy; it's just a figure of speech."

"Yes, the cowboy one. Coming to terms with a loss that terrible is not an easy thing. Sometimes we need a bit of magic to tell us that it's okay to feel what we feel."

"You seem to know a bit about that." I watched him, realizing I'd tapped into some hidden emotion. He sounded like he had lost someone. A parent? A girlfriend?

He smiled again, sadly this time. "I think the scene was beautifully made."

"Which arrondissement did you live in? Was it in the movie?" I asked hopefully. I'd hoped the short films would act as a catalyst to propel Zayed to start talking a bit more about his home and family.

"It was not."

I was going to push further when I realized the weather had changed dramatically during the movie.

"Oh wow."

We stopped at the big windows in the lobby and stared outside. It was hurricane-like on the street. Tree branches were whipping by, carried on winds so strong we could practically see the currents. The angry clouds hurled down a heavy spray of rain.

"Why don't we wait out the storm at my flat? It's nearby. If you're comfortable with stepping outside, that is," Zayed said absently, glancing up the street.

I was pretty sure he wasn't aware of the cultural implications of a guy inviting a girl to his place, alone, and I wasn't going to tell him. It was only fair that I should see his place after he'd seen mine under the most stressful of circumstances.

He took my arm as we pressed ourselves against the side of the buildings. "It's there." He pointed at a majestic brownstone down the block. "Let's run."

Clasping hands tightly, we ran the short distance, laughing. We reached the awning of the apartment building, breathless.

"You're fast in those shoes!" Zayed said in a playfully accusatory tone.

I pressed against the stone wall, catching my breath. Zayed didn't take his eyes off me as he retrieved his key from his pocket and fumbled with the door. The way he looked at me—God, no one had ever looked at me like that before. I didn't want him to stop looking.

He held the building door open for me. I paused in the doorway, not moving. Staring up at him, daring him to make the move we both knew he wanted to make.

He leaned forward, his shoulders pressing against mine. I felt him breathing into my wet hair, the warmth inviting me in closer. "Let's go inside."

The full-body shiver traveled all the way down into my pointy-toed shoes.

I shook water out of my hair as he turned on the lights in his apartment. "Shall I take your coat for you?" he asked, gesturing to a quaint coat rack with only his black pea coat hanging from it. He hung my Burberry raincoat next to it.

I didn't tell him this was my first time visiting a guy in his own place. There were no parents to chaperone us here. I shivered a little at that thought. I had made the decision to come here alone, without knowing too much about Zayed or even telling anyone where I was going. My father would not approve. I put these thoughts out of my head.

His studio was sparse, but extraordinarily orderly. A much-loved coffee table and bookshelf were both stacked with books to the point of bursting. The two-person couch's back was pushed up against the bed, giving the illusion of separation between the "rooms." The bed itself was a fairly majestic-looking four-poster that was perfectly made up with pillows and sofa cushions. I didn't let my gaze linger too long on the bed.

"Mostly everything was left behind by the previous tenant or for sale in the building. I'm very fortunate to have found so much," he said from the hearth. Garage-sale furniture. I loved that he didn't look one bit ashamed of anything at all.

I was surprised to see a fireplace in such a tiny apartment, but he expertly lit a log and added a few sheets of newspaper to inspire the flames.

A tiny "mew" surprised me when I went to take a seat on the couch. I glanced down at someone who had to be Coconut, the kitten who had adopted Zayed.

"Hey, there," I held out my finger to the little fur ball. She was adorable, fluffy and white with brown spots. She batted at my finger with her paw and hopped on my leg.

"I will serve you tea today. Please take a seat."

The apartment smelled like Zayed now, the smoky burning of the wood in the fireplace simmering with the fresh smell of bright tangerines arranged in a shallow bowl on the coffee table. A stack of index cards sat next to the bowl. The top card said, "1846." I flipped it over, "The start of the Mexican-American war," Zayed had written in his tiny, neat handwriting. So he'd taken my advice after all about using flash cards to learn dates. That flattered me, no matter how silly it seemed. I liked that I was able to teach someone something.

Zayed spent a few minutes in the kitchen boiling water and assembling a tea tray, Coco following him every step of the way on the counter. I sat still and watched. He stopped and stroked her ears every few minutes, talking to her softly.

The pot and cups were from the tea house we'd been to. I recognized the distinct style and sturdiness as he poured the hot water.

"And Russian tea cookies as a special treat."

They looked like closed seashells coated with a dusting of powdered sugar and nestled on a small red plate.

"Russian tea cookies with a handsome boy from Paris, what an international way to spend an afternoon in Seattle," I commented.

"Try one, they're amazing. I did not make them." He seemed to ignore my comment, but found him glancing at me from behind his thick curtain of eyelashes.

The crispy shell gave way to the creamy bath of Nutella. Then came the crunch of walnuts.

"Where did you get these?"

"My secret." He grinned, looking carefree and young. I could hardly believe this was the same guy who'd been so cold to me the first day we'd met. "The tea is a crème de la Earl Grey. It's the standard Earl Grey with a creamy vanilla undertone. We can only steep it for a few minutes or it'll become bitter."

I had never taken a formal tea before, but I loved the ritual of it as I followed Zayed's lead. There was something so classic about waiting the three long minutes for the tea leaves to finish steeping before pouring the liquid into a warmed teacup and adding a little splash of cream and sugar. Then taking a little bite of the cake-like cookie, along with a sip of tea. Coconut became less wary of me and curled up on my knee, batting at my scarf.

"This was my family's tradition every afternoon, the one time of day we were all together," Zayed said in a rare moment of speaking of something personal. "It's not the same when I'm alone. Thank you for joining me."

It felt a little strange to share a family tradition with someone I was not related to—a good kind of strange. I'd never believed a "perfect moment" could exist, but here it was. I realized we were both lucky, he and I, to have this moment.

"Can you tell me what happened with your father?" he asked after almost a minute of easy silence.

The wind outside rattled the windows of his studio, sheets of raining continuously pounded against the building, diagonal and relentless.

"What do you mean?" I set my teacup down as it started to heat up a bit too much in my hands.

"Your friend Jason said over and over that your father wasn't coming back. Why is that?"

I swallowed. "I don't know."

"Yes, you do. You have that expression that you get sometimes, Mars. Like you're desperate for the moment to be over so you can escape."

"I don't want to talk about this."

"I understand. But you can. I am here only to understand and listen, not judge. You know that."

"Okay. Then understand that I don't want to talk about it."

"I felt it was disrespectful of him to have that conversation with you within earshot of others and especially after he came to realize he was upsetting you."

"Thanks. I appreciate that."

Zayed got up and put another log into the fireplace, breaking the discussion. The wood immediately started to smolder and crisp, giving way to a spray of ashes. "You don't have to be so formal with me, Mars."

Ashes to ashes.

"You're not telling me things about yourself," I said.

"What do you mean?" he immediately pounced on that statement.

"You know what I mean. There's something. How can you expect me to share my deepest thoughts when I don't even understand why you're here in Seattle? I know it can't just be your dedication to the SAT or your desire to get a degree in Near Eastern studies."

Silence.

"Zayed, please. I know you're keeping something when you press your lips together. Like this," I demonstrated. "And you do this all the time."

More silence.

"I can't tell you, Mars."

And there it was. The truth. I swallowed a last bite of cookie, watching him. He was intently stirring his tea, glancing around the room, at Coco, anywhere but at me. I felt an overwhelming, irrational urge to jump on top of him and tickle him until he told the truth.

Did he just not trust me? Did he think I was some stupid kid who would go and tell Lana or whoever?

"You can't. Or you won't?" I held out a finger to the tiny kitten, and she busily started grooming it.

"Cannot. It's beyond me. I will be in trouble if I do. You have to trust me when I say I am not keeping something from you that will hurt you. I need to keep this to myself for the protection of people I meet."

"Who told you to do this?"

Again, silence.

"Police?"

The rise of his eyebrows and widening of his eyes told me I was not completely wrong.

He wasn't even denying it. This was bad.

"Are they protecting you from something?"

Nothing.

"Tell me something then. Anything. Something true."

"My brother passed away." He stood up and turned around so his back was to me.

Passed away. The word hung there, between us. It sounded so insignificant compared to the reality of what *passed away* meant. His brother was gone; he was physically never going to be with Zayed or any of us again.

"Zayed, I'm so sorry."

"I am too. Jamal was older by two years. He was killed in a terrible accident."

"And your parents?"

"Were devastated." I could hardly hear him over the crackling of wood and paper. "Seeing me reminded them so much of—him, and everything. They were unwilling to accept his death. My mother called me by his name, talked to me as if I were him. I knew I had to leave."

Like Angel from my therapy group. People in grief saw what they wanted, believed what they wanted, if only to keep themselves sane and functional. I bit my lip. Poor Zayed. He hadn't even been able to mourn his brother properly because he'd been too busy taking care of his parents' grief.

"Are they still in Paris? When will you see them again?"

Zayed didn't answer as he stared into the fireplace.

"Zayed?"

"I miss them very much. But I don't believe I can go home. Maybe ever."

I was by his side before he finished what he was saying. I pressed my shoulder against him as I slipped my hand into his. "You can always go home."

"Or build another home." He smiled sadly at me. "You've made such an impact on my life. I hope you're aware of how grateful I am to you."

We stared at each other. I wanted to say something. Anything. I wanted to tell him how I'd never felt this crazy, terrifying feeling before. That no matter what happened, I would flash back to this moment for the rest of my life. Tell him how right it felt standing here side by side, fingers entwined.

Our lives entwined, I wanted to believe.

He was running away, and I was looking for somewhere to run to. We'd found one another in a storm, during the most helpless times in our lives so far. Now I couldn't imagine not being with him.

That last part scared me more than anything.

We finished our tea. We talked. We held hands. He read me poetry by Theodore Watkins that I had never heard before.

"This is one of my favorites," he said, glancing up at me from his book with the burgundy cover.

"Can you recite it without looking?" I grabbed the book from him and pressed the open pages to my chest.

"What will you give me if I do?" he asked, arching one eyebrow in my direction.

"A secret."

"*How did you sneak underneath the stone walls that I built so carefully?*" he said softly.

"Then?"

I read ahead the next few lines, feeling that incredible, deep longing again.

"*You dug, you burrowed, and you found me. The real question that remains is why I allowed you to stay.*"

I closed the book. He knew the whole damn book.

"You owe me a secret." Zayed gently took my book from my hands and set it aside.

"Later," I whispered, moving forward so our knees were touching.

Zayed reached around the sides of my legs and pulled me closer, trapping me between his knees.

"Now."

"I know how you feel about me." I didn't let my gaze waver from his face, though I could feel my cheeks getting hot. It was a bluff. I was starting to develop some ideas, but he hadn't said anything for certain.

"I don't think you do." He released my knees and leaned backward into the arm of the couch, eyes on me.

"Yes, I do. We're friends. Acquaintances, actually. You don't trust me enough to be even a friend." I bluffed, inviting Coconut to crawl back into my lap and make her way up my arm to my shoulder.

He laughed softly, ironically. "You don't know. Seeing you, Mars, is the best part of my week. I look forward to it like nothing else. That day I saw you on the street and . . ."

I didn't know how to tell him that seeing him was the best part of my life. I petted the kitten behind her ears after she had started to chew my scarf and purr softly, kneading me like bread dough. "You don't even trust me enough to tell me the truth about who you are or why you're here, so how can I assume you feel anything for me?"

"Wait here." He stood up with a sigh and walked over to his bookshelf, returning with a blue notebook.

"After I saw you on the street that first day, I didn't want to forget your face," he said, turning the book around and around in his hands. "So I did this."

"What is it?" I gestured toward the book.

"My journal."

Before I could react to the thought of Zayed having a journal that would be the key to all his secrets, the book fell open on my lap to a page with a rough pencil sketch of a face.

My face.

"I created this sitting in that coffee shop. I wasn't able to help myself. I didn't want to forget your face. How was I to know that you would be here with me one day?"

I sat stunned, staring at the angles of my jaw, the swish of hair across my cheek. My eyes looked haunted and sad. I looked vulnerable. Beautiful even.

"I couldn't stop thinking of you. I felt as if my dreams brought you into reality."

I ran my finger over the sketch and flipped the page, hoping for more. Lots of scrawled words that I didn't get a chance to read.

"That," he said, reaching out and removing the book from my lap, "is personal."

I was going to get my hands on that journal.

As if he could read my thoughts, Zayed quickly changed the topic. "Will you help me with my flash cards?" He reached for the stack of index cards on the coffee table.

I held up the first one. "1783."

"Um . . . next."

"That was the end of the Revolutionary War. Next is 1759; this one is international."

"Um, French and Indian War?"

I laughed. "No! It's the beginning of the French colonization of India. Completely different kind of 'Indian.' "

"Ugh." Zayed groaned, sitting down. "I'm going to fail this midterm, I imagine."

"No, you're not. What are you doing tomorrow? I can help you study. We're going to get you an A, damn it."

"I teach every weekday until about nine. On Tuesdays and Thursdays, I also teach the verbal SAT class in the mornings. I have school every other time between eight and five. And then I need to meet my adviser three times a week."

"Why do you need to meet him so often?" I was genuinely surprised he needed so much advising. I would be pretty annoyed if someone was telling me what to do every step of my major.

"I must be a hopeless case." Zayed smiled.

"I doubt that—"

Zayed's cell phone rang, interrupting. I waited for him to get it, but it stopped ringing before he could. "Are you going to check who that is?"

He shook his head. "It can't be as important as what's happening here."

I blushed.

"Tell me about Lana. Why do you call your mother by her name? My mother would slap me if I did that." Zayed leaned forward and took my hands in his.

There, cradled under his arm, my head on his shoulder, I told him many things. About how Lana and I were always up to mischief against my father's better judgment. How things changed so quickly after his deployment. About how she suddenly wanted to be a real mother to me after all these years. About why I was so hostile to Vivek. Yes, I felt Lana was trying to replace my father, but also trying to replace me as her number-one confidant. I hated that she'd already talked to Vivek about deeply personal things—like my father being gone. He hadn't been there with us throughout the years. He wouldn't understand.

I told Zayed things I hadn't even realized myself until I said them aloud.

As the rain subsided, I realized I had to get home before it got too dark and the storm picked up again.

Zayed seemed to see the sadness on my face as he walked me to my car.

"I will see you tomorrow," he promised.

In a room with twelve other students, just one in a crowd. I was cradled in the warm cocoon between Zayed's body and the Corvette as he shielded me from the wind and rain. I couldn't imagine getting into the car and driving home and leaving him standing on the sidewalk. I tilted my head back and felt the drops splash across my face.

Zayed kissed his thumb and pressed it to my cheek. "You're lovelier now than I've ever seen you. What have you done to me?"

I felt my heart beating wildly, and every part of my body pulsated with the energy that fueled through me. Why didn't he just kiss me and get it over with?

"Zayed, come home with me."

CHAPTER 12

The Night

"He stayed over? Seriously? You're not messing with me?" Erica's mouth hung open. "Has *anyone* ever stayed over with you before?"

"Shhh." I glanced around the hallways. I didn't want this news getting out. I still didn't want anyone to know or speculate any more about Zayed.

"Nothing like that happened between us."

"Nothing *never* happens, Mars. What happened?"

So, lots had happened, but nothing I was willing to share yet. My night with Zayed had felt like a dream or hallucination. I couldn't distinguish the events of one moment from another, but I could recall how I felt every second of it.

It had taken half an hour to convince Zayed to come home with me. Finally, I'd had to resort to the excuse of being afraid of the storm. We arrived home before Lana returned from her date with Vivek and retreated into my loft fairly quickly. I was *not* going to try and explain this to her.

I'd never had a guy in my room. Dad had always strictly forbidden it. I knew it was wrong to break my word to him when he was gone, but I couldn't not be with Zayed that night.

I hadn't known what was going to happen, or how the night was going to play out. All I knew was that I had to know more about him and was not willing to lose the opportunity.

"Your room is beautiful," Zayed had said from my bed, where he was flipping through my photo albums. They were childhood pictures of my parents and me during birthdays, vacations, and school plays. I'd set the plate of grilled PB&Js I'd made quickly down on the nightstand. I'd joined him on the bed, and he had immediately retreated to the window seat.

"Don't worry, I won't hurt you." I had laughed. "I never thought the guy I was seeing would react this way to being on the same bed as me."

"Seeing each other? As in?"

I'd suddenly become very busy with choosing the biggest sandwich off the plate.

"Mars?"

"As in, seeing each other outside of class," I'd said lamely. I hadn't meant to let that slip. Seeing each other was such an overused term. What we had seemed so much more special than that. More meaningful. Were there words to describe being unable to imagine a day without him?

I held out the sandwich as a distraction. He stretched his neck forward like his cat and took a bite. He chewed thoughtfully.

"What is that?" he finally asked.

"The magical peanut butter and raspberry jelly combination." I took a bite of the same sandwich and savored the melting-in-my-mouth feeling. Dad's recipe tasted even better when shared with someone.

"That's wonderful."

"Told you."

"It might be my new favorite food."

"That's what you missed out on that morning when you stood me up," I couldn't help but add.

"Will I ever hear the end of that?"

"Nope."

"Didn't I make up for it with scalloped potatoes?"

He had, but he didn't need to know that. "Not yet."

We both lay on our sides, staring at each other, his hand possessively on my hip. His eyes were grayish blue, I'd decided, the color of a dolphin's skin. His mouth was amazing, with a ripe, rounded lower lip, like a wedge of tangerine, and a perfect Cupid's bow on the upper.

"I told you I would keep you the whole day," I said shyly, gazing into his eyes again.

"You can keep me for longer. As long as you'd like. And you haven't done anything unmentionable to me either," he reminded me.

I blushed. The things I'd dared to say in email.

I'd run a finger over his lips, wondering why he didn't kiss me. I wanted him to. I knew everything would change the second he did, but I very much wanted him to. I considered making the first move, but it didn't feel right to do so. He was as skittish as Coconut. I would wait for him to be ready and not rush anything.

"What's that?" Zayed asked, breaking the tension that finally got to be too much. He was gesturing toward the painting Erica had started and I had finished. The angry red brushstrokes. I had rested it against my dresser with a plan to hang it above my bed.

"History," I said, staring at it. That day, I had been so uncertain about my feelings for Jason and the budding ones for Zayed. How things had changed so quickly. Everything that had seemed so important just a few weeks ago, I couldn't even remember what they were anymore. "Come back here."

He'd obliged. He rested his chin on my shoulder. I felt myself warming up under the weight of his body. After fifteen minutes of stillness, I thought he'd fallen asleep but then felt his lips caressing my neck. His hands and arms slipped underneath my hips, bringing goose bumps to my skin.

"Have you been with another man like this?"

"Yes." I had answered truthfully, despite my instinct not to. Thinking of my relationship with Jason now seemed ridiculous.

"Is it shameful that I hate that man?" Zayed had mumbled into my neck.

"No." I had to laugh.

"I want to kill him."

"It's ancient history."

"Have you done more than this?"

"No," I said truthfully. It had bothered Jason that we never had, but I hadn't cared. "Have you been with someone else this way?"

"No," Zayed said.

"And I won't," I thought I heard him say, but I couldn't be sure.

I closed my eyes as he kissed my neck, my jaw, and then the corner of my mouth. I waited, eyes closed still. Eventually I felt the lightest of grazes across my lips, or perhaps I imagined it. The deep desire in my core wasn't imagined, though, and I wrapped my arms around Zayed and pulled him even closer.

He sighed my name, and I could feel the effects I was having on him. He rested his head on my heart, his lips exhaling on my bare skin. We stayed that way for a long time. I didn't dare to move, didn't want to break the beautiful tension of that moment.

We'd both dozed off at some point.

"How long have you been keeping a journal?" I had asked dreamily around two in the morning, letting locks of Zayed's hair curl around my pinky.

He lifted himself on his elbow. "Almost my entire life. I always felt like I had so much to say, but no one to really listen. So I started to write."

"Do you plan to share them someday with someone?"

"No. Who would be interested in each and every one of my inane thoughts? I have all of them from when I was five years old."

He sat up and paced the room, stopping at the wall-sized window. "The fog. It's almost magical here."

The quilted fog wrapped its way around the trees and buildings on the waterfront. Silent and cool, it coated the window with a mystical haze. I could make out the glow of streetlights speckling the peaceful night like a paint-by-numbers coloring book. It felt like we were the only two people awake in the world.

"I want you to share your journals with me," I said, sidling up behind him and wrapping my arms around him.

He wiped some condensation from the window before covering my hands with his. "If I do share them, it will be with no one else."

I was warmed by the statement but had to know, "When?"

"I don't know, Mars." He turned to face me, searchingly staring. "Why?"

I shrugged and started to edge backward on the bed. "I want to know what you think. How you think. Is that weird?"

He crossed the room and was hovering over me within seconds. "You will have plenty of time to read them. I promise to be with you as long as you choose to have me."

"You don't know that; you can't promise that." Even though I was starting to actually believe him.

"Yes, I can. I promise it." He laughed, not in a "ha-ha" funny way, but almost desperately as he slid down to bury his head in my chest.

"You are frighteningly beautiful with your moods and tantrums. Your smile makes me forget everything and not care. Do you understand? I don't ever want to forget that look in your eyes, like you're not going to let me go—ever. I don't want you to let me go."

I never believed anyone, but I believed he meant what he was saying.

Before I knew it, the sun was coming out, and our night together was over. Absolutely nothing had happened; we'd only eaten PB&Js and talked, yet it had been the most intimate night of my life.

I watched him walk down our driveway to the bus stop, my heart doing something that could only have been described as breaking. Even though I knew I'd see him in a few short hours, I stood in the doorway for who knew how long, wishing he would come back.

I knew I had to go to school. I knew I had to concentrate, but my mind and soul were with Zayed, following him back to the U District to attend a full day of anthropology and religion classes.

"There was something about seeing my Burberry raincoat hung up next to his simple one on the coat rack. There was symbolism there," I said almost absently to Erica as I got my English notebook out of my locker.

"What are you talking about?"

"I don't know what I'm saying." I leaned against the locker and wondered how this person had completely infiltrated my thoughts. How could it have only taken the weekend for him to become such a permanent and *necessary* aspect of my life?

"I can see that you're completely over the moon right now."

"What do you mean?" I grinned. I knew exactly what she meant. That morning, everything seemed brighter. The school building suddenly seemed beautiful, the sky lit up by a thousand clouds, every car I'd passed on my way vibrant with color and light. It might have been the sleep deprivation, but I knew it was much more than that.

For the first time, I had a connection with another human being, the thing I'd longed for. I felt like I could tell him the thoughts from the deepest corners of my mind and he wouldn't think me insane or ridiculous.

"Mars, I've never seen you like this. You're . . . glowing!"

I laughed, attracting the attention of several people who exchanged looks.

"You've lost so much weight it's getting a little scary though, babe."

I still didn't stop grinning. It was no wonder. It felt like my heart was beating faster constantly, and my appetite was completely shot due to the never-ending fluttering in my stomach.

"Is he an amazing kisser? I bet he is."

"I wouldn't know." I laughed again, seeing the look on her face.

"Okay, let me get this straight." Erica tucked one of her pink spirals behind her ear. "You are completely, totally head over heels in love with this guy, Mars. And you've never even kissed him?"

"Love?" I stopped mid-step. "What do you mean?

"Oh, honey, you didn't know?"

"No. I don't think—"

"This is it. The feeling where you can't believe you went this long without him and know you can't go back to the world where he's not with you?"

Exactly my feeling.

"The feeling where you want to share everything with him, no matter how trivial?"

Exactly that.

"The feeling where you can spend hours just staring into his eyes to decide what color they are?"

I'd done that last night.

"This is love, babe."

Oh, God.

"Oh, you didn't know. Yeah, you're screwed." Now it was Erica's turn to laugh, seeing the look on my face.

Lana was sitting at the kitchen counter when I arrived home. Alone. No laptop in front of her or any other distraction. Lying in wait for me.

"Hey," I said hesitantly. Her normally pouty lips were set in a tight line.

"I saw Zayed leave the house this morning."

Damn.

"You sure?" I tried to sound casual, and I flung my coat off and threw it on the countertop.

She crossed her arms, pulling them tightly around her. "I pulled into the driveway as he was leaving through the back gate."

"Where were you coming from?" She hadn't even been home last night, and she had the nerve to judge me.

"Mars," she said in that newfound "Mom" warning tone.

"You can't stop me." I cut her off. "I can see him as much as I want."

"Having a boy stay over and do God-knows-what is completely unacceptable. What are you thinking? I—"

"We didn't do anything. We just talked."

She, of course, didn't believe me, and her eyebrows said it all.

"There is no way this is acceptable. You're still living in my house, and while that continues, you'll do what I say."

"Then I'll go live with Zayed."

I was not going to do that, though it did sound tempting after the previous night. I wasn't sure if he'd mind or not, but I didn't want to know if he wouldn't want it. That would be beyond humiliating.

Her eyebrows came together. "Don't you dare try and black-mail me."

Mine came together as well. "I'm just telling you what's going to happen. Don't try to make a bunch of random rules. How is what I'm doing any different than you?"

"Mars, I'm an adult."

It was pretty funny to hear her say that, as if she was trying to re-assure herself.

"Well, so am I."

She made an exasperated noise.

"I'll be eighteen in three months. I'm an adult."

"When you're on your own, you can do what you want, but you don't know anything about him. I don't know anything about him."

"He's been in our house before. We didn't do anything last night. I wouldn't—"

"I just can't believe you think this behavior is acceptable. If your father was here, he would have—well, I can't imagine."

"Well, he's not here, is he? Whose fault is that?"

She was silent, and we both stared at each other.

No, he wasn't here. She didn't know what to do with me in a situation like this, and we both knew it.

"I love Zayed," I said without thinking, hoping maybe she'd understand. I stunned myself at how right the words sounded out loud. It was as if they had always been true.

"What?"

"I do."

"You don't know what that means."

"Yeah, I really do." I grabbed my purse. "Leave it alone, Lana. You're not Dad. Don't try to be."

CHAPTER 13

The Gazebo

"Where are we going, Mars?"

"You'll see." I glanced over at Zayed, sprawled comfortably in the passenger seat of the Corvette, his feet crossed and resting on the dashboard. He looked so at home in my world, it was strange. As if he'd always been a part of it and I'd never noticed.

I guided the car onto I-5 from the U District and proceeded south. "I wanted to share something with you. Something I've never told anyone."

"Are there ghosts involved this time?"

I had to laugh. He had the ability to make me do so even when I was bracing myself for something somber. "No ghosts. I promise."

"Then?"

"Wait and see," I replied, squinting through the pelting rain on my windshield. Traffic didn't look too terrible despite the evening rush hour. We would be there in twenty minutes.

I had decided it was time. I would tell Zayed the one secret I kept from everyone, even Lana. I would show him where I went every Friday afternoon and what I did there.

I needed Zayed to know I trusted him, and in return I wanted him to trust me with his secrets.

"Tell me what happened that morning."

He glanced quizzically at me, playing dumb.

Seattle downtown whizzed by on the right, the top of the Space Needle barely visible from under the low-slung clouds protecting the city from the chill on the mountains. This was the kind of afternoon to spend curled up indoors nursing a hot cup of coffee over a good conversation. But I had to do what I always did on Fridays, and though I was nervous about Zayed's reaction, having company during the routine was actually reassuring.

"The morning we were supposed to meet and you stood me up. Why didn't you come? And why did you change your mind later?" I said, spelling it out for him.

"You won't understand." He looked away this time, all traces of levity gone.

"I won't, huh? Really, after everything, that's your cop-out?" I was starting to get angry at these dead-end answers.

I wasn't a stranger anymore. We'd spent a night together. He owed me some answers, and I was not going to back down. "You're going to tell me, or I'm taking the West Seattle exit and leaving you on Alki Beach."

The beach, while beautiful in the summer and a primary spot for diving in the Puget Sound, would be freezing and deserted now. There was also no easy way to get back to the University District from there for Zayed.

"You'd make me walk home and ruin our afternoon?"

"You bet."

He turned and stared at me for a second in silence. I set my mouth in a thin line, hoping he realized I was not kidding.

"I don't want to be left on the curb, so I'll tell you something. I need to know that you will never talk about this with anyone. I'm asking, Mars, for you to forget I even said this."

"Do you see lots of confidantes around?" I asked sarcastically.

"Where *are* all of your friends, Mars?" Zayed asked, casually flipping through the music playlists and selecting a new song. An old Coldplay song came through the speakers. "According to American television, a beautiful teenage girl like yourself should have a group of friends always surrounding her and a line of suitable young men a boyfriend should be having to fend off every day. Where are they?"

I peeked at him out of the corner of my eye at the boyfriend remark. So he considered himself my boyfriend. The thought thrilled me despite my frustration.

"Have you always been a lone wolf?" he asked. "So secretive and private?"

"Why, kettle, you're so black," I said, knowing he wouldn't get the reference. "My name is pot." I found it almost funny he thought I was the secretive, mysterious one when he had openly told me he had secrets that he would never share with me.

"Why do you have no friends who are wondering where you are right now, Mars?"

This was one of the reasons I appreciated talking to Zayed; he had no preconceived notions of what I had been before. He had no qualms about asking intensely personal questions because he didn't worry about how I would react or what was appropriate. He asked because he wanted to know.

"You're not going to be able to get off the subject of why you stood me up that easily, you know. I'm not stupid," I said sternly, knowing what he was trying to do.

"That I'm completely aware of." He grinned. "Sometimes I wish you were less intelligent so I could 'get away' with some things at least."

"Well, you're out of luck. According to you, I'm Ivy League material, remember?"

"That you are, my darling." He reached across and brushed a strand of hair back behind my ear, letting his fingers linger on my earlobe.

My darling? I didn't move. Every touch. Every moment with him. I savored each one in my mind at night while I tried to sleep.

"I'll tell you a piece of my story, but then you have to answer my question. Deal?" I pulled my head away reluctantly. No distractions.

"Deal."

"I used to be that quintessential American girl," I said with a smirk. "Something happened at school a while ago that made everyone think I was crazy."

The familiar whirr of airplane engines roared overhead as they made their descent into the Seattle-Tacoma airport. I watched the underside of the plane arc forcefully through the air. Would that be the plane?

"What happened at school?"

"You first. What happened that morning at the U?"

I didn't expect him to answer, honestly at least, but he spoke up at once.

"I met with someone earlier in the day, someone who is . . . guiding me. And he advised me not to get involved with someone like you. An innocent person."

"Who did you meet with?"

"I cannot share that."

"Why not?"

"Please don't ask me to."

"Why?"

"Please drop me off by the side of the road," Zayed said quietly.

I sighed. Clearly he was done. Very annoying.

"Fine, why did you change your mind and come to my house?"

"Because I realized I was . . ."

I looked over at him. He was biting his lip, measuring his words. I hated when he did this. Why couldn't he just say it? I knew, he knew. He knew I knew. Everyone knew.

"I realized I had romantic feelings for you. I admire you, respect you. I want to be with you all the time. For good."

"I want to know where you disappeared off to for those two weeks last month. When you didn't teach class and left us with that horrible substitute. I want to know where you go and who you talk to."

"I'm not allowed to speak of it, Mars."

"Why not?"

He was shaking his head, and I knew I wasn't going to get anywhere. "I'll tell you someday, but I can't right now. Please trust me."

I slowed the car down, earning a honk from a Prius behind us. I didn't want the ride to end so quickly. I had to know more.

"How can I trust you when you don't trust me at all?" I tried to hide the hurt in my voice, but it came across much stronger than expected.

"Every night I wish I was with you. Holding you in my arms as I did in your room."

I still didn't say anything.

"Every day. Every minute. I want to tell you everything, but I am obligated not to."

"When will you tell me?"

"Soon. Maybe before the year is up. Maybe before I ask you to spend your life with me. Please be patient with me. That's all I ask of you."

Damn! We drove in silence.

I felt a light flush on my cheeks. "I guess it's clear how I feel about you."

"How?"

"You're just a friend." I looked away. I wasn't going to say it. Not now.

"You're the world's worst liar, Mars."

"What?"

"You get this snooty, arrogant look on your face and your whole face changes."

"Does not." I glared at him. He didn't know me well enough to know when I wasn't being completely honest. He couldn't. That would be terrifying and impossible.

"And there it is now. That look."

I veered the car into the exit more callously than I'd expected to.

"We're here," I said, ending the conversation.

"The airport?" he glanced at the ARRIVALS and DEPARTURES signboards. "You're sending me somewhere?"

"Alaska."

He looked at me, alarmed. I'd thought about it actually. Getting on a plane and dragging Zayed with me. Disappearing to someplace other than Seattle for a few days and demanding every bit of truth out of Zayed.

I knew Lana would call the Army Reserves to find me, though.

"No one is going anywhere. Relax."

I parked the car in short-term parking and held out a hand for Zayed's.

"Come on."

We walked across the sky bridge and into the arrivals hallway. I guided us to a waiting area, where we took seats. Travelers passed us lugging suitcases, snowboards, and guitar cases. Every single one of them with a purpose.

"What are we doing here?"

"Waiting." I crossed my legs at the knee and watched the time.

It was exactly six o'clock when they started to come out. Troops. Marines. Army. Navy. Air Force. In their uniforms, looking exhausted, they came into the arrivals hall, and most were greeted by tearful family and friends.

I clutched Zayed's hand, threading my fingers through his. Maybe he would bring me luck and this would be the day.

"Mars?"

"I come here every Friday. I always hope that he will be one of them."

"Mars Alexander Senior?"

I nodded.

He slipped an arm around me, and we waited. I rested my head against his chest, feeling hopeful. The soldiers were still coming out. Any minute. How happy he would be to see me, how surprised. He would like Zayed, I knew he would.

A young woman in combat boots came into the terminal and looked around the hallway. There didn't seem to be anyone waiting for her. I bit my lip. Where was her family? Her friends?

She stood, waiting, looking sadder by the second. I almost stood up and went over to her but didn't know what I would do after that. What was wrong with people? This girl was home from a nightmarish place, and there was no one to show her she was loved and missed.

My father was never going to be in that situation, I had vowed. I would be here every Friday, whether he called ahead to let us know he was coming or not.

The young woman finally realized no one was coming and headed toward the taxi stands. I watched her leave the terminal to look for a taxi.

A few minutes passed, and we watched the arrivals dwindle down. Then no one came up the escalator at all.

"I don't think he's coming today." Zayed's arm around my shoulder tightened.

I allowed myself to bury my face in his shoulder to stop the tears that I knew would come next.

"Why not?" I whispered.

"I don't know."

"Where is he?" I asked needlessly, the tears starting, though I'd promised myself I wouldn't cry today in front of Zayed.

Zayed continued to hold me and let me cry silently.

"I don't know, but we'll be waiting here, both of us, when he does come."

"There you two are!" Vivek exclaimed. "We were about to give up on you."

Vivek had insisted that Zayed and I join him and Lana for a late-evening dinner that night. He was making Indian-Italian fusion cuisine and wanted an honest audience, he'd claimed. Lana wanted to keep an eye on me and Zayed, is what I thought the real motivation was.

I hadn't wanted to go, given my fight with Lana and the emotional afternoon at the airport. Still, I knew how much Zayed had enjoyed breakfast at our house and hadn't wanted to refuse the offer of dinner after seeing his eyes light up. I understood it must be incredibly lonely for him to go from being with such a close-knit family to where he was now, living alone with only a tiny kitten as company.

Vivek ushered Zayed and me into his downtown Seattle condo. I stared at the 360-degree view of the city from the twentieth-story windows. The panoramic vision could've easily been frozen in time, creating a perfect postcard of all the Pacific Northwest had to offer. Still, I was astonished at how spectacular and new the snow-covered peaks of the Olympic Mountains, the blanket of silvery-blue lake, and an up-and-coming downtown area looked even to me.

"Your condo is gorgeous," I said as I glanced around the foyer, which had clearly been done by a professional decorator. There was no way a twenty-something guy could have picked out the perfect wall-hanging and rug combo that showcased his place.

"This is my weekday home. My other place is a mansion." Vivek nudged us toward his living room.

"Really?" Zayed whispered, tightening his grip on my hand.

"Probably." I muttered back, loudly enough for Vivek to hear.

"No! I'm obviously kidding," he said, laughing at the look of disgust on my face. "I did this whole place myself, from the floor plan to the décor."

I couldn't help but raise an eyebrow at that.

Lana was already in the kitchen, pouring a glass of wine. "Hello, kids. I'm glad you both could come on such short notice."

I frowned. Kids? She was the one dating someone a whole teenager younger than her.

"Thank you for including me, Mrs. Alexander."

"You're most welcome, Zayed. I knew if I wanted to see my daughter, I would have to lure her here." Lana gave him her fake smile. This evening would end very quickly if she continued with her snide comments. Clearly, Zayed made me happy. I was giving her new boyfriend the benefit of the doubt; she owed me the same in return.

"Tonight's specialty is ravioli stuffed with butter chicken served in a rose alfredo sauce, a cold potato curry salad, and for dessert, panna cotta infused with ground cardamom powder," Vivek announced, presenting each dish on the table with a flourish.

Tall candlesticks graced the ends of the table, which featured asymmetrical dishes and flatware unlike any I'd seen before. I smoothed my napkin on my lap and watched Vivek pull out Lana's chair for her. She rewarded him with that smile that I knew would make him crazy. He stared at her long after she turned her attention to the serving dishes.

It was already happening. He would be moving in in no time, and this downtown condo would become our weekend home.

"Where did you find this ravioli?" I took the first bite. Delicious. The butter chicken was creamy, spicy with just a hint of rosy milky sweetness.

"Vivek and I gave the pasta maker a run this afternoon to roll out the dough for the ravioli. I made the alfredo sauce." Lana watched me eat. "You like it?"

"You made this?" I asked incredulously, taking a second bite of ravioli.

"I've never had anything like this before." Zayed commented. "I'm accustomed to spicy food, but the potato salad has a definite bite to it. It's excellent."

I took a small forkful of the potato salad, which was sprinkled with crushed serrano peppers to add some heat. "Wow."

Vivek smiled with satisfaction, glancing over at Lana. Even I had to give them credit. The food was delicious, and it was a rare thing to see Lana participate in cooking anything. My father had long ago banished her from the kitchen, having grown impatient with her experiments gone wrong.

"If you like spicy food, I will make my mother's recipe for khoresh anaar for you all soon," Zayed promised. "It's a famous Iraqi dish that everyone says is the best they've ever had."

"I'm going to hold you to that," Vivek warned.

So was I. After tasting the infamous Anwar family scalloped potatoes, I would love to try something authentically Middle Eastern.

"What is your family like, Zayed?" Lana asked. I realized now that she was digging for information rather than asking out of politeness. I was annoyed but didn't intrude or change the subject since I wanted to know as well without seeming like even more of a snoop.

"My father is an engineer, a top hydraulic engineer. He helped design the water system where we live."

"In Paris? He must have done very well for himself," Vivek commented.

Zayed went on as if he hadn't heard Vivek. "We also own a villa outside the city that we rent to tourists."

Vivek raised an eyebrow at this. Zayed's family appeared to be very different from what I'd imagined. They were undoubtedly well off and educated. No wonder he had such beautiful manners and knew so much about the world.

"My mother is a homemaker, though she's always longed for a career outside the home. She didn't have the opportunity for further education since her family stressed the importance of being married rather than having a career. She used to teach young girls verses from the Qur'an, but that was all."

Zayed's cell phone rang just then. He reached for it just as it stopped. I was surprised that he didn't even check to see who it was. Then I wondered who it was that always called and hung up so quickly.

"You'd said earlier that your family are progressive Muslims. What does that mean?" Lana pressed on.

"Progressive Muslims don't have one central authority, but we believe that independent reasoning is preferable to blind faith in religious leaders; in the importance of safeguarding human rights; and in determining the value of a person based on his ethics and values, rather than how rigidly he follows religious rituals."

I nodded, urging him on. "And this is how you were raised?"

"Yes. This is how my father has always explained Islam to us. Teaching tolerance is most important, above anything else. He says that the young people of today harbor a passion unlike anything he has seen before, and if harnessed correctly, it can be used for the advancement of the whole human race. He also says something we all know, that this passion can be used for good, but also evil."

"Extremists," Vivek said knowingly. "This happens in India too. I've had relatives who—" he stopped. "People do bad things, and they actually believe they're doing something that will benefit the people they care about."

The table was silent for a few minutes.

"So what can be done? Can teachers and other people in positions of power do more to prevent extremists?" Lana took a bite of her ravioli and made an "mmm" noise. I had to agree; the sauce was delicious. I had no idea she had the potential to be such a good cook.

"I think so," Zayed said. "Eventually I would want to teach high school kids and college students these kinds of lessons. As I grow older, I realize I can't just talk about the problem; I have to get involved and help stop it. This is part of the reason I am pursuing my field of study."

I paused in mid-bite. He was not in it alone. I was going to be there with him and for him, no matter what Lana or anyone else had to say about it.

"My brother and sister shared everything with each other," Krish, the heartbreakingly pretty girl, said in therapy group, her eyes filling with tears. "Ever since she died, he's been so different, like—"

"How do you feel about that? Not how your brother feels, how do *you* feel?" Stephanie, our group leader, to the rescue again. She had been especially pushy that Tuesday evening to get each person to share their feelings and nothing more. I had the feeling of being measured against some bar she'd set for us. Krish, Octavio, and Erica were all looking a bit uncomfortable at her forcefulness, and Ken had just tuned out and was playing with his lighter again.

Krish looked around the room and bit her lip. "Well, I'm hurt most of the time because my brother doesn't talk to me the way he used to talk to her. I can't blame him, though; he has these dreams where he's watching her get shot. He runs to her and—"

"Again, let's keep the focus on you." The leader interrupted again. "Please don't make me ask again."

I had been examining the red sole of my boot and looked up just in time to see Krish crossing her arms and pursing her lips. She was done. Shut down.

This was enough.

"No. Stop. Please tell us about your sister and brother and anything else you want to share," I requested of Krish. "I have no siblings and love to hear about the relationships between others,"

She opened her mouth and started to say something.

"I think the discussion has gone off topic today," Stephanie interrupted the dialogue again. I gave her a look in an attempt to shut her up, but she carried on.

"Let's all go around the circle and say one thing we're thankful for, and then it's time to go." Twenty minutes earlier than scheduled, at that.

I rolled my eyes. "I'm thankful I met so many great people in this group." Except you, I thought silently in her direction. Everyone followed suit with an equally feeling-less sentiment.

After the circle was complete, we all stood up and left the old building in clumps, Krish and Octavio leading the way, their heads together, a word or phrase shared between them fading as it reached us.

"I feel like we were really talking today before you-know-who cut us off," Ken offered, walking with me, as he flicked his lighter for the millionth time. "I wanted to hear what she," he said pointing to Krish, "had to say about her brother. It's probably hard for her to feel so helpless. I mean, both her dad and sister gone and her brother falling apart."

I knew *exactly* how she felt. She wanted to talk about her loss; she didn't want to pretend it didn't exist like everyone else seemed to assume she wanted. Why people were so afraid of grief and talking about it was beyond me.

I looked over at Ken, who didn't seem to be in any hurry to leave. But then all of us were walking fairly slowly, possibly reluctant to leave the sanctuary of the group and return to the real world.

I had an idea. "What about all of us who want to, let's finish what we were talking about. Let's keep having our session, just without you-know-who."

"What? Where?"

"The gazebo." I gestured in the general direction of the waterfront.

The Kirkland downtown gazebo is the central, sparkling jewel of Kirkland's waterfront park. It hosts concerts and performers all year long as well as being the destination spot for late-summer weddings. It was the perfect place to sit and talk about what was on our minds.

Ken hurried to let Krish and Octavio know the new plan. I was really starting to like this kid. I had been amazed to see the difference in him from a month ago to now. He'd gone from silent and brooding to being willing to listen and help anyone he could.

I sidled up alongside Erica, who'd been very quiet all evening, barely acknowledging my tap on her shoulder.

"Do you need to tell Chad where you're going to be if I keep you out a bit late?"

She shook her head, staring at the sidewalk as we walked.

"Why?"

"We're not talking right now."

"You guys? You're always talking. I don't believe it." I almost stopped in my tracks. I hadn't seen Chad in a few days, actually. I hoped it wasn't serious.

"Believe it."

"What's this about?" I matched her step for step, realizing she wasn't effervescently bouncing down the street like always. Something was very wrong.

"Traditions."

"What?"

"Things that everyone else does that Chad refuses to do. Dinner with my family, stuff like that." She hesitated as if she was going to say something else but seemed to change her mind. I wondered what was really going on. She was obviously keeping something to herself, with no intentions of sharing.

That annoyed me. She always insisted I tell her everything, and I felt like she was putting up a wall to keep me from doing the same. It was like we had hit the ceiling of our friendship and she was not going to let me know any other layer of her personality other than the friendly, funky artist she portrayed.

"Do you think he doesn't want a long-term commitment? That doesn't sound like him. You guys have been together longer than most people have been married."

"I just know that he thinks some of the things I want are silly, and he doesn't take them seriously."

"Like what?"

"Like regular things. Like going to homecoming."

"The dance?"

"Yeah."

"You know how he is. He thinks homecoming is for the 'mainstreamers,' and it's not his thing. I've never gotten to go, and this year is the last chance. It's the one time I get to wear the dress, get my hair done, rent the limo. All the things you've always done."

"Are you sure Chad won't go?" I felt bad for Erica that she'd never been able to experience basic high school drama.

Erica blinked those enormous, glimmering eyes of hers, looking hurt and betrayed. "He said absolutely not and that I was being stupid for even wanting to."

I had never heard her tone so biting. Wow, it was serious. And, come to think of it, I hadn't seen Chad's Mini Cooper around in a few weeks. Had they broken up for good?

"Erica, listen to me. What you guys have is special. I think you're both mad at each other right now. I think it's going to be okay." And I was convinced it was. She would go to homecoming in the princess gown and, for one night, be like everyone else in school. Then she would realize how lonely her night had been and everything would be okay.

"I'm sorry, hon." I couldn't think of anything else to say to make her feel better.

"Can we talk about something else?" Erica sighed, glancing up and seeing Ken and the couple heading toward the gazebo.

"How's Ricardo?"

"He's having nightmares."

I didn't know what to say to that either. There went Zayed's theory that I would make a good therapist. I didn't even know what to say to a good friend when she needed me, much less a group of strangers.

Instead, I took Erica's arm and guided her across the street to the gazebo, where Ken, Octavio, and Krish already waited, sitting cross-legged on the ground. I activated the backlight on my cell phone and held it in my hands. The others followed suit, and soon the five of us were sitting in a semi-circle, the glow from our phones lighting up our faces.

"Why is our group so small?" Ken asked after a few minutes of silence.

"He's right. We can't be the only kids in school affected by the war, right? Where is everybody else?" Krish piped up. "My sister and brother, your dad, your mom," she pointed at me last, "and your dad. Are these the only people from Kirkland who are deployed right now? I don't think so. Where are their kids and siblings? Where did Angel go? He hasn't been here in weeks."

"I think," I said slowly, "people want to move on with their lives without having to be part of groups like this." I hated saying this because this is exactly what I had done up until a few weeks ago.

Heads swiveled in my direction.

"Think about it, you guys. So many people just deny this grief; they don't want to deal with it . . ."

I was starting to get choked up at this point.

Erica took over, "She's right. People don't want to look weak, like they need help. Like they need to talk about this stuff. Especially people our age that get made fun of for showing any kind of real feelings."

People wanted to go on like nothing had happened and forget about mourning what our families used to be. I had done this. Lana had done this. Zayed had forced me out of my shell by needing me to be there for him. I had shared so much of myself in an effort to get him to open up. And it had worked, kind of.

"Well, I feel like the war has affected my life a lot, and I want to talk about it," Krish said. "Nothing will ever be the same for my family again. And I know it's the same for him," she pointed at Octavio. Even in the dark, I could see the two of them touching hands. The war did bring some people together.

"Me too. I want to talk about how I'm going to take care of my brother," Erica said with a shrug. "Maybe I won't even go to college. I might have to get a job so we can pay for his expenses."

I stared at her. No way. I wasn't going to let that happen. She'd worked too hard all through high school for her perfect grade-point-average that would take her directly to an Ivy League university.

"Me too," Octavio said. "I need to stay home with my dad. How can I go off to college? I won't put him in a home. And I haven't seen my mom in years; she ran off when I was five. She's not going to take care of him."

So many families were less fortunate than mine. Yes, Dad was off in Afghanistan, and who knew when he was going to come home, but Lana and I were safe and taken care of, thanks to her huge inheritance. We didn't need to worry about money or our futures. We had each other, and we had our comforts. I could attend the college of my choice, and Lana could continue to host parties and galas without second thoughts.

How ridiculous all my talk of designer clothes or my Louboutin shoe collection must have sounded to Erica. What had I been thinking? Lana and I had an obligation to do something for others who didn't have those luxuries. I was starting to have the earliest inklings of a plan, but I needed Lana's help.

We sat there, the five of us, and talked in the darkness. We were virtually strangers, most of us not even knowing each other's last names. That semblance of anonymity made it easier for us to talk openly about the one thing that bonded us together, the war, its effects on our families, and how it kept us awake every night.

Joggers passed us with dogs; couples looking for a private spot and even a friendly squirrel went by, but we kept talking, desperately almost, like we had so much to say and such a limited time in which to say it.

"This was a great idea," Ken said after we'd been sitting for over two hours and a silence had fallen over our group. "Thanks, Mars, for organizing it."

Krish said softly. "I was able to share a lot more with you guys here than I've ever been able to in that building."

I smiled in her direction.

"You're good at this," Erica whispered to me as she stood up. "I need to go."

I was the last to leave the gazebo. I sat there on the cold ground, enveloped by night, surrounded by fireflies and serenading crickets, wondering. Zayed did have a point.

I wasn't able to help these kids yet, but I had a sense that maybe I would be able to soon. Sharing my story seemed to have opened the floodgates of our group. Maybe I would have to do it more and see what happened, for the group and for Zayed.

CHAPTER 14

The Rejection

"The chicken is going to overcook unless I tend to it. You have to stop distracting me. Or at least do so less." Zayed swatted me playfully with a dish towel as I leaned over the counter and fluttered my eyelashes at him.

I purred, similarly to what Coconut had been doing a few minutes prior.

"You're bad," he said, cupping my face with his hand.

"I try." I was grinning like a fool. I never acted like this. Giddy and silly and flirty. Laughing at everything.

Things had changed between us after the trip to the airport. The innocent touches were no longer that; both of us were ready for more. He told me often about how beautiful he thought I was. He looked at me in a way that I knew he thought about me at night when he was alone.

"The chicken," I reminded Zayed.

"I can't think with you around." Zayed sighed and turned back to the stove.

Khoresh anaar. That was what Zayed was cooking for dinner. He wanted to do a practice run of cooking it before attempting to make dinner for Lana and Vivek. I tried to assure him that he didn't actually have to fulfill his promise to make dinner for them, but he'd looked at me solemnly and assured me that he always kept his word.

"I hope you didn't mind all the questions at dinner the other night," I said, referring to Lana's hundred questions about his family, his life, his schooling. He had perfect responses to everything, but even then she hadn't been satisfied. She'd squeezed my arm as Zayed and I had left Vivek's apartment, letting me know she would be home in an hour. Translation: don't try anything funny.

"Your mother does not trust me. She believes I am hiding something that will hurt you," Zayed responded easily, not sounding surprised or hurt or any other emotion I would expect.

"And you're not?"

"Can you get the bag of flour from the pantry, please?" He changed the subject just as easily.

I scowled a little as I did as he asked. Helping in the kitchen was not the only thing I intended to do this evening.

So far my help had included sitting on the counter, playing with the cat, while asking him why he was adding pomegranate seeds and walnuts into a chicken curry. He had sliced the onions and sautéed them in oil before adding the chicken. After adding water and cooking the chicken for over half an hour, he'd added various herbs, spices, and garlic. That was when the walnuts and pomegranate seeds had gone in, earning a raised eyebrow from me.

"Tell me more about your mother," I instructed him as he added in some flour to thicken the curry and covered the pan.

"She would like you very much. I would've liked to take you home with me and for you to meet her if it was possible." I smiled at that. *Home with him* sounded magical.

"Although she was raised in a traditional house, her family was very progressive and believed that women should have choices," Zayed said, turning the heat down and stirring the chicken. "She is also an extraordinary cook, and this dish is her specialty."

"Do you make it as well as your mom?" I teased, as if I had room to talk with my specialty PB&Js. I scooped up Coconut in my arms and showed her what was happening on the counter, answering her insistent meows.

"As you would say, hell no!"

I laughed. "I like a man who's self-aware."

"Can I assume that means you like me, even a little?"

I love you.

I didn't say it out loud, though I wanted to. I loved the way it sounded. *Not only can I not be without you, I don't want to be.*

"I didn't make that clear?" I hopped off the counter, depositing the kitten safely on the floor. I slid up behind Zayed, wrapped my arms around his waist, and rose to my toes to brush the back of his neck with my cheek. "What about you?"

His skin was like velvet. Smooth, golden velvet.

"I like you too much." I could barely hear the words, just his breathing and the strong rushing of his heart.

"Why?"

"Because you are very clever with words. More clever than I ever will be." He glanced at me while tasting the chicken one last time.

"That's the only reason, huh?"

"Unfortunately."

He carried the dish of chicken to the coffee table while I served the white rice he'd prepared in the microwave onto two plates. He served me a spoonful of chicken over the rice.

I dug in before it was polite, unable to resist the tangy smell of the curry. The dish was tart, yet spicy with a sweetish aftertaste. It was exquisite.

"This is unlike anything I'd ever had."

"Good unlike?"

"Very good unlike."

"I hate when people watch me eat," I mumbled through a bite of chicken. "But you can."

"I'm honored."

We ate in silence for a few minutes. Again, it was a comfortable silence that I was used to now.

"I think it's nice your mom let you help in the kitchen. When my father cooked, he never allowed anyone in the kitchen during the elaborate affair."

Zayed glanced at me, biting the corner of his lip. I knew that look.

"What happened to him, Mars? Why does everyone avoid the subject?"

I set my fork down and wiped my lips. "I already told you."

"Please. I want to know you."

I hesitated. I wanted to tell him. Everyone else knew. How could he not?

"I won't repeat it to anyone if that's your concern. I'm also unpopular."

My concern was much more than that. To him and only him, I was normal. Once he heard the story, I would be one to be pitied, someone fragile and delicate who could fall apart at any moment.

"You could have, and should have, left me on that roof along with everyone else. You stayed. And I want to know why you're so brave."

I remembered the therapy group session where I had first shared Zayed's email about me being a hero and how that made me feel. Remembered how much everyone had appreciated it and how good I had felt afterward.

"My mom and I got a letter delivered." I started before I changed my mind, reaching for Coconut and pulling her into my arms for comfort. She nuzzled my cheek as if encouraging me to continue.

Zayed sat perfectly still, not eating anymore, just staring at me, which made me even more nervous.

"It said, verbatim, that my dad's truck at the head of his convoy had exploded. Blown up. He is listed as missing, presumed dead." I rushed through that part. People were ridiculous, completely ready to dismiss his life and everything he'd done in mere seconds.

"Then?"

"The next day, I was in the girls' locker room after gym—at school—and everyone started consoling me, acting as if he was dead, telling me they know a therapist I could see, a support group I could join. I lost it."

"You lost it?"

My cheeks burned, remembering. "I ran into one of the shower stalls with a pair of eyebrow scissors and I hacked off my hair. To get them to stop. To get them to talk about something else. I cut my cheek by accident. There was some blood. That's all."

I'd been hauled out of the locker room on a stretcher and to the hospital in an ambulance after someone called 911. Lana sobbed through the whole event, not being one bit supportive. I'd slept for days after and, upon returning to school, found myself a pariah.

"But you believe him to be alive. You go to the airport to wait for him, and you get very angry when anyone says he's gone."

"We fought the night before he left."

"About?"

I remembered every detail. I had brought up the idea of doing a semester abroad in Paris in the spring as a foreign exchange student.

"You're not going, Mars. End of discussion." Dad didn't glance up from the bag he was expertly packing for his deployment.

"Why not?" My arms had been crossed. I was going to get my way this time. *"Why are you being a pain about this?"*

"A pain?" he'd finally looked up, his dark eyes flashing with anger. "Do you actually think you're going to talk to me like that?"

I had seethed silently.

"I said no already. You are not responsible enough to be in a strange city by yourself. And don't try and convince your mother to let you go. It doesn't matter what she says. The answer is still no."

"You're leaving tomorrow. Do you really think you get to control what I do? I'll go to Paris if I get into the program." I slammed the door to the bedroom.

"Mars, I'm warning you," he yelled after me.

"Warn all you want, I'll be gone by the time you get back!" I'd yelled back before storming out of the house and had spent the evening at Jason's complaining about how impossible Dad was and how he was done controlling me.

"He doesn't get to go away forever when we didn't get to finish the fight."

"That was the last conversation you had with him?"

I nodded. He'd left early the following morning, and I had been too angry still to go downstairs and say good-bye.

"And now everyone is saying he's dead. Even his regiment."

"They didn't ship anything back. How can he be dead if there is no body? Lana had a funeral, and she buried an empty casket."

I'd refused to attend and had claimed hysterics. I'd told her I wouldn't have been able to deal with the crowd of people sure to be there. I'd told her I would have another breakdown if she made me attend.

She'd left me alone that day.

And all the days after, never talking about it again.

Zayed was silent. He didn't look one bit surprised. He should've looked more surprised.

"Did you know that already? About the funeral?"

He nodded without hesitation. "Vivek told me while we were preparing breakfast."

I bit my lip, now feeling my cheeks heat up with anger. That morning had been one of the most horrible in recent times. I'd been trying to work through my anger at Jason and had appreciated all the support Vivek and Zayed had given me when in actuality they had been talking about me behind my back. Worse, Lana had told Vivek everything. The letter, my breakdown, everything.

She had let him in completely.

And all this time, Zayed had been pretending he didn't know what had happened or why I was so angry at Lana.

I was betrayed by everyone again.

I grabbed my plate off the table and started to stand up.

"Wait, wait. Mars, are you angry with me?" Zayed reached for the remote and muted the volume on the television, washing the room in silence.

"No." I didn't look at him and instead stalked into the kitchen.

A minute later, I felt his hand on my shoulder.

"We were both concerned for you."

"Yeah, I bet."

"Please." He gently removed the plate I was gripping to the point of shattering it and set it in the sink. He then pulled me into his arms. "I didn't know the details of the letter that came to your house. All Vivek knows is that there was a funeral. Your mother does not speak to him about it."

We stood there, my arms uselessly by my side and Zayed holding onto me too tightly.

"I'm glad you cut off your hair. It's beautiful this way."

I smiled into his chest. "I know hacking it off like a crazy person was a clichéd move. I watch movies. I know what it symbolizes. It was an excuse to be crazy, and honestly, I was sick of my hair."

Coconut had followed us to the kitchen and was now trying to stick her paw into the sink to investigate. I reached out and batted at her playfully, trying to keep her off the dishes.

Zayed was watching me when I raised my head to look at him. "You had to cut it off in public?"

"I didn't want anyone else to talk to me about my father, so I acted insane. People mess with a tough girl, but no one messes with the crazy girl. I wanted Lana to know that I was not okay. But she ignored it."

During the funeral, I had called Dad's cell phone repeatedly, leaving one frantic message after another begging him to come home.

Ever since then, everyone had referred to him in the past tense. I wasn't going to do that. He was out there. I knew it. I could feel it. If he really was gone, I wouldn't feel his protective presence around me all the time.

Now I buried my face in Zayed's chest and waited for him to tell me I was insane. That it wasn't possible. That I needed to move on. He would be joining the ranks of everyone else in my life to believe so.

He continued to stand silently, just holding me.

"Say something." I finally insisted, punching him gently in his side.

"You must protect yourself," he said quietly. "I understand that. I'm sorry to hear you feel you're alone in this."

"I do feel like I'm the only one waiting for him." That was clear from the fact that only I went to the airport. Only I called his cell phone.

"I'll wait with you, Mars. I don't know where he is or why he's not here, but I'll wait with you for as long as you want."

Tears sprung to my eyes. The one person who'd never met my father was willing to believe in him. Why couldn't anyone else?

Zayed and I washed dishes together, me drying and putting away while keeping Coconut from ending up in a pile of soap. He was very quiet, a pensive look on his face as he scrubbed the pan.

I wondered what he was thinking. That I was crazy. That this, whatever *this* was, was over. Or that what we were doing was beautiful and magical and he couldn't live without me. I knew telling him was the right thing to do, but I feared I had jeopardized what we had.

I tossed a soap bubble at him to break the silence. We'd never had that long of a silence between us. He swiped it out of his eye like the cat and blew one back at me. I splashed some soapy water on his shirt and, laughing, ran into the living space quickly before he could drench me in return.

I watched him pull the black V-neck sweater over his head and toss it aside. He walked toward me with his perfect martini-glass-shaped silhouette. No hesitation. He was coming straight in my direction.

I felt my heart do the clichéd speeding up again. So, this did happen in real life. He pulled me roughly to my feet and into his chest again. This time, it wasn't for comfort and safety. I breathed in that scent of firewood and oranges again. His skin was warm, hotter by the second.

"What are you doing to me?" he whispered.

"Nothing."

"What are you to me?"

"A tour guide and a friend," I said breathlessly.

"If only," Zayed sighed. "You're all I think about. The thoughts I had that night in your bedroom." He didn't say anything else, just ran his hands down my back and stopped on my hips. "I wanted to wait until after we were married for this, but I don't know how we can . . ."

Marriage? He was ready to discuss that kind of commitment to me and yet couldn't tell me what his giant secret was? That was ridiculous. I spun him around and threw him on the couch. The look of surprise on his face urged me on. I placed my knees on either side of his legs hovering, not touching him.

"Tell me what you've been hiding."

"Mars, I can't. You know that."

I pinned his arms against the back of the couch. "Now."

The dance was over. We'd gone as far as we could without things changing to become more serious. Things were going to change tonight.

I eyed his bed, perfectly made. Like my life had been before he'd arrived in it. Perfectly calm, waiting to be mussed. One way or another, everything was going to change.

As if he was reading my mind, he broke free of my bond and wrapped his arms around my waist, hands grazing the sliver of exposed skin. He slipped a hand under my sweater and traveled up my back as his lips found my jaw.

I closed my eyes, hoping to feel his lips on mine.

Nothing.

I opened them and he was inches away, his gaze roaming over my eyelashes and lips.

I love you, Zayed Anwar.

"You're so very beautiful."

"You look like a prince." I retorted softly, stroking my thumb over his lower lip.

"That I'm not." He continued to gaze at me while he kissed my fingertips, then hand, then arm, then shoulder. Then he reached behind and lifted my sweater. It went up, up, up, and over my head. The shiver went straight through my spine.

Tonight, he wanted more.

"You might be. What do I really know about you?" I lifted myself onto my knees, pushing him back against the arm of the couch. I hovered over him again, enjoying the amazed look on his face as he gazed at me.

"What do you wish to know?" Now his eyes closed as I adjusted myself on his lap. "Keep doing this and I'll tell you more than I should."

"Who are you?" I whispered, my lips close to his ear. "Really. Why are you here?"

"I'm yours. I'm only here for you," he sighed. "I'm someone you've saved over and over again. Someone who is ready to spend the rest of his life serving you."

He wanted me. I knew that. I could feel the heat coming off his body.

I also knew that if I kissed him now or did anything else, I wouldn't be able to stop. I wouldn't get the answers I wanted, and I wouldn't care. I would have him finally, and nothing else would matter.

I'd never felt this kind of longing for another person. It was terrifying, empowering, and not at all something I had ever done or felt I should do.

And I no longer gave a damn.

I ran a finger down his throat, into the hollow. I gently scraped his chest and trailed down his stomach to the buckle of his belt. I finally kissed him, below the throat. I felt his hands on the tops of my thighs, pushing me down gently so I straddled his lap.

He tilted my head back and pressed his lips on the edge of my mouth. "I read that when you save someone they belong to you. I belong to you, Mars. I hope that's not too much for me to say."

I knew he was mine from the first night on the roof. The way I thought about him constantly, the way I wanted nothing other than to be with him twenty-four hours a day. The way his lips were about to meet mine for our first, long-anticipated kiss.

"I'm in love with you," I whispered. I hadn't wanted to be the one to say it, but the words came out anyway. It was as if a spell had possessed the two of us and I had no control of what my body or mind was doing.

He froze as my lips pressed against his.

Damn.

I'd made a mistake. It was too soon.

"I'm sorry." He pulled away, staring at the television.

Embarrassed, I quickly moved to the other end of the couch, pulling my knees to my chest. I realized Zayed was still staring at the television, frowning.

Television, really? My love for him made him crave the news?

I felt a sudden chill at the caption on the news story he was so intently watching, TRASH BOMB DETONATED AT WAR RALLY AT THE UNIVERSITY OF WASHINGTON. SIX INJURED.

CHAPTER 15

The Suspicion

I sat in my therapy group the next day, staring at the wall. Erica might have whispered a comment about Chad or something, but I couldn't be sure. All I could think about were the events of that night, repeating themselves over and over in my mind.

The whole night had felt like a dream. From the touching and whispering to that ill-fated kiss.

"Would you like to share another event that's happened with you lately?" Stephanie pressed me again, giving me an almost-dirty look.

"No." I passed the flag to Erica. These sessions felt hollow and superficial compared to how much we'd all shared a week ago in the gazebo. I noticed everyone was staring at the ground a lot more and saying a lot less, and Stephanie didn't seem to notice or care.

Too many events lately. Was it only a month or so ago that I'd been sitting here contemplating the first night on the roof with Zayed? It had only been a short amount of time, but for me it had been a lifetime and a half ago. Everything was different. Everything that had been vital before no longer was, and things I'd never thought about were frighteningly real.

I couldn't stop seeing Zayed. Despite all the red flags about the secrets he was keeping, despite my father never having had known him, I couldn't stay away from him. I couldn't stop thinking of his smoky-gray eyes probing mine. His trembling lips underneath my fingertips. The magical second when our lips had met.

But the way he'd been staring at the television, no shock, no horror, no surprise. Just matter-of-factly watching the news of a sudden tragedy in Seattle. He'd been distracted and distant as I'd packed my bag and kissed Coconut good-night. He'd squeezed my hand at my car and said good-night quickly. Something was happening, and Zayed knew a lot more than he was letting on.

What did he do when we weren't together? A little nagging voice asked. Where did he disappear off to sometimes?

"I'm worried you're not progressing at the same rate as everyone else, Mars." Stephanie halted the discussion with a dismissive move of her hand. "It feels like you're not moving toward acceptance or any other resolution. Let's talk about this."

Talk? Now she wanted to talk? Fine, we would talk.

"What do you mean?"

"You don't share anything with us. I don't feel that you're a very valuable member here."

Ken was about to say something, but I held my hand up to stop him. This was not his fight.

"You don't know anything about me or my resolution. Do you know what's going on inside my head? Do you have some barometer?" I jerked my head away from her, knowing I was about to snap. "Or have you become psychic?"

She bristled. "There is no need to—"

"Then how do you know I'm not 'moving toward acceptance'?"

"I can only assume from my past experiences with these groups," she said in that snooty voice that made me crazy.

"Past experiences? *Past experience* is knowing and feeling what I or anyone else in here for that matter are going through. *Past experience* is *not* nodding and pretending to understand six grieving kids so you can check off the five stages of grief on a worksheet! We've all lost someone, and you're going to have to accept that not all of us are going to get over it as quickly as you would like."

Suddenly four pairs of eyes were watching me. I knew I'd helped them the previous week at the gazebo. I'd seen it in their eyes, and I'd known it deep down. I had to stay strong for them.

"My job is to facilitate the discussions, not relate and relay. Also, not everyone in here has *lost* someone, so please don't—"

"Yes, they have," I snapped. "Even if people have come back from the war in one piece, the person they used to be is *gone*. Do you even get that? Erica's brother is not the same person he was before. She has lost him. Will she find a better, different version soon? Hopefully. But in the meantime, please do not belittle what she's feeling!" I could feel my voice rising uncontrollably. I didn't want to cause a scene, but I was tired of wasting my time in these group sessions if I wasn't even allowed to talk about my feelings unless it was on some agenda.

I was finally starting to realize that yes, I had lost my father. I had no idea when he was coming back and why he was gone, but right now, he was lost to me. I wanted to talk about that, to express my sadness for as long as I wanted. I didn't want to be told how I was "supposed" to feel by a certain week.

I felt like I was having a déjà vu moment. I'd had a conversation about this with Zayed at the tea house. He brought out a passionate argument in me about it, and I felt the same words slip out of my mouth now. "This therapy group needs a leader who can relate to our experiences of loss. You have to have gone through it! You have to understand that people take different amounts of time to heal." I took another deep breath.

"Does everyone else feel this way too?" Stephanie stood up and glanced around the circle.

Krish raised a hand. "Sometimes, yes. I don't feel like you really understand what we're going through. You tend to hurry us through our discussions."

"Then why are you here?" Stephanie snapped at her, clearly not having expected anyone to take my side. "Why are you wasting my time?"

I almost gave her a piece of my mind just then but decided to take the Zayed approach of trying to explain my point of view. "Listen, it's not personal. It's about empathy versus sympathy. Right now you may feel sorry for us or sympathetic or whatever, but do you really understand what we're going through? Do you really understand that even if someone knows they need to move on, it doesn't mean they can just do it? That acceptance isn't one step?"

"Well, aren't you the expert?" Stephanie didn't take too well to my explanation. "Would you like to sit here," she gestured toward her chair. "Would you like to lead these sessions?"

I remembered Zayed's words. *You understand what those other teenagers are going through. Because you feel a deep empathy for them. Because you "know."*

He'd taught me that we have to take chances sometimes, even though it might seem like a risk. Otherwise how do we learn anything?

I decided to take that risk.

"Maybe. Are you offering to let me try?"

Every eyebrow raised at the same time. Mutiny. That's what I was staging here.

"Mars, I'm going to have to ask you to leave because you're interrupting our work here." Stephanie's tone was cold, and I knew my time at these sessions was officially over.

"No problem." I stood up. "I won't be coming back. Sorry, guys."

I breathed a deep sigh of relief after I'd stormed out of the building. Finally. I'd spoken my mind about *something*. I'd known it probably wouldn't end well, but at least I'd tried.

The familiar jasmine perfume that followed me out of the building reassured me that Erica was right behind me. "I'm so proud of you," she said as she hugged me close. "I am so, so proud of you."

Truth be told, I was too.

"At least look at their program details. Please, Mars." Zayed clearly was not going to give up.

I finally relented. I wasn't going to attend the University of Michigan, so there was no harm in appeasing Zayed. He did have to understand that my mind was made up about staying close to home. Besides, I was hardly special enough to travel across the country to attend a top psychology undergraduate program. He was convinced I could perform well enough the first few years of college to qualify for the specialized, exclusive Honors Program.

Zayed and I were sitting on the roof of the College Prep building long after the last student had left, enjoying the unseasonably warm evening. I had put aside all of my thoughts about the bombing on the U campus and his interest in the news when he had mentioned nothing about it and acted completely normal during class.

He was probably just surprised that there was so much violence in Seattle. I realized I was hurt by his reaction to my proclamation of love and was choosing to suspect him of something ridiculous to make myself feel better. I had to stop making my feelings for him so obvious. I sounded desperate and silly.

Now he perched at the ledge of the roof, and I sat near the stairwell. He had that evening's practice exams to grade, and I had yet more practice exams to power through. I felt as if my essays were improving, but Zayed didn't share my opinion. He claimed I could do better, be more honest with my writing.

How can humans not be fearful of the mistakes of their past? We are conditioned to learn from past behavior and evolve. This is why my stance is that memories should always be important as people make decisions.

Like I should have known better than to tell Zayed that I was in love with him. I was sure he'd heard me and had freaked out. Then I had to go and kiss him. I knew it was too soon; Zayed and I had been together for such a short time. It had been in the heat of the moment, and I hadn't meant it anyway. What did I know about love?

"You're positive you want to stay here rather than go to my apartment?" Zayed asked for the sixth time. "You look cold."

I was, a little bit, but was not going to admit it. Instead I pulled my scarf tighter around my neck and glanced up at the overhead light on the roof. It wasn't the best environment, but it would do.

It had been my idea to stay at the College Prep Institute rather than the alternative of going to his place. I couldn't think clearly when he was so close to me, smelling delicious and inviting when there was nothing stopping us from continuing what had almost happened that night.

I trembled, remembering. How I felt like I belonged with him in his world in front of the fire. Like there was no other place I wanted to be. I was scared at how easily I'd bared myself and my soul to him. I was scared at how incredible his lips had felt on my skin and how much I wanted to touch him again.

"When I get home, I'll look up Michigan's psychology program. Happy?" I shook the thoughts out of my head. I wouldn't go there again. I couldn't afford to with the next SAT exam just a week away.

"Here, please use my computer." He nudged his laptop in my direction.

I rubbed goose bumps off my arms as I got up and retrieved the laptop. Even being near him for a moment had disturbing effects on me. I didn't like it one bit.

"I can start the fireplace in my apartment. It's much more comfortable." He glanced up over the stack of practice exams he was working through.

"Uh, I'm okay here. Besides, I need to be home early. I have a calculus exam tomorrow morning."

"You don't have to sit so far away from me at least."

Yeah, I really did.

I had to give myself some time away from him. I was scaring myself with my vulnerability. I was scared I'd tell him I loved him again or touch him in a way he wasn't ready for.

"I was scared about what happened the other night," I said changing the subject. "The bombing at the war rally. Things like this never happen here."

Zayed didn't react, but he did set his lips in that thin line. I watched him. So he wasn't as unaffected as he let on.

"This happens in Afghanistan or Pakistan or somewhere in the Middle East, right? What do these terrorists want from us? You're studying topics like this in your class. What do you think?" I knew I was crossing a line here, but I wanted him to talk about it. I would push him if I had to.

"You have to understand that they don't think of themselves as terrorists." Zayed set down his pen.

I tilted my head, surprised at how certain he sounded on the topic.

"What would they think of themselves as then?"

"Insurgents. Militants. Pursuing an idealized version of their old world, perhaps?"

"How? By hurting people for attention?"

Zayed cracked the knuckles in his fingers, clearly buying time. "You can't expect such logical thinking. People who are in desperate situations . . ."

"Desperate situations like what?"

"Terrorists, as you say, are created, not born. They are people who have nothing, are uneducated. They do not know any other way."

They went after children, Zayed had said at dinner with Lana and Vivek. These terrorists were taught from childhood that hurting others for a specific purpose was okay.

"They want to attain the first four levels of Maslow's Triangle, you mean." I recalled having studied this exact concept in psychology class the previous year.

"Whose triangle?"

"Abraham Maslow. He was a researcher who studied human motivation. Maslow believed there was a hierarchy of human needs based on levels broken into two groups: deficiency needs and growth needs. He believed humans were not able to understand growth needs until all of their deficiency needs had been met."

"Food, shelter, and such?" Zayed asked.

"Something like that. Think of being stranded on a desert island. The first thing you'd try to take care of are hunger and thirst. The second is seeking out safety and a shelter. The third is belonging and love, being accepted by others in society." I was impressed that I remembered so much. I had thought that the topic was interesting, but it had clearly stayed with me more than I'd expected.

"And this is the level these insurgents are operating in. They will do anything to be part of a group, a community of sorts. They just want to belong. Even hurt others. They don't understand what is right or wrong or why," Zayed said, resting his head against the wall he was leaning on.

I understood their motivations. People did terrible things to fit in. Any high schooler would be able to understand that. I didn't understand what people were hoping to accomplish by bringing fear into a normally peaceful city. What did we have that they wanted?

"You seem to know a lot about human motivations. This may be an excellent area for you to focus your college studies in, don't you think?"

There he went again. He had to get over this fascination with my future.

"What do you mean, 'human motivation'? Is that a field?"

"Human behavior or maybe child psychology. It's the perfect entry to graduate work. Michigan also has an excellent medical school if you were to pursue the field of psychiatry. You would do exceptionally well in either."

These topics did interest me, but I could just as easily study this field from the U. Before I'd met him, I hadn't thought about what I would do. I did know that I didn't have what it took to go to medical school like he was convinced I could.

I searched for the University of Michigan on Zayed's unwieldy large laptop. I was glad I had been researching newer, sleeker laptops as a Christmas gift for Zayed. It reminded me of my plan to ask Lana if Zayed could spend Christmas with us. No matter what was going on with him, I felt an overwhelming urge to take care of him, be his family. And I couldn't imagine a better gift that waking up on Christmas morning to find Zayed by my side.

I scrolled through the campus maps, course information, and student life details of the beautiful University of Michigan. I'd seen pictures of their majestic campus before, in glossy brochures showcasing one of the top ten loveliest college campuses in the country.

I could easily picture myself there, walking across the bustling Diag, cup of steaming espresso in one hand, Zayed's arm in the other. He could pursue graduate studies in education while I studied psychology. We would share an apartment on the picturesque Main Street in Ann Arbor and spend our nights talking about everything over tea and lavender shortbread cookies.

Unfortunately, I didn't have the grades, exam scores, or any other qualifications to go there, and wished Zayed would realize it. Zayed believed I could do many things that I knew I was not capable of. I hadn't told him about quitting my therapy group or how I had stormed out.

I landed on the developmental psychology page and skimmed the course work. The entry-level courses were focused on baseline stuff like directed experiences with children and teens, and the 300- and 400-level courses focused on specialized areas; each sounded more interesting than the last.

We'd talked a lot about topics like these in both my psychology classes as well as in the therapy group. I'd always participated in those discussions. In another lifetime, I would have loved to be the girl he thought I was.

After I was done looking at the page, I opened Zayed's list of stored bookmarks scrolled along the bottom of the screen. I was snooping but couldn't help wanting to know the last site he'd been looking at.

I almost gasped out loud when I saw what it was.

He looked up from his practice exam stack with a questioning eyebrow.

"The campus is really nice-looking," I said weakly.

"I knew you would appreciate it." He smiled, incredibly striking and angelic at once. At that moment, I knew there were many things he was keeping from me. Dangerous things. I also realized that, as much as I would have liked to believe otherwise, my first instinct had been correct.

I didn't know Zayed Anwar at all.

CHAPTER 16

The Secret

I hadn't been in Dad's office since I'd moved all his books into my room. This time I realized how diminutive the space was compared to the rest of the house—a narrow, dark room lined on both sides with bookshelves, now mostly deserted. A Turkish rug pulled together a burgundy wooden desk, a leather love seat, and an overhanging lamp.

I hadn't allowed Lana to give or pack away a single item, and now I was very grateful because Dad's presence hung so strongly in the air, I could almost close my eyes and pretend he was there. I settled into the love seat with a flannel throw to ward off the chill in the room.

I was in over my head.

All my searches on the internet for "Zayed Anwar" had resulted in absolutely nothing. Usually this wouldn't draw much suspicion from me. He was young, a student; I'd assumed he didn't have a website or social network page, but the content I'd found on his laptop made me rethink my nonchalance.

His bookmarked sites list read like an inventory and accomplishment list of Islamic insurgent groups. Suicide bombers and kidnappings in the Middle East. Bombings in Iraq, Afghanistan, and London; the most recent one was about the trash-can set on fire in Seattle in early October, the day I'd first seen him, calmly sitting in the window of Sureshot drinking coffee when there was chaos all around him.

Honestly, I wouldn't have thought anything of it. After all, he was studying Middle Eastern culture; he would need to research these kinds of topics. Then I'd found the forum he was participating in.

Jihad. Fighting for the cause of Allah. He was logged into the site, and his last message had been sent the night before, in Arabic. I told myself he was just chatting online with other people about what was going on in the world. He was just curious. The graphics of guns and other artillery told me this wasn't just a common discussion site. The messages that kept coming through with exclamation points and inflammatory words reiterated that theme.

I wanted to believe that he wouldn't be so stupid as to give me his laptop to use if he had incriminating information on it. His fear the night of the blackout on the roof had been genuine. He'd been afraid of something. He had to have a good excuse for what I was seeing.

The intuitive part of me that had been overactive lately told me not to just brush this off. That there was something going on here. That either Zayed knew about these threats that had been taking place in Seattle . . . or he was a part of them.

I felt my heart slam against my chest again, thinking of the moment I realized there was something more behind those soulful eyes. A secret, possibly an incredibly dangerous and treacherous one. I cursed myself again for being such a fool and putting my trust in a man whom I knew nothing about.

We'd spent the night together, become an "us." I'd fallen in love with him and his cat, and I'd never known him at all. He knew everything. What I wanted out of the future, how I felt about him.

My dance with the mysterious dark prince was over, and I realized how silly my dreams of fairy tales and happy endings had been.

He knew so much about the bombings and insurgents. He knew so much about their motivations. How had I not seen it?

Pulling my knees into my chest and hugging them did nothing to numb the dull pain.

I missed him.

I missed the way he said things, using every word he knew. I missed the way he made me forget what I'd been thinking and not even care to remember. I missed the look in his eyes when he told me how brave he thought I was.

Every song that came on the radio reminded me of him, no matter how obscure. Suddenly all those words I'd thought were stupid made complete sense. How could I have developed such strong feelings for him . . . convinced myself I was *in love* with him, when I'd never known him?

The best night I'd ever had was staying up with him, talking, only talking, in my room. Him blinking those curly eyelashes, like flowers unfurling, shadows sweeping his cheeks.

My hand resting on his chest. His hand covering mine and pressing against his heart. The solid, purposeful beat of his heart. The heat radiating off his warm center.

It was the closest I'd ever been to another human being. In those short hours of the night, I'd known that everything was right in the world and I was exactly where I was supposed to be.

I could have lain there next to him every day and every night and not run out of things to say. Now it looked like that night, and the past few weeks, they had never been real at all. Our beautiful relationship had never been anything at all.

"Hey, Mars." Vivek was sitting in the kitchen, nursing what smelled to be espresso, when I left Dad's office. I hoped the fact that I'd spent a good part of the afternoon crying wasn't obvious. "How was school? Everything okay?"

I hadn't seen him around in a few days, and although Lana talked about the dates he'd taken her on to the local wineries as well as the symphony, I'd been wondering how things had been really progressing between them. I didn't want to admit it, but I kind of liked having Vivek around sometimes. It gave Lana something to do besides obsess over what I was doing.

"How's it going with you?" I sat down next to him and peeked inside his cup. It looked fancy and foamy. Seemed like he had figured out how to use the thousand-dollar espresso maker in our kitchen that had been unused since the day it had arrived.

"Your mom is getting changed for a hike at Tiger Mountain this evening. I'm taking the bear spray, so don't worry." He stood up and poured me a cup of whatever it was he was drinking.

"Lana is hiking?" I almost choked on the caramel-blended coffee.

"Sure, why not?" he said in a nonchalant tone that suggested that Lana might as well have been a nature-trail guide on weekends.

"She doesn't own flat shoes."

"We bought her some great hiking boots at REI this afternoon." Vivek continued to look pleased with himself.

Hobby of the week, I presumed.

"Can I ask you something?" I hooked my toes under the railing of the bar stool I was perched on.

He took a sip and nodded.

"How serious is this thing between you and her?"

The grandfather clock ticked for a few seconds. When someone else was around to talk to, I realized how empty our house was the rest of the time. I could literally hear every creak and tick and rustle. I remembered how lively our house had been the morning the guys had cooked breakfast. The smell of bacon and waffles, the warmth of the stove, the laughter and conversation echoed through my mind.

Stop, I ordered myself, hating the stab of nostalgia.

"Define serious," Vivek said finally, openly stalling.

"Casual dating? Marriage on the horizon?" I asked, hoping for the former, but knowing Lana, they were probably choosing an engagement ring after their hike.

He laughed. "Lana told me she plans never to remarry."

"What?" I almost choked on coffee again. Classy.

"She said she only believes in marrying once, and that dream ended."

"Oh." I was shocked into silence. Had she really said that? It didn't sound like her at all.

"So, yeah, we don't talk much about marriage."

"Have you thought about why she refuses to marry again?" I couldn't help but take a dig, though I knew this whole thing wasn't Vivek's fault. He'd just gone and fallen for a pretty woman with baggage. A whole trunk full of it.

"She doesn't believe your father is still alive, Mars, if that's what you're insinuating."

So they had talked about him. I hadn't expected Lana to talk with Vivek about her former life. I had expected that she acted like a coquettish ingénue who had never known anything before she'd met him.

"She might. You don't know that." I shrugged. He thought he knew Lana, but he did not. No one really did, except for Dad. Vivek certainly didn't know her insecurities or that this confident, fun woman she was portraying was just a farce.

"She had a funeral to say good-bye to him."

"She had to, to appease people." I retorted. I hated when someone said this. *Your father must be dead; we had a funeral.*

Lana might've had a funeral for me too in that case.

"She wouldn't be seeing me if there was any hope left for her that he was coming back. She's told me so much about him and how he was everything to her. He was, and always will be, the love of her life. She would do anything for him."

"Except give him a chance to come back," I said bitterly, grabbing my coffee cup and getting ready to leave. "No one believed they would last, not even my grandparents. I guess they were right."

"She told me that everyone asked how she could marry someone who killed other people as part of their profession. Someone who would never be able to share himself completely with her. There was so much he kept from her, to protect her."

I swallowed uncomfortably, staring at the swirling granite countertop. I had never thought about it. How hard it must have been for her all those years when he was gone for six months at a time. How hard it must've been when he wouldn't tell her what an ordinary day was like for him.

"Where are you headed now?" Vivek asked.

"Just . . . figuring some stuff out."

"Anything I can help with?" He gave me a knowing look. It said everything he wouldn't say: *I know you're up to something, but I won't snitch.*

"No."

"How's Zayed doing?" He reached over me to the espresso maker and refilled his cup.

Normally I would've become indignant at the thought of this man trying to interfere with my life, but I was fairly devastated by my findings on Zayed's computer and wanted to talk to someone about it, and not someone who would fly into a fit of protectiveness.

"What did you think of Zayed?" I asked before I changed my mind.

"He cares about you very much."

I listened to the sounds of Lana's footsteps walking back and forth upstairs. She would be down any minute now. I lowered my voice slightly.

"How do you know that?"

"He was extremely worried when Jason said those terrible things to you. He said you're very strong inside, but still very susceptible to being hurt."

That hadn't stopped him from hurting me in the worst possible way, though, by making my love for him mean nothing. By lying to me about everything.

"He told me you're afraid of leaving the past where it belongs. That the only thing holding you back from happiness is you."

"That's pretty heavy for a first conversation." I tried to sound casual, like these words didn't mean everything to me.

"He told me you've given him what he needed most. You've clearly given him something he's longing for, someone to talk to, someone to belong to. He seemed to want human contact more than anything else. He's lonely."

Someone to belong to? That's what the insurgents wanted as well, to belong. Zayed wanted to belong. No wonder he'd stayed behind that morning to help make breakfast. No wonder he didn't mind spending time with Lana and Vivek.

No wonder he hadn't made a move when we'd been together. He didn't understand the games we played with the opposite sex. He wasn't obsessed with when a kiss was appropriate or when it was time to take the next step to more intimacy. He only wanted my company. He wanted to be near another human and have basic interaction that went beyond his formal teaching relationship. This was why he'd been so satisfied to stay up and only talk for a whole night.

I was just another warm body to him. It wasn't me he wanted. It was a human being. Even if I'd been anyone else, the story would have ended the exact same way.

Somehow that made me even sadder than before.

"Is he dangerous?" I pressed. I wasn't getting a straight answer, and this was not acceptable to me. I had to know, no matter what the truth was.

I'd left a message for Bree on the phone several hours ago, requesting information about Zayed Anwar, and she had finally called back. Her tone had been reluctant from the first moment. She clearly knew more than what she was willing to share over the phone. I was prepared to go to her house and demand she tell me the truth as a next step.

Lana and Vivek were still out, and I had the kitchen to myself—to pace and ponder questions to which I needed answers. So far, I hadn't gotten any that made any sense.

Bree had started off by asking me questions about how I knew Zayed, why I was so involved with him, and how had I come across the information that led me to believe he was involved with the latest incidents in Seattle.

I had answered none of them and instead had fired off a series of questions of my own.

"I can't share this information with you," Bree snapped. "Please just listen to what I'm asking you to do—"

"What did he do?"

"This isn't something you need to get involved with. Do not talk to him about it. I think it would be best if you enrolled in another SAT class altogether if you've grown attached to him."

Attached. I was much more than attached, unfortunately. I was already involved, and there was nothing I could do about it other than to understand what I was involved in.

"Tell me what he's done. I'll ask him myself otherwise," I threatened. If I was going to do that, I would already have by done so by now. Fortunately, Bree had no kids of her own and didn't understand idle threats.

"It doesn't matter. It's over. We are on top of things, as are the Seattle police, so you don't need to play vigilante."

Vigilante? Who used words like "vigilante"?

I had suspected the worst, but hearing it from someone who knew for sure hit home harder than anything else could have.

God. What had he done? The teakettle I'd set to boil whistled readiness. I reached across and turned the gas off.

"I need to know more. Why aren't you just arresting him if you know what's he's done. Define 'things.'"

She said nothing.

Trash-can fires. Power outages. Bombs at war rallies that hurt people. I waited for her to say these things, preparing myself for the worst.

"He cannot go back to his country," Bree finally said.

"France?"

"What? No."

I didn't think so. His indifference during *Paris, je t'aime.* His knowledge about happenings in the Middle East. I had to sit down at the kitchen counter as I digested the information. He was from the Middle East, that I was sure of.

"What did he do? Did he kill someone?"

"Mars, this is classified information, and you have no reason to know it. Please forget this and forget him. Where is your mother? I tried her cell phone and got no response."

I took that as a yes. He'd killed someone. Zayed, *my* Zayed had killed someone. Those gentle gray eyes had looked into someone else's as he'd taken their life.

Zayed, what have you done?

Despite everything I was finding out, I didn't know how to stop thinking of him as mine. How did I stop thinking of his problems as our problems? I had brought him into my life, my home, my entire world. How could I throw him out now without knowing anything concrete?

Yet deep down I knew it was over, that the innocence in our relationship was gone. We would never again sit in his apartment, holding hands, talking about anything and everything. I would never see Coconut again. The realization was almost enough to bring on the onset of sheer mania.

Why had he done this? Why had he made me fall in love with some illusion of who he was?

"Will he hurt me?" I had to know.

Bree hesitated. "I'm not saying any more. I do know that you need to stop your involvement with him. I need to speak to your mother. Do you know how I can reach her?"

"He won't hurt me, will he? Come on, Bree, he's an SAT instructor. How is he still working there if he is capable of hurting someone?"

Silence.

She wasn't going to tell me anything more. I tried one last bluff. "Shouldn't someone let the Institute know? I can talk to the receptionist tomorrow."

"No!" Bree quickly cut me off.

"Why not? Do they know?"

"There is nothing you need to do, Mars."

"You should just tell me. Did he cut some kind of deal? Did the police set him up with a job and a place in return for something?"

Silence. Again.

"That's it, isn't it? He killed someone, and you guys are willing to protect him if he does something for you." My imagination ran wild as I starting pacing frantically. "What is it? Is he bait? Tell me he's not bait."

"I can't talk to you about this; you have to understand that. All I'm asking is that you stay away from Zayed Anwar."

I wish that was so easy to do, I thought bitterly.

I stopped walking as Bree said her final words. "Promise me, Mars. This is what your father would want. Promise me."

CHAPTER 17

The Confrontation

I knew it was dangerous. I knew it was risky and stupid and my father would be horrified if he knew what I was doing. I also knew Zayed had had plenty of opportunities and he would never hurt me.

It took me three tries to make it past the front door of the College Prep Institute. The roof had seemed like the best place to meet. I didn't trust his apartment. I didn't trust myself to be alone with him.

I didn't know how to begin or what to say after. I wanted to know the truth, but I wanted to hear his story, too. Had anything he'd told me about his family or past been true? I needed to know if he was even capable of being honest with me.

I wanted to know if it was ever *me* he'd cared for.

Zayed was already waiting, legs hanging over the edge of the building, leaned back on his elbows. He didn't make eye contact, and he didn't smile as I took a seat a few feet away from him. He knew something was up, and I had a feeling Bree Nguyen had gotten to him first.

"You missed class last night. And you should be in school right now," he said after I arranged my hands on my lap. His voice was low, casual, like we were two strangers making conversation in the grocery line.

"You should be in jail right now," I retorted.

Zayed didn't look surprised or shocked or any of the things I'd expected. "I asked you to stay out of it."

"Then you shouldn't be in my life," I stammered as I saw the look in his eyes, sad and defeated when he finally turned to me. "That's how this works. This relationship business."

He gave me a look that was half hurt, half annoyance. My hands were trembling, betraying my bravado. I didn't have a very good escape plan if I was wrong and he tried to hurt me. The thought of throwing him off the roof wasn't appealing at all to me, but I knew if it had to be done, I would do it.

I wrapped my hand around a stray brick, ready if I needed it.

"Tell me the truth, the whole truth, and nothing but the truth. You'll be doing that soon enough if I understood Bree right," I demanded.

He glanced at my hand clutching the brick and, I thought, almost smiled. "Mars, I can't involve you in this."

I loved how everyone kept saying that. I couldn't be involved. I was too delicate, too naïve, too so-many-things to be involved. I was *already* involved. More than I'd ever imagined or wanted to be.

"After everything we've been through, you owe me the truth. You're in trouble, Zayed, with the law and your country. You have nowhere to go. Now I expect you to tell me what's going on. It's the least you can do after all the lies."

"If I involve you, we can't go back to what we were before."

His eyes were closed, as if he was resigned to whatever fate awaited.

"The *before* was a lie, right? So why would I want to go back?"

He tapped his fingers on a large cardboard box that I'd just noticed sat next to him on the ledge. I wanted to ask what was inside but wanted other answers more.

"Talk. Do it now. The truth can't be worse than what I've imagined."

He only stared out into the city, the shadows of an early sunset creating spirals across the planes of his face, brooding and beautiful all at once. He was a broken prince in my short-lived fairy tale.

It was every girl's dream to meet a dark, mysterious stranger and fall hopelessly in love. It was no girl's dream to discover that her stranger was in fact a criminal, a violent one, and that every magical moment they had shared was a lie.

"I'm an informant," he said.

"A *criminal* informant?" I'd spent the sleepless night doing frantic research on the internet about spies and informants and whistleblowers. None of them sounded like a good person to be.

"Yes."

"To the Army?"

"The Marines. They sent my case to the Army Reserves of Washington. The Seattle police are involved too. This," he said pointing at the gorgeous silver watch on his wrist, "is my father's watch, but they planted a tracker in it."

"Where are you really from? Do you even have a family?"

"I've lived in Iraq my whole life. My parents are exactly as I told you before. Educated people. We aren't wealthy, but we are very comfortable, and we are good people."

I didn't understand how he could say this. He was a criminal. And a liar.

"Why is your English so good? And why do you speak French? And why do you know about Paris?" I knew I was rambling and these weren't questions that mattered. I had yet to process the full extent of Zayed, *my* Zayed, being an informant.

"I attended a very exclusive school run by a French family for expatriates. In return for the cost of the tuition, which we could not afford for both my brother and me, I tutored their youngest sons. I was invited to go along on family vacations with this family to Paris once a year."

I raised my eyebrows thinking of Zayed being an au pair.

"So you really have a brother?"

"Jamal was killed during an altercation in Iraq."

I watched him. The same faltering in his voice, the same flutter of his eyelashes. This part was true, I was sure of it.

"Why was he killed?" I asked, lowering my voice from the shriek it had been raised to a moment ago.

"Mars, you're going to not understand this." His voice wavered again.

"What have you done, Zayed?"

"You're not going to understand."

No, I really wasn't. I already had a feeling I knew, though.

"I already don't understand. But you owe me the truth. You insisted I tell you the truth about my past and everything I've been through. Now you need to do the same."

He didn't look like he was going to say much more.

"This is different. You needed to share what happened to you to heal."

"It's not up to you to decide what I need to do or not to heal," I retorted. "What I didn't need was to be lied to and used. You owe me the truth. Now."

"Jamal and I were approached a year ago at the Abu Hanifa Mosque by the older brother of one of my friends. He talked to us over the course of several weeks about our country, our pride, and how it needed to be protected."

"No," the words came out of my mouth silently.

This was a textbook example of how terrorists recruited new people. I couldn't believe Zayed had been naïve enough to fall into the trap. He had talked so much about insurgents and their need to belong and have a group of people to call their own in such a clinical, textbook manner. He had been no better than the ones he had talked so theoretically about.

"He was a part of a cell of the larger militant group al-Talle. We were told there were enemies among us, people who were here to destroy our country and challenge our culture. People who believed themselves to be superior."

"The Americans. And you listened to these *insurgents*?"

He sat up and hung his head. "I am an educated man, as was my brother, but these men, they were not all insurgents or criminals or terrorists. They were military. They were people like you or me wanting to protect their country."

"By hurting others? Is that what you did?"

"I didn't. But my brother did. And I didn't know how to stop him. It's as if he was someone else. Possessed. Brainwashed."

I observed the tracker watch on his wrist ticking ten seconds. I didn't know what to say now that my worst suspicions were becoming real. Deep inside, I'd been hoping that Zayed would say that he'd been framed or there had been a terrible misunderstanding. I also knew if he'd told me that, I wouldn't have believed him. This was the only truth I would accept because I knew, from the beginning, that Zayed had been hiding something big from me.

"Tell me what happened."

There was no going back now, and no stopping the words that he couldn't help but say out loud.

"Al-Talle inducted Jamal and me slowly, telling us Americans didn't discriminate. They told us about how only thirty-five of the seven hundred animals at the Baghdad Zoo had survived after the

Americans attacked in 2003. All those innocent creatures killed. How this was nothing compared to the hundreds of thousands of military and civilian casualties in the decade since then."

I felt a deep sadness for Zayed and for his friends and his family. How terrible to live knowing that you and the people you loved were always in danger; that the very people who had come to liberate the country you lived in would be the ones to destroy it.

"They told us stories of brothers and friends who'd been killed in battle trying to defend their country. Al-Talle had formed to fight back against the strangers who fired an aerial attack on our city. Baghdad was destroyed, Mars, when the Americans came. You've never seen it beautiful. It was an incredibly modern, cosmopolitan city with every comfort a person would need. Now, dust, rubble, death. That's all."

"What did you do?"

"Al-Talle had information that the Marines were seeking out the Abu Hanifa Mosque and were planning an attack on it during Friday prayer in the next few weeks. This was where my brother and I had prayed every Friday our entire lives."

"And you believed them," I said in a voice that didn't sound like my own. I felt like I was floating above, watching this interaction between two strangers.

"I did believe them. They asked us to protect the area surrounding the mosque. To scare off the solders by putting a few explosives into the ground. Ultimately, I couldn't do it. My brother and I agreed we wouldn't do it. But he lied. He did it. And I couldn't stop him."

"He planted IEDs," I said. Like the one that had taken Ricardo Esteban's legs. Like the ones that had taken so many people away from their families.

He didn't need to say anything more.

"What else did he do, your brother? Kidnapping? Car bombs? Did you detonate a bomb on a bus where you knew a convoy of Americans would be?" I whispered. I knew my father was in a completely different country, but I had to know.

"He did nothing else because I . . . I saw the faces of the people whose death and mutilation he was responsible for in my dreams. I learned that the largest number of people who died at the hands of al-Talle were Iraqi civilians. Children. People like my family. People he'd been trying to protect and was in turn putting in danger. I found the Marines based in Baghdad and told them everything. I gave the Marines the information on al-Talle and where the next meeting would be. They stopped the next attack by posting guards at the next location."

"Then?"

"Al-Talle thought my brother had told and they . . ."

I braced myself against the ground I sat on.

". . . killed him. Because of me. They killed him publicly. They said he had brought shame on our country. And that I was next."

My head jerked. Zayed, *my* Zayed was in their crosshairs.

"I'd been taken into custody and wasn't there when he died. I had to leave Baghdad immediately so they wouldn't hurt my parents. All I could take were my journals and the watch my father gave me."

"Why are you here?"

"There is a militant cell in Seattle now. They are associated with the al-Talle. Their primary targets are the airplane hangars. To destroy the warplanes."

"Oh, God. In Renton or Everett?"

He didn't say anything.

The hangars were barely half an hour away from Seattle and were in very densely populated areas. There would have been hundreds, maybe thousands, of people hurt or killed.

"I was to engage with the cell and discover information, relaying this back to the local police team. In return, I was provided with this apartment, an opportunity to attend the University, and a job at the Institute. I was assigned a case officer who meets me several times a week to give me my orders. The first and most important order was to tell no one."

"And the bombs that have been going off in the area?"

"That is the work of al-Talle."

"You had nothing to do with them?" I asked, feeling a slight relief despite my best intentions.

"Of course not. They were warnings. Signs to other members of insurgent cells. I was to stay out of sight and only engage with them through online forums. A few days ago, I gave my case officer information about where I believe their location to be."

"And then?"

"I'll give anything to have this group caught."

"What happens to you now?"

"I'll testify against al-Talle on counts of murder and terrorism once they are caught. I'll probably move on then."

That I hadn't expected to hear. I knew after today I wouldn't see him again, but knowing I would never even have the choice, would never be able to find him again, that realization seemed to punch me in the chest on top of everything else.

"You're going to leave Seattle?"

"I think so. I can do good against other cells in other cities. I'm sorry I didn't tell you. I couldn't. My case officer—"

"So you lied. About everything." I set the brick down. He wasn't dangerous to me. He was a sad little boy who'd built a delusional little world and pulled me in.

"I had no choice. And I had to protect you."

He slid the box in my direction, and almost against my will, I picked it up. It was surprisingly heavy.

"What's this?"

"My journals. All the ones I brought from Iraq. All the ones about my life here."

The truth.

I had been looking for it for so long, and now I held it in my hands. How little it seemed to matter now that the greatest truth— that Zayed had never loved me and didn't even know what that meant—had been revealed.

"What happened that day on the roof?" I ran my fingernails under the rim of the box, wondering if I should take it home with me or not. What had been real to me was over; there was no longer anything more for me to know.

"I had a flashback to the aerial bombings in Baghdad. I was trapped in the attic of my house for hours because our staircase collapsed. I was finally able to escape to the roof."

I was silent.

"Please say something."

"I need to go." I shook my head. I didn't want to hear any more.

"I have to tell you something else, Mars. This is about you."

I stood up, box in hand, ready to leave. I'd gotten what I'd come here for. And it had been much worse than I'd expected.

"You are so special that if there was any chance that your father was alive, he would be here with you."

"You shut the hell up." I glared at him. I was not going to listen to this. Not from him. Not from someone who was *related* to the kind of people who had taken my father from me.

"Mars, I've seen a convoy explode." He hesitantly stood up and approached me. "You need to understand what that means in that part of the world."

"There was no body." I stared past his shoulder beyond the city, beyond the lakes to the mountains with the crisp, white peaks. I longed to be able to run away, disappear. Not have to hear this.

"I'm afraid there would only be ashes—scattered ones, at that. There would not be a body left. Not with that kind of explosion. I'm sorry, Mars."

"He's not gone. I know he's not. I would know if he was—-I would know it."

"He's with you, always." Zayed's hands were on my shoulders. "I feel like I already know what a good man the senior Mars Alexander was from being with you. You're just like him. Kind and generous. Giving. You have so much to offer. I can't watch you trapped here, not being able to believe that he would want you to move on."

"Get your hands off me."

"Mars."

"Listen to me because I'll just say this once. I hate you. I will never forgive you for what you and your family have done and for lying to me. You've betrayed me, deceived me, and believe me, you are going to hell for what happened to those innocent people. And for what you've done to me." I harshly shoved his hand off my shoulder.

I didn't wait for him to follow me. I let myself into the building through the roof door, walked myself to the car, and locked the door behind me. Only after I realized his journals were still in my hands did I allow myself the bittersweet release of tears. Our perfect love affair had been built on a pillar of scattered ashes, and now it was completely and truly over.

CHAPTER 18

The Days

I didn't attend another SAT prep class. I had the option of switching to another instructor, getting my deposit back, and several other alternatives. I did none of them. I didn't write another essay, didn't complete another practice exam.

I couldn't. Didn't want to. Didn't care.

I also couldn't stop hearing Zayed's voice in my head. Seeing his face in my dreams. Reliving that last conversation over and over again.

I'm afraid there would only be ashes.

I didn't listen to the dozen voicemails he left on my phone each day. I deleted the twenty-four emails he sent me each day. I ignored the forty-eight questions I got about him from Erica, Lana, Vivek, and even Bree Nguyen, who came all the way up to my room to check on me.

Bree let me know several members of al-Talle had been caught during a raid on their hideout in Everett. The local leader had escaped and hadn't been heard from since. Zayed was scheduled to testify at the arraignment, which was set for a few weeks away. I listened silently to the news and thanked her quietly before hanging up.

Zayed would be fine. Just a little while earlier I would have been terrified at the thought of my Zayed dealing with a group of very dangerous men and challenging them head on. Now, I realized he had been related to, and *almost had become*, a part of that dangerous group of men. He didn't need me or anyone else worrying about him.

The unopened box of his journals sat on my desk. I stared at it day and night, wanting to know, but wanting to forget at the same time. Every day I considered going to him, wanting an explanation. A different explanation.

One Saturday, I got into my car and made it all the way to the University. I parked outside Zayed's apartment and stared at the window to his living room, wondering if he could see me sitting out here, wondering if he would come out if I waited long enough.

I sat in the silence of the car and considered retracting everything. I wondered why he hadn't fought me on that day and had let me go so easily. At the same time I was grateful he didn't because I wouldn't have been able to go through with it.

Feel the loss, Mars. Don't shut it out. I tried to lecture myself with all the lessons I'd learned in our group sessions. But still, I felt nothing. Just numb.

I drove back home, not having accomplished a thing.

The day of my final SAT exam was set for early December, and each day passed as slowly as the last. I spent the majority of the month curled up on my window seat. The leaves sputtered, then disappeared for the winter. The lake grew progressively more choppy and windy. There had been talk of snow, but there hadn't been a single flurry yet. Seattle was not a city that was well-equipped for snowstorms, and I was secretly hoping for a blizzard to shut down school for weeks. I had missed so many classes; even when I was physically in the school building, my mind was ten miles away, sitting on the roof, reliving that horrible conversation over and over again. I found myself frequently leaning on various surfaces: walls, desks, my hand, and staring into a corner. Before I knew it, half an hour had passed.

Erica and I hadn't been speaking much either. She'd called almost every day and stopped by several times, but I hadn't been terribly responsive. She was convinced Zayed had done something stupid and childish to hurt me. I didn't tell her the truth. I didn't want anyone else to know what the guy I'd fallen in love with had done and how stupid I had been to not see it earlier.

After the initial numbness and shock of my conversation with Zayed started to wear off, I let my thoughts wander to those places in my mind I'd blocked off before. Things he'd said, things he could never take back. Things I could never get out of my head.

I've seen a convoy explode. You need to understand what that means in that part of the world.

I couldn't stop visualizing it. The convoy exploding, rupturing into pieces in the air, slamming back down to earth. No one left. Only ashes.

He was right. I could deny it all I wanted, and when other people said Dad was not coming home, I could brush them off as being ignorant about what war meant. When Zayed said my father was dead, I knew it had to be true. He had seen people die with his own eyes. People he had known.

There will not be a body left. Not with that kind of explosion.

Everyone else had been right all along, and I had been the crazy one. The funeral had been real. I hadn't attended, had never visited the grave. Still didn't want to.

I couldn't believe the things I'd told Zayed, the parts of my soul that I'd bared to him. All those moments, what had they ever meant?

I'd wanted to know Zayed, the real him, for so long, and now I did. I wished I didn't. I wished I'd never probed and snooped and found out the truth. I knew I was being ridiculous, but I had been genuinely and truly happy when I'd been with him.

Some days, I was almost happy my Dad would never know about Zayed. He would be so disappointed that I'd turned my back on everything he'd taught me was right to chase after the shadow of a person that Zayed was.

Now I would never be able to tell Dad that I was sorry, that I had never meant to disappoint him the way I had my whole life, that I'd been planning to be a better person if he'd come home, that I never should have fought with him the day before his deployment about something so silly, that I missed him so very much and was lost without him to guide me. I called Dad's cell phone every day. No answer. I called twice more, each time cut off by the voicemail.

Finally I left a message, "Where are you?" I whispered, though I now knew he would never answer again.

After much debate, Lana decided to have Thanksgiving dinner at our house. Vivek headed up the cooking, my mother acting as line chef. I had nothing to do with the preparations and spent the day in bed until I was called down to dinner.

I thought I would protest more, but I realized we'd all missed several Thanksgivings the past few years due to my father's deployments.

Having Vivek cook for us was better than having a lonely dinner for two at an upscale French restaurant like we'd had the previous year.

I stared at the empty chair to my left as Lana stood up to carve the turkey. I'd never seen her at the head of the table before. It was startling to see her taking charge of something that traditionally my father would always have done, but I was starting to realize that she had known all along that he wasn't coming back. She had made peace with it and had somehow achieved that magical closure everyone talked about.

I hated her for being able to move on, hated her for not missing the closeness we had shared before, hated her for being happy with someone else, but mostly hated her for not feeling any of the pain I was suffering now.

I pushed a piece of turkey under the mound of mashed potatoes on my plate and covered the whole thing in real cranberry sauce. Everything looked delicious, but I couldn't muster anything close to an appetite. I gave up and set my fork down, unable to recall how happy I'd been the last time we'd all been at this table together. Zayed had been by my side and . . . I shut my eyes. He didn't deserve to be in the thoughts on this day.

"Mars, your mother and I have something to tell you," Vivek announced after raising a toast.

Just as I'd predicted. I glared at both of them. I'd known this was going to happen, despite everyone's assurances it was not. He'd proposed. She'd, of course, said yes. All the talk of her not wanting to get married again was unlike her, and I'd known it all along. I glanced at her ring finger, where her wedding ring still sparkled brilliantly under the chandelier's light. Replacing one with another.

"I asked Lana to marry me."

I didn't even blink. I knew he would. He wouldn't have been able to resist.

"She said no."

"What?" I glanced at Lana to see if he was being serious. "What do you mean?" I practically barked.

"She said your family isn't ready for another upheaval right now. We've been rushing into this a bit, and we both realize we need to give you and Lana some time to adjust to life before I come in and everything changes again," he continued calmly.

Neither looked upset, neither looked angry. Lana sipped her wine and smiled in Vivek's direction.

"Really?" I asked finally. "But you guys are still together? When will you get married then?" I was completely confused. She'd rejected him. Why was he still sticking around?

"Maybe never," Lana said nonchalantly. "I realize I need to make sure you and I are okay before changing our family in any way."

"We're both here for you, Mars," Vivek added. "No matter what happens. Both of us."

We continued on with dinner after that as if nothing at all had happened. Lana and Vivek made easy conversation, trying unsuccessfully to include me. I excused myself before dessert, went back up to my room, and buried myself under the covers.

The sad thing was that my first instinct was to call Zayed to share the news. Knowing I wouldn't be speaking to him again seemed to be a lot easier than actually accepting the knowledge.

I heard Zayed's voice guiding me as I took a seat on SAT day in the deserted high school classroom. I knew this was my last chance for success at this, and though I no longer had to go to the University of Washington, I'd worked too hard to throw away the opportunity to score high.

I heard his voice instructing me to spend a few minutes thinking about the topic: Progress is not possible without sacrifice.

I felt him coaching me with every line I wrote.

Be honest, Mars. Write about something real. Write with emotion, but not emotionally, he would say.

I twirled my pencil in the air.

As much as I wish progress was possible without sacrifice, I know it is not so. My father has lived this concept through his actions by serving in the U.S. Army Reserves for the past twenty years.

I felt Zayed's presence nudge me when I hesitated to write the next lines.

Now it's my turn to do the same and make a sacrifice to come to terms with his death. I need to sacrifice that protective, welcoming shell of denial I've lived in for so long and move forward with my life. I need to make progress in accepting that my father is gone but that the impact he's made on both my life and the world lives and will

*always live. I was so afraid of facing this reality for so long, but now
I realize that he's gone and . . .*

I heard Zayed's voice in my head again. "It's time for me to allow
myself to grieve."

I set the pencil down and stared at the words. That was about as
honest as emotions could get. It was the best thing I'd ever written, I'd
known that from the first word. I closed the booklet before I could
change my mind about sharing those deeply private words with a
group of unknown SAT graders.

Lana was waiting when I left the high school. She reached across
and opened the door of her black Escalade. I slid into the passenger
side wordlessly.

She had been unconditionally supportive through the past few
weeks, even after I'd told her everything. Zayed, his past, the journals.
She hadn't said "I told you so" even once and had seemed to understand my pain at loving someone who was not capable of ever feeling
the same way. She'd called Zayed a "lost boy" and told me I would
recover someday but needed to take the time to do so.

"Let's go home." As she started the car, I brought up the topic of
a fund-raiser. Something to help the children and families of those
killed or hurt in war.

"People like Erica and . . ."

"And?"

"Us. Dad is gone. This is what he would want us to do since he
can't."

Lana squeezed my hand as she pulled away from the curb.

"Let's do it."

I lay in bed that night, unable to sleep. I picked up the book that
hadn't budged from the nightstand and flipped through the pages.
"Mine" was the name of the poem I chose to read. It was as if Theodore
Watkins had known this moment would come:

> *I wake up nightly, wrapped in bedclothes. Not in you.*
> *If you think of me, I'll feel it, a sunburst, a moment of solace.*
> *My mind, silent and demure, listens for the sound of your*
> *heart's drumming; the utopian dream of your body that*
> *has haunted me for so long.*

*You are both novel and familiar, like a childhood friend who has
grown into an interesting adult.
The way you move, deliberately. Always deliberately hypnotizes me.
Your mind, your thoughts, your obsessions have become mine.
The desire to possess you as an equal.
Knowing you is powerful, but being able to touch the vulnerable is
my ultimate aphrodisiac.
You are mine.*

. . .

CHAPTER 19

The Scene

I'd had no desire to go to the homecoming dance that Lana had convinced the school board to magically convert into a war relief fund-raiser, but knew I had to, given that it was kind of my idea. All proceeds from the tickets, plus donations, would go to the community to bring opportunities to families affected by the war. And the best part was that it was being held in the infamous all-ages club upstairs in the Kirkland Teen Center. It was the grand opening, and City Hall had high hopes it would be a place teens could get together.

Lana surprised me with a gray, beaded strapless number from Italy in an attempt to cheer me up. She'd ordered it online with help from Erica. A few months ago, I would have been thrilled to wear the dress, which highlighted my tan shoulders and arms along with a pair of brand-new silver cutout sandals. I spent a few minutes flat-ironing my hair and applying dark, smoky eye makeup. I left my lips pale and marveled at how much I had started to look like Lana.

Lana insisted on taking a picture of me before I left, and I stood alone, next to the grand fireplace, expressionless. There was worry in her eyes as she asked if I wanted her to come with me. I'd laughed then, thinking that taking my mother as a date might actually be a better option than going alone.

Erica had also called earlier and asked if I wanted to go with her and her fake date, some random freshman she was tutoring. I still couldn't get over the fact that she'd broken up with Chad over homecoming and told her I'd meet her there.

I entered the Teen Center's new club alone. No limo, no corsage, no posse. I had never arrived at a dance this way, but never before had I cared so little about this so-called rite of passage, which suddenly seemed so insignificant.

I wove through the crowd of my classmates, looking for a place to sit. I couldn't believe how anxious and overwhelmed I'd been at the thought of not being accepted anymore just a few short weeks ago. It didn't matter what these people thought of me; it had never mattered. I'd thought that being envied had made me happy, but it really had only made me feel secure and like I belonged somewhere, never happy.

I was starting to truly understand Maslow's hierarchy of needs and how I'd considered myself so far above the insurgents in Iraq, but all I had wanted was to belong, just like them. I'd never reached that level that would set me free.

I felt a tap on my shoulder.

"You look *amazing!*" Candace Littlefoot shrieked.

"Oh," was all I could muster. She'd startled me. "Thanks, Candy, you too."

"Dolce. The new collection."

I nodded politely, though I didn't even know what that collection looked like or why we actually had conversations about these things. We were in high school. I couldn't believe we were so fascinated by what designers we were wearing rather than what we planned to do with the rest of our lives.

"I love what they've done with this place, don't you? I can't believe it's so gorgeous. Totally thought it would be lame. I heard this has become a thing to benefit the families who've, you know . . ." her voice trailed off.

"Lost someone in the war? Yeah, it is. It looks amazing in here." I had to admit. Lana had made a sizable donation to transform the upstairs of the Teen Center into a wonderland of fall colors. Swaths of cloth in every color on the trees outside scalloped over the ceiling of the ballroom, covering every inch and creating a dusky, mysterious atmosphere. Completing the cozy alcove were dried crimson and orange leaves clustered on each tabletop, enhanced by the glow of a thousand tea lights.

The atmosphere was romantic and magical. Zayed would have loved it. I sighed. I'd promised myself. Not tonight. I wouldn't let him ruin this night.

"Come sit with us. Did you come with someone?" Candace glanced around to see if someone had stood up to claim me yet.

"I think I'm done with boys for a while." I smoothed the silvery glove on my left hand to check the time on my watch. I would give myself till midnight, but then it was time for Cinderella to dash back to her castle for the night.

"Us too. We're done with boys. High school boys are so . . . juvenile. I think we're all ready for the college guys, right?" Candace nudged me as she led me back to the table, where she and Kendall were sitting and, of course, gossiping.

College boys were fairly juvenile too, with all the lying and deceiving, but I resisted throwing that in. There was no need to add any fuel to the gossip fest already erupting at the table.

"I cannot believe she's dancing with some freshman guy. What's she thinking?" The conversation was already in full flow when I took a seat at the table and we'd exchanged formal pleasantries. They were watching Erica and her tutee. I thought it was smart of her to bring someone she knew nothing romantic would happen with, though I still thought breaking up with her kind, *honest* boyfriend was a dumb move.

Erica did look beautiful, though, in a black-and-white ball gown, her pink highlights flying gracefully through the air. She was living out her fantasy of being a princess for the night, and I didn't have the heart to tell her that the morning after was not always happily-ever-after.

"Oh, there's Jason!" Kendall nodded pointedly at me. He had escorted in a tall model of a girl I didn't recognize. I didn't think she even went to our school.

"That girl looks anorexic," Candace sniffed as if she was offended by the girl's tiny figure. "What's he thinking? I bet he pays her by the hour."

Kendall snickered.

"He's thinking he needs to show off to everyone that he can come with any girl he wants. That he was not dumped by me," I said, as Jason whirled the girl by our table, staring pointedly at me. I knew I was being petty, but still, that's what the night was for.

Both Candace and Kendall stared at me silently, exactly the reaction I was hoping for.

"You broke up with him?" Kendall asked at last.

"Of course. He's not a good guy. And I don't want to be with someone like that. That girl's probably with him because she feels sorry for him."

"Wow, that's really brave of you, Mars," Candace said. "He seems like a great guy. I don't know if I would have had the guts to do that."

"I'm a brave girl." I smiled a wistful one. "And there are far better guys out there for me."

A mild commotion at the other end of the gym interrupted our conversation as if planned. An unrecognizable man had entered, handsome in a slim white tux, graceful, debonair almost. He looked like the guy-next-door-cleaned-up on all the teen-friendly television shows. I watched him cross the room. It couldn't be, but it was.

Wow.

He ignored everyone else and walked straight up to my table. "Hello, Mars. Would you care to dance?"

Kendall and Candace stared at Chad Winters. I knew for a fact they had no idea who he was and they regretted it.

"Um, sure." I stood and took his outstretched hand. Chad and me, dancing at homecoming. Stranger things really had not happened.

"What are you doing here?" I whispered as he pulled me close and whizzed me across the floor. "And where did you learn to dance?"

"I've been taking lessons. I'm here to get my girl back."

"Despite her insisting on coming to homecoming without you?" I stopped moving, getting my feet stepped on. "Ow."

"I love her. You can't love someone without letting them do things they want to do. You can't just love someone temporarily. They become a part of your family, a part of your life, a part of *you*. She hurt me by coming here without me, but I love her, and I'm going to fight for us."

I stared at him in disbelief.

"What?" he asked, staring back.

"That's incredibly stupid. She broke up with you over a homecoming dance."

He laughed. And laughed some more. He was seriously weird.

"Love is stupid. People are going to disappoint you, even people you think very highly of. And you're going to disappoint people. I was just being stubborn, and Erica decided she'd had enough. You have to deal with things if someone is worth it. What's more important at the end of the day, being right or being with the one you love?"

"I . . . I—" For once I was speechless. I didn't know.

"I'd rather be miserable with Erica than be without her. Even if I have to change some parts of myself." He swayed me around, giving me a chance to think about what he was saying.

"Hypothetically speaking, why be miserable at all? Why not just move on? You're in high school. There will be plenty of girls. Why do you need to change to be with her?"

"Without her, I can't be anyone or anything," Chad said, watching Erica and her friend sweep by us, a whirlwind of white gauze and black silk. "Go after him if you love him, Mars."

"I don't love anyone," I retorted.

"Yeah, okay. Now, please excuse me." He left me standing where he found me, back at the table.

I stood in the corner of the Teen Center and watched Erica spot Chad and do a double take, watched him wave shyly in her direction, watched her fly into his arms. Watched them kissing passionately.

Watched the freshman kid walk off the floor, looking terribly disappointed.

Wow.

Toward the end of the night, Jason appeared in front of me. His date was nowhere to be seen. He took a second to wave hello to the girls behind me. I heard them snicker again.

"Hey, Mars. I know we left things—"

"I know." I cut him off before he could launch into a recap.

"Do you think we could—"

"We could?" I was enjoying this.

"Try again? I'm sorry for what I said." He gave me his best smile. *That* one. The one that had always melted me and gotten him his way.

"You know what, Jason?" I fluttered my eyelashes at him, putting a hand on my hip.

"Yeah?" He looked so hopeful, so sweet, so handsome.

"You're the one who's crazy if you think I'll ever speak to you again."

With that I walked away from him, with the laughter from the girls at our table as my soundtrack.

CHAPTER 20

The Trial

L ana and I waited outside the courtroom in downtown Seattle. Zayed's testimony was to be given in a closed courtroom, and although Bree had made it clear that I wouldn't be able to sit in, I had to be there. We sat on the hard wooden bench generally reserved for the press and stared at the door as if that would make the two hours pass more quickly.

"Will you speak to Zayed today?" Lana asked me after ten minutes of silence. We'd already talked about the weather and the traffic and about what a pretty dress Bree had worn to court. Things had been less awkward between Lana and me recently due to her best attempts. She was at home a lot more and spent all her time looking concerned for my well-being and working on our fund-raising project.

I shrugged. "I don't even know why I'm here."

Lana put an arm around me and held me close.

"You'll talk to him, I think."

"You don't know that," I muttered.

"Yes, I do."

"Maybe I won't."

"You will." She squeezed my shoulder again. "It's okay for you to want to. You have a lot to say to him."

I was silent after that because most likely, yes, I would talk to him. I was here to say good-bye. Most likely we would never see each other again, and I needed that amazing thing my therapy group had harped on for so long: closure.

"What happened at the homecoming dance?"

"Lots of people attended, so we should have some really great proceeds for our fund."

The newly founded Families of War Fund that Lana had started with several members of the school board was one of the most successful fund-raising efforts Kirkland had ever seen. The dance alone had already raised over a hundred thousand dollars in donations, and there didn't seem to be a dip in sight as local millionaires continued to make donations.

There were plans for the usual bake sales and car washes, but also free tutoring for kids who were too distraught to make it to school and special scholarships from local businesses for kids who didn't think they could go to college. Lana had spent the weekend drawing up a business plan and nominating members for the fund's board. I knew that Erica, as well as the other members of my therapy group, were getting letters delivered to their homes, offering help from the fund. I had done my part to make up for leaving my therapy group.

"The fund is not what I'm talking about."

"Then?"

"Word's gotten around about the drama. I heard about it at my book club."

"The Jason thing?"

"And everything else. Erica and her boyfriend."

"I actually had a pretty good time going alone," I admitted. "I danced a lot and caught up on the gossip. There was no pressure, no nervousness, and no issues. I could arrive when I wanted, talk to who I wanted, and leave when I wanted."

Lana kept her arm firmly attached around my shoulders. "You're going to be just fine. Trust me."

The familiar stab of pain was back. I thought that by now every time I thought of him and that desperate look in his eyes it would hurt less.

It didn't.

"Mom, why did you and Dad fight so much?" I asked abruptly as a few men in tailored suits entered the courthouse, letting in a swish of cold air though still no snow had fallen on the ground.

Her look was of surprise. I thought it was about the question.

"You haven't called me Mom since you were a little girl."

I thought about that. She was right, but it felt okay to do so today.

She was sitting with me at a courthouse, supporting me in something she didn't believe in. She wished I would forget about Zayed and focus on college applications and our fund. But she was here, holding my hand. This was something a mother would do.

"I always felt like we were more than that." I tried to be tactful.

"You mean you never saw me as a mother."

I didn't say anything, not wanting to hurt her feelings. Things were going well today, and I didn't want to cause a scene in a court of law.

"It's okay. Your father didn't either. It was one of the reasons." Lana had a faraway look in her eyes as she gazed at the closed door of the courtroom.

"What were the others?" I finally asked, genuinely wanting to know this time.

"When we got married, no one thought it would last, so we worked extra hard to make sure it did. I think, over the years, your dad felt like I wasn't happy anymore."

"Were you?"

"More than anything." She wrapped her arms around her waist and smiled almost to herself. "Up until I met him, I didn't feel like I meant anything in the world. I didn't know my place. When we started seeing each other, I realized I meant everything to him. All he wanted in the world was to be with me and make *me* happy."

She sounded like a love-struck teenager, and I realized how hard the past few years must've been for her. His pulling away, going away for months at a time, and then never coming back.

"Why did he think you weren't happy?"

"He let insecurities and what other people said and thought get to him. People, my parents, my friends kept saying that being married to an Army man wasn't what I signed up for and I was disappointed in my life. And he started to believe that."

"But you weren't? Not ever?"

"I have not had one moment of regret about marrying your father, Mars," she said to me. "Even if we weren't always together, even if I stayed up so many nights worrying about him being overseas, the moments we shared together and the daughter we have is more than I ever thought my life would be. I tried my best to prove that to him, and I hope he knew that at the end. My only wish is that I'd told him more often how happy he made me every day for the past twenty years."

So many regrets. So many missed opportunities. I leaned my head against her shoulder. "I love you, Mom."

"I love you too, baby."

"I feel like he and I never said good-bye."

"You don't need to."

I waited as she put her arms around me and pulled my chin into her shoulder.

"Do you know he was so proud of you?"

"No way. He thought I was stupid and immature and selfish, remember? He was so angry with me for wanting to go to Paris for the semester."

She laughed. "He never thought that. He always thought he wasn't enough of a father to you. He always felt guilty for leaving you alone so often and letting you figure out so many things on your own."

"No, he didn't."

"He was so proud of the independent woman you were becoming in his absence. He told me the night before he left this last time that you were starting to stand up to him, to show him the error in his ways, and that you were not afraid anymore of making decisions. He told me you were going to be more of a hero than he ever would be. He was going to tell you to go to Paris."

I sat, mostly shocked, but also disbelieving. All this time, I'd thought . . .

I pulled out my cell phone. "Do you know I still call him?" I had never admitted that to anyone, not even Zayed.

"I do too. Every day." Mom slowly took the phone from my hand. "What number is the speed dial set to?"

"One."

She pressed a few buttons.

"When you press one, it will call me. You can call me anytime, and I will always answer. I'll change my phone's speed dial to call you. Deal?"

I didn't know if I would call, but it was enough to know I could.

We sat in silence, and I pondered how she and I had been going through the same thing all these months. Calling my father, even though deep down we both knew he was gone. Just thinking that he could hear us was all we needed to get through the moments of darkness.

"They're coming out." My mother stood up and reached for my hand. "It's going to be okay."

Bree came out first and headed straight for us. "You guys didn't need to stay. I could have called."

"What happened?"

"Zayed is free to go. His testimony and the details he gave are enough to hold that group."

"What will happen to him?" I asked, looking over Bree's shoulder.

I didn't hear the answer, but I heard Mom making a concerned "hmm" noise. I was too busy watching Zayed come out of the courtroom. He looked tired, like he hadn't slept in days, dark circles under his eyes. His blue shirt's collar was uncharacteristically wrinkled. I felt like I hadn't seen him in lifetimes and wanted nothing more than to go to him. I knew that would be the worst thing I could do. That would mean I forgave him for what he had let happen to other families, families like mine, where mothers and daughters stood alone and were afraid of what they would all have to face now.

I couldn't do this. I thought I could. I thought I could be strong and say good-bye like an adult and wish him well, but seeing him again was too much. Every moment of that last day on the roof came rushing back. The despondence in his eyes as he begged me to understand. How could I understand the death of innocent people?

"Should I come with you?" my mother asked, looking from me to Zayed, observing my hesitation.

I shook my head. "I'm ready to go home now."

"Okay. Bree, thank you. We'll call you later."

"Take care, ladies. I'll be coming by to check on you." Bree waved good-bye to us as we started to walk away.

"Mars, wait," the familiar voice called. "Please wait."

I turned around. He stood only a foot away. I could see the velvety gray of his eyes, his rumpled collar exposing his neck, his hair unkempt.

He was beautiful. Still so beautiful to me, despite who he was.

"Please. Just one minute."

I wanted to go to him. It was such a strong physical pull he still had over me. The same one that had kept me on the roof with him, the one that had encouraged me to forgive him after he'd stood me up that rainy afternoon. I needed to break it, once and for all. I needed for him to know that he could no longer have any control over me.

My mother squeezed my hand tightly, unwilling to let go.

"It's okay," I whispered to her.

I allowed Zayed to lead me a few feet away, within earshot of Bree and Mom.

I could see Mom watching me, Bree standing next to her, with a hand on her shoulder. I knew she wanted to come over and interrupt and take me away before something else happened. Dad's role. She had officially stepped into his shoes, and it was not strange anymore.

I would pretend to hear what Zayed had to say, and then I would tell him what I needed to say. And then I would be free of him.

"I'm sorry."

"You've said that already," I said, not looking at him. I was so afraid that if I did, I would fall into his arms and hold him and tell him I would never again let him go.

"I thought I was dreaming when I saw you here," he made a noise that sounded like a laugh.

"I came to make sure the right thing happened," I said, realizing my tone was colder than I'd thought it would be possible for me to fake.

"You came to make sure I was okay."

I stood silently, not bothering to deny it. He knew when I was lying.

"I've missed seeing you."

"Are we done here?" I pulled my purse onto my shoulder and wrapped my arms tightly around myself. I needed to say what I had to say and then leave. Now. This was much harder than I'd imagined.

"Have you read my journals?"

"No reason to." I shook my head, not telling him I'd taken them all out of the box and willed myself into putting them back in. Despite my best intentions, I wanted to know. I knew I would read them. I wouldn't be able to resist.

"There's something that you should know then. Please take this." He held out a sealed envelope. "Please. It says everything I don't have the words for."

Some force possessed me to reach out and take the letter from him. I then stared at the floor, wishing he would stop talking and at the same time wishing he would never stop so I never had to leave.

"I've never experienced this feeling before, Mars. I've only read about it in all my books and all my poems, but never have known it firsthand," he rushed on as if he would run out of courage. "If it does exist, what I'm feeling for you is surely it, because Mars, I cannot imagine that I will have to go on without you. I cannot imagine a life worth living without you. I love you so much."

I wanted to tell him that I continued to love him. I wanted to tell him I'd known it for quite some time, and I ended up tracing the words on any surface I could find countless times during the day. I wanted to tell him that when I slept it was only him I dreamt about anymore, and I hated waking up because I knew he wouldn't be there by my side. I wanted to tell him that I wanted to forgive him and be with him, but I didn't know how.

"I'm sorry, but I don't feel the same way," I said instead, looking him straight in the eye. "No matter what you do next, you can't escape where you come from or what your family has done. Good-bye, Zayed. Don't contact me again. I mean it."

CHAPTER 21

The Faith

I contemplated throwing the letter away. I told Lana I had burned it in the sink. I told her I didn't want to hear anything Zayed had to say ever again.

I hid it under my mattress for half a day before giving up. I sat on the floor and smoothed it out:

My dearest Mars,
Theodore has the words which express my feelings today and for always. I love you. I'll wait for you no matter how long it takes.

We had such little time
Compared to other foolish lovers

I would set my skin on fire
For the chance to have our most terrible night

For my best moments without her
Are still far inferior to my worst moments with her

She was not my first love
But she will be my last.

I know you will never understand and never forgive me, but I am yours, Mars. You are my first love and my last. I vow to have you back in my life.

Yours in love and friendship.
Always,
Zayed Anwar

I stayed awake all night that night, reading Zayed's journals at a feverish pitch.

His entries during his life in Baghdad were light and innocent, talking about what he learned at school and what his mother had cooked for dinner. The entries had stopped suddenly two years ago and resumed only after he moved to Seattle, leaving out the entire part of his life when he'd been converted.

And then there was me. He wrote about me for one entire journal:

When I'm with Mars, I feel as if she has been waiting for me her whole life. She has, without realizing, been waiting for someone to love her this way. Unconditionally and forever. I have never known a love like the one I feel for her. I would commit any crime for her, any sacrifice. When we spent the night together, my thoughts were altogether impure. I was ashamed. It would have been a disgrace to compromise her honor.

So he had wanted something to happen between us. I had a feeling it had something to do with the mysterious "adviser" he met with and I was right.

I met with Stephen again today. He wants to start meeting thrice weekly as we start closing in on the insurgent group. I asked if he could meet on campus so his role as my academic adviser can be believable in the event we are seen together. Stephen believes al-Talle will strike again soon more publicly, and I will have the opportunity to be used as their plant. I told him about Mars and my breakfast with her family. He made it very obvious that if he found out there was something more than friendship, he would have to report who I was to her parents. This is not how I want Mars to find out. I will hold back on my feelings for her. I don't know how long that will be possible.

That's what he'd been doing when he'd disappeared for two

weeks. All those times he'd gotten those phone calls that only rang once.

She has everything that would make her happy, and yet none of it does. She tells me many things that I suspect she has never thought of telling anyone else. Her father is gone, and I believe she understands that . . .

He had known all along that Dad was gone. That day in his apartment when he'd said he'd wait with me. That had been a lie. He'd been humoring me. Mocking me. This angered me all over again.

She cried in my arms at the airport, and at that moment I wished more than anything that I had the power to reverse time and stand in the way of her father's convoy the day it happened. She is heartbreaking and powerful without realizing. With a single tear, she brings me to my knees to pray to whoever is watching. Please God, bring her father back. I will do anything if you only bring him back to her.

I'd had to shut the journal. I didn't want him thinking about Dad. He had no right to after what his brother had done to innocent people much like my father.

My SAT scores had come back, and I'd submitted my application to the University of Washington. A ten out of twelve. I wasn't surprised; writing the essay had felt like an out-of-body experience. I didn't experience any elation. I mailed the neat package to the U and got back into bed.

As I mailed the letter, I realized that I was not doing this for my father anymore. He wasn't coming back; he didn't matter in this particular decision. This was for me.

I was changing, becoming my own person. I could feel it happening more and more as the days went by. Zayed had helped me see that I needed to live for myself. My thoughts continued to turn toward him whenever I was idle.

I thought so much about his situation, and what he must have gone through during that terrible time in his life. How alone he must have felt. How, like me now, he'd had no one who would understand.

I analyzed his journals with more depth with each read. I found myself understanding him more each day.

I realized I didn't need to go to college or do anything at all, for that matter. I could hide in my house, living with my mother until I was a hundred years old, throwing fund-raisers and raising cats. But that would remind me of Zayed, as I thought about events benefiting children who were victims of war, like naïve Zayed, who had wanted nothing more than to belong and do the right thing. The cats . . . well, I missed little Coconut and her tiny mews. And her owner. I missed him most of all.

"Get up."

I pried an eye open, not knowing how long I'd been drifting. Erica hovered over me, a disembodied head. Fuzzy and confusing.

"Now. Get up now."

"Go away." I pulled the covers back over my head and waited to be disrupted again. What day was it? Wasn't it a weekend?

Nothing.

Good, she'd given up.

"Ahh!" I shrieked a few minutes later, feeling cold hands on my feet dragging me off the bed. I landed on the soft carpeting with a thud.

"What the hell!" I crab-walked away from the two pairs of feet that stood threateningly in front of me.

"Get up." Chad stood next to Erica; they both looked solemn and fairly no-nonsense.

I grabbed the duvet and wrapped it around myself. "Why are you guys here?"

"Lana sent us up. She said you won't listen to her, and you won't listen to Mrs. Nguyen. You won't get out of bed. You won't do anything. You're being horrible."

"I'm not being horrible. I just want to be left alone."

"Wow, she really has regressed," Chad said to Erica.

"Told you. We thought homecoming was a turning point. You were so amazing that night, arriving alone, wowing everyone and leaving alone. People have been talking about you for weeks!" Erica tried to grab for my duvet. "Come on, Mars."

"Will you two please go away?" I was in no mood to be around the lovebirds or their school gossip or anything else.

"Our therapy group needs you," Erica said, flopping down next to me, shaking the mattress violently.

"I quit, remember?" I mumbled, wishing they would leave. Chad leaped onto the bed on the other side of me and both proceeded to continue to pelt me with information.

"So did Stephanie," Erica continued.

"What?" That was enough to get me to peek over the duvet. "When?"

"She got into grad school. She quit."

"What the hell," I muttered. Just as I'd thought. That woman hadn't been even the slightest bit invested in us or our progress. She'd just been using our sessions as fodder for her grad school applications.

"We need a new leader." Erica continued to bounce on the bed.

"So go find one." I retreated under the covers again, eyeing the foot of the bed. I suspected I could make a run for the bathroom and lock myself in there till they left.

"Everyone voted. And they chose you. They want you to come back." Chad said. "Hell, even I've been going to therapy lately since there's so few people left."

"You guys are insane," I muttered, edging toward the foot of the bed.

"They're on their way over."

"Who?" I paused.

"Our therapy group! We're meeting here today. They're going to be downstairs in ten minutes. Lana said it's fine."

Traitor. She knew how I was feeling and she was subjecting me to this. I would never forgive her.

"So? I won't come down. They'll get hungry and leave eventually. We just have a bunch of ice cubes in our refrigerator."

"They'll wait five minutes, and then they'll be in here. They'll see you in these cute little leopard-print pajamas." Chad realized my plot and grabbed at the leg of my pajama pants.

"Yeah, we can meet in here. I'll let Lana know." Erica got off the bed.

"Okay, that's it. Out. Both of you." I rolled off the edge of the bed, pulling the duvet with me.

Chad jumped off the edge of the bed, straight on top of my legs, pinning me to the ground. "Either all three of us leave this room, or none of us leave."

"I hate you guys," I muttered.

Their argument worked, and within ten minutes I was showered, dressed in the first thing Erica handed me: skinny jeans, riding boots, a tunic sweater. After Chad's ribbing that I looked like a labradoodle, I pulled my hair back into a mini-chignon.

I could hear the congregation of the therapy group downstairs, and I brushed on some lip gloss to counteract some of the pallor of my face. They were all here, expecting something impossible of me.

"Hey, Mars!" Ken practically threw himself into my arms as I descended the stairs.

"You look pale."

"We missed you."

"Stephanie quit. We want you to be the new Stephanie. Except not such a bi—"

"Hey, hey. Let's watch our language in front of Mrs. Alexander."

Everyone stood in the parlor and talked at once as I glanced hopelessly at Mom, who didn't even bother to hide a smile. She retreated into the kitchen with the promise of cocoa for everyone.

"You guys." I sat down and motioned for everyone to do the same. "I can't be this group's leader. I don't even know what I'm supposed to do, much less what *you're* supposed to do."

"Why don't we talk about it?" Erica perched on the arm of the love seat next to me. "What are you confused about?"

I glanced around the room. Everyone looked eager to listen, and no one seemed like they were ready to pounce on my emotions or judge.

"Someone told me my father wasn't coming back. That he was dead. And now I don't know what to do because—"

I noticed Ken flicking his lighter and started to yell at him, but then realizing he was using it to light the remaining paper and wood in the fireplace. Soon a bright flame was burning, the first that had been lit in the room since the night Dad left.

"Because I realize that Zayed is right. Dad is not coming back. And now, I don't know what I'm waiting for. I've been waiting for so long for him to come home and fix things for me. Now, I don't know what to wait for anymore. Now I feel like I'm just making things up as I go along."

"What if you are waiting for nothing?" Ken asked.

"Which is probably weird to think about after doing it for so long," Krish suggested.

"Is it terrible that I want to ask you if you feel relieved?" Erica asked.

I almost jerked away from her. How had she known? Ever since that fateful conversation with Zayed, I had felt almost relieved that I knew. I'd been hovering between denying it and moving toward acceptance for so long that having an answer was almost a reprieve.

"It's okay to feel that," Ken said. "You told me so yourself. It's okay to feel whatever you feel. It's okay for me to love my stepmother. It doesn't mean I loved my mom any less. You said that, remember?"

Yeah, I had said that. And I had meant it. But for some reason I wasn't allowing myself to feel the same thing.

"Did you not mean it?"

"I meant it."

"Then please mean it for yourself, too. It's okay. You can move on with your life now. Isn't that what Mars the First would have wanted?" Chad, who'd been sitting quietly this whole time, piped up.

I thought about the conversation Mom and I'd had at the courthouse. How Dad was proud of the independent woman I was becoming. He would have wanted me to be happy, make my own decisions, and he certainly would have wanted me to help these people in any way I could.

"Thanks, you guys. I need to think about this some more," I finally said.

"And you should think about it for as long as you want. There is no deadline," Krish said. "You said that to me, Mars."

I blushed.

"Let's talk about you, Erica. How are you doing?" I pulled my friend close to me. "What are you doing to take care of yourself?"

"I'm letting myself be myself. I'm not letting myself hide what I want anymore." She smiled at Chad. "No matter how stupid it may sound. I talked to my mom about my art and how it's a part of me and how I can't give it up for something practical."

"And?"

"She agreed. She was horrified I'd even contemplated it."

I laughed. "Told you."

"See, this isn't bad. We can have these sessions and then hang out in the 'all-ages club.'" Erica did air quotes.

We all laughed. Who would have thought the all-ages club would get some use after all.

The six of us and Chad. We were strangers, really, yet we were bonded in such a way that we knew exactly what we were all going through.

I could trust and help these people. We would help each other, *together*. It was my duty to facilitate that, and I was not going to run from it anymore.

Lana and I pulled up in Dad's Corvette to the flawless green meadow. It was one of the last sunny days of fall, and other than the sounds of a few insistent seagulls, there was silence.

"Will you come in?" I asked hopefully, staring into the seemingly endless rolling hills in front of me, dotted by blooms of flowers and stones. For the hundredth time, I wondered if I would really be able to do this.

"I'll give you some time with him," Lana said. "You'll be fine."

I waited for another few minutes in the driver's seat, fiddling with the silver box I'd brought with me.

"Okay. I'll be back." I summoned my bravado. It wasn't going to get easier. "Don't drive off and leave me." I pocketed the car keys to make sure she didn't.

This time it was me who was visiting my father's grave while Mom waited behind the wrought-iron fence. I could feel her watch me, and that gave me a sense of accountability. Now I had to do this. If I ran away, she would fret and worry and call Bree, and we would have another talk about acceptance and such.

I found the grave almost as if by instinct.

I approached slowly and read the simple printing on the headstone. "Mars Alexander."

Now I was the only living Mars Alexander. For so long I'd begged and pleaded with the universe to send Dad home so that this truth wouldn't be real. I was scared, absolutely terrified of having to be strong for my mother. I wanted him home so I didn't have to be strong anymore.

Now I realized there was no going back. I'd been strong for Lana for long enough. She didn't need it anymore. She never really had. Now, I just had to be strong for myself.

"Hey. How's it going?" I said after standing there for a few minutes. "I brought you some of your stuff."

I'd been talking to him for so long and not getting a response via voicemails that this wasn't even strange for me. It was almost a relief to have something to talk at versus thin air.

"If you've been listening to my voicemails, you know what's going on, so no need to recap."

I opened the silver box.

"So, here's *Les Misérables*, your favorite. And here is that book of poems you really like." I showed the headstone both books. "Theodore Robert Watkins. That's some heavy stuff. I really got into it because of . . . well, you know. Him."

I swallowed. It was weird. Despite everything, I really believed Dad would have liked Zayed. Liked his honor and, yes, his desire to protect his people. I understood that now.

"And here is a picture of you, me, and Mom. I thought you'd want it. I don't know if you took a good one of us when you left last time. One where I don't look like a dork, I mean."

I was rambling. I couldn't believe it, but I was rambling at a gravesite. I now stared at the picture I'd framed this past week. It was not a candid one; it was very posed, but still funny. The three of us had been out at brunch the previous year, celebrating Easter or Mother's Day or some holiday where all the restaurants were over-crowded, and we all went out anyway because we were too lazy to do anything else.

Only Lana and I were looking at the camera, posing with pouty lips and arms bent at flattering angles. Dad was looking at us, with the smile I remembered the most, of amusement mixed with pride. That seemed fitting. He looked so peaceful that day, relaxed and happy.

Now this was getting hard. Fighting back the fresh tears that threatened to drain what bravado I had left, I placed the lid on the silver box and closed it tightly. I knelt next to the grave and started to dig.

Not caring that my fingernails snapped or that the knees of my leggings were shredding, I continue to dig until I had created a hole that would safely cradle the box. I brushed my lips over the seal of the box, saying a good-bye and a thank-you at the same time. I gently lowered the box into the hole and tossed the single white rose onto it.

Tears were threating to make an appearance again. I'd promised myself I wouldn't fall apart here.

"Hey, I'm taking care of your car. I took it for an oil change and got the tires rotated. I even told the guy not to overcharge me because I was a girl. I negotiated. You would have liked that. I'll take care of it for you."

I glanced behind me. I couldn't see Lana behind the tinted windows, but I knew she was still there. True to her word, she was letting me do this on my own.

"I didn't get to finish that fight with you. I'm still waiting to hear if I get into that study-abroad program. We can argue about it later."

Okay, that seemed to be good for the day.

"You never said good-bye to me, and now I get why. There never really will be a reason for us to say good-bye to each other."

I then refilled the hole I'd made with the mound of dirt. "I'm sorry for what I said. I'm sorry for the mistakes I made," I said as I let the last crumbles of dirt cascade back into the earth, where it belonged.

I waited for some sort of sign, but there was nothing other than the powerful breeze, which enveloped me tightly and carried away the last of fall's leaves.

CHAPTER 22

The Acceptance

"Mars, you need to look at this." Lana stood in my doorway for the tenth time the following Saturday. She'd been up to bring me soup, then tea, then just to chat about going to a movie that night.

This time she was holding a thick white envelope.

"What is that?" I barely took my focus off my computer screen. I was working on a yearlong plan for the therapy group as a part of my new role. I had an outline of what we would cover in each session and each person's individual goals. I had started with what I wanted to accomplish this year, to talk openly about Dad's life and what he had wanted for me. I was planning to present my plan to the board of the Grief Therapy organization as a template for other groups like ours to use.

"It's from the University of Michigan." Mom rattled the envelope.

"What?" I stopped typing. I hadn't thought of Zayed—much—that day, but now that memories of his insistence that the University of Michigan was *the* school for me came rushing back, I sighed. Would his ghosts haunt me forever? "Why did this come for me? I didn't apply there."

"Just open it."

I tore the thick envelope open.

We are pleased to inform you that you have been accepted into the University of Michigan's undergraduate program . . .

"How did this application get sent?" I asked suspiciously. I had been practically sleepwalking the past month, but I was pretty sure I had not sent this application in.

"I have no idea." The snooty little smile on Lana's lips was familiar. This was how I looked when I lied, Zayed had said. Wow, it really was obvious. No wonder he'd always known when I was keeping something from him.

"Did you send this in? Why?" I read the rest of the letter. Fall admission. I needed to choose my dorm and a roommate, if necessary.

"Zayed sent a package to me a few weeks ago. It had some sample essays you'd written in class and this application. He said in his letter that he would be doing you a disservice as a friend if you didn't apply. That you were incredibly talented and had potential to help many people with the same kinds of sorrow you've experienced. He was right. I filled out the application and sent in all the info that day."

"That's illegal. And corroborating with *him*?"

"Well, he was right. You did get in. And I did some research. The child psychology program at Michigan is really wonderful."

"I can't go." I muttered. "It's too far."

"Oh, you're going. I'll send in the acceptance and drive you there myself if I have to."

"Why? I can just go to the U and live at home."

"Oh, you'll be a real winner then. Living with your mother forever."

I didn't answer. Yes, that had been my plan, actually.

"Zayed asked me to give you this also." Lana set a small envelope down on the bed next to me. "You should open it."

I eyed it as if it was a poisonous spider. Another letter. He was still in my life, despite me having ordered him to get out of it. I was tired of thinking of him all the time. I knew if I went to Michigan, I would think about him every day, about his belief in me and his unending persistence in pushing me to be better.

"Should I read it aloud to you?" Lana reached for the letter.

I grabbed it, giving her a dirty look.

Mars,

You'll be angry at me for many things, my lies, my past, my interference. These things you have a right to feel. One thing I wish you would not hate me for is my belief in you. You are the strongest person I've known. You deserve happiness. Please don't deny yourself that. I will never forget you or the magic you have brought into my life. You are my hero, the one who has made me realize I have the opportunity to live again, even if it's not by your side.

You have a desire to change the status quo, to not be like everyone else. You said it then, and I believe it now. Please accept the change in your life and do the extraordinary things you were meant to.

This is good-bye. I am leaving Seattle to start over some-where else. I will respect your wishes and not contact you again.

Yours in love and friendship,
Zayed Anwar

He was leaving. He was leaving me. He was *such a liar*. He'd said he'd wait for me, but he was leaving me forever.

I felt Lana watching me, waiting for some kind of reaction. I felt the heaviness again of ending our relationship. That feeling in my chest. The realization that I would never see him again.

I wasn't clueless. I knew I had the choice to forgive him and make things okay between us. I had the option of staying with him and dealing with all the lies and mistrust and not knowing what he was thinking. I wondered again if I would feel less alone and helpless than this. Would it be better to be miserable with him than without him?

"He represents everything I hate in the world," I said at last. "I can't forgive him."

She said nothing. Just sat and watched me.

"Say something, please."

"Listen to me for once." Lana slid down on the bed next to me. "I saw the way you lied to him at the courthouse. You wanted to hurt him, and believe me, you did. Is this the way you want it to end?"

"I don't know what to do."

"This is one of those times I'm going to tell you what to do, and you're going to listen," Lana said firmly, putting her arms around me. "Go to him and give him a chance to explain."

"There's nothing to explain."

"Everyone deserves that chance, Mars. What are you gaining by not giving him that chance? Do you want to live with regret for-ever?"

I was silent.

"He's changed you. Anyone can see that. You need to let him know how much before he disappears and you never see him again."

"I don't know what to say to him."

"You need to tell him what he means to you. Trust me on this one, Mars. You don't want him to go away without him knowing that. That is one regret you will carry forever if you let him go like this."

CHAPTER 23

The Proposal

I watched the sun rise the next morning, remembering the night I had spent with Zayed. I had been so afraid to ask him the questions I had that night. Afraid of ruining what we had, afraid to know the truth. I was no longer afraid. I knew what I had to do and that there really was only one possible outcome. There had only ever been one possible outcome, no matter how much I had fought it.

I got dressed and reached the U before any college football traffic could clog the bridge. I tailgated my way into Zayed's apartment building behind one of his neighbors and knocked on his door. The apartment door flew open as I stood by, stunned.

It was empty. Everything was gone. The furniture, the books, Coconut, Zayed. Only spotless hardwood floors remained. It was all gone. I realized with a sense of dismay that he had meant what he'd said. He really was leaving Seattle.

This was still not going to deter me; I was going to talk to Zayed today. Not bothering to move my car, I ran the few blocks south to the College Prep Institute and found my administrator friend at the front desk.

"Hey, Mars!" She was just as perky at this hour as she was at the end of the day.

"Do you have Zayed Anwar's contact information?" I knew I was probably being rude, but I needed to find him, and he needed to hear what I had to say.

She gave me a strange look. "Why?"

"I need to . . . tell him something. It's about my score." That was a half truth. I did want to tell him about my score and my admission into Michigan.

"Well, I can give you his email information." She looked on her computer screen. "But I don't have his phone number."

"You don't have his new address? He moved."

She shook her head.

I turned to go. I would get Bree to find him. I couldn't believe he had really just disappeared and had left no information as to where he was going. "Thanks. I'll find him."

"Mars, he's upstairs if you want to talk to him."

I was halfway up the staircase before she could finish.

For once I knew what I was doing. I knew exactly what needed to be done and how I was going to do it. The previous afternoon, the conversation with Lana, it had been pure clarity. I realized that I could control certain things, but the rest had to happen as it would.

I saw Zayed across the room, setting a cat carrier down on his desk. Just moments later, he looked up and spotted me. He stood staring with a look of disbelief. I heard a tiny "mew" from the carrier. Coconut!

"I need to talk to you."

He walked toward me and then past me. "Let's go to the roof."

This time he lead me up the flight of stairs and pushed open the creaky old door.

"Is this real—" he started to say.

"*Sit down,*" I practically yelled, gesturing toward the edge of the roof, the exact spot we'd become so familiar with during the blackout. "Where is all your stuff? Why is your apartment empty? What the hell is going on?"

Zayed looked confused. "Mars, there's so much I have to say to you."

"Are you leaving town?"

He took a deep breath. "Yes, I am. This is my last week before I leave for San Francisco."

"You're running away? That's your solution to your problems? Just pretending it never happened? Do the lies never end for you?" I sounded harsher than I'd meant to, but it hurt me deeply that after everything he and I had shared, he would just leave town without telling me where or when.

"I'm sorry for not telling you the truth. By the time I understood your story and the loss of your father, I'd . . . I'd fallen in love with you. I was afraid that you wouldn't speak to me if you knew," he rushed on. "My case officer also told me I shouldn't involve you. That it was dangerous."

"You were right to think that. If you had told me, it would have been over on day one. I never would have fallen for you."

Zayed's expression was sorrowful. "Is that what you wish?"

"Sometimes." I answered honestly.

"I was hoping . . . I don't know. That if enough time passed, you could forgive me. That was stupid." Zayed sighed, rested his chin in his two hands. "I was cherishing each day because I knew that the moment you discovered who I was, it would be over. I wanted to tell you, more than anything, but I couldn't. I couldn't lose you."

"But you did. Lose me, I mean."

"Did I?" His eyes darkened, closed, then opened again, this time averted from my gaze.

"Absolutely you did." I was firm in the response. He had betrayed me and deceived me, and though I had told him everything he'd asked, he had done nothing but lie to me in return.

"Oh."

I could see that I had dashed whatever hopes had propelled him to the roof that quickly.

"I was ready to cut you out of my life. I was well on my way. But then I got this." I pulled out the acceptance into the University of Michigan and set it down next to him.

Zayed broke into a smile as he read the first few lines. "I knew you would get in. I knew it. What was the score? Are you going?"

"We're talking about you right now," I reminded him. "I realized so many things when I got that letter. You knew I would never speak to you again, but you still didn't give up on your belief in me."

"And I never will."

"I need you to do something else now, Zayed."

"Just tell me."

"Now you need to believe in yourself."

He seemed to hang his head.

"You have to. How can I, or anyone else, if you don't? You're running away to another city to catch another terrorist. What will you do there? Lie to some other girl?"

He looked shocked. "There will never be anyone else."

"You don't know that."

"I do know that. In my nineteen years, there's never been anyone else. And there won't from here on out."

"Zayed, you need to have a life of your own. Put down roots and start being honest with people around you."

"I have so much to make up for."

"You need to make peace with what's happened. You need to understand that your brother made mistakes and hurt many families, some Iraqi and some American, but there was nothing you could have done. He wouldn't have listened to you."

"I should have turned him in earlier. I should have been able to stop it. I could have saved those people."

"You can't blame yourself for his actions."

"But I do," he said.

"I know."

I sighed.

"My father, he . . . he's taken lives in the name of his country."

Zayed gazed at me, those stormy gray eyes full of sadness.

"He did those things because he wanted to protect his country and his family."

"He was a good man."

I nodded, agreeing. "You thought you were doing the same. You are a good man too."

I suspected those were tears in Zayed's eyes. "I went about it the wrong way. I was stupid and—"

"I forgive you. I realized I was blaming you for things that I believed you represented. All I wanted was to feel safe, and I blamed you for taking that away from me."

"And now?"

I bit my lip, ready to take the next step.

"I want more than just to feel safe. I want to help you." I hurried on as I saw hope and light on his face. "But things can't be like they were."

"Anything."

"You have to trust me. You have to tell me what you're going through."

"I will. I promise I will."

"You'll do better than that. You'll continue to write in your journals."

"Did you read them?"

"Every one."

"I want you to continue to read them. I want you to know everything."

I lowered my eyes. Suddenly, I felt awkward, uncomfortable. Now what? We couldn't go back to where we had been. That was impossible.

He held out his hand for mine. "Please?"

As on that first day, saying that our gazes met was a complete understatement. There was promise of a future, as long as I was able to leave the past where it belonged.

There was only one way for me to find out. I reached out and took his hand.

A sea of visions blurred my eyes: my father and me fighting the day before his deployment, the day the letter arrived in the mail, Zayed telling me there were only ashes left.

I knew Dad was gone, but at that moment, I felt him with me. Peaceful and hopeful, urging me to move forward, to take a chance on someone who loved me and was willing to give me what I wanted.

I twisted my hand, firmly encapsulated inside Zayed's. The hand that belonged to my nightmare. The hand that belonged to someone who came from a world that had taken my protector from me. The hand of someone I couldn't be without.

"I have a proposal for you." I watched our fingers, entwined together. They looked right. Complete. "I want you and Coconut to come to Michigan with me."

"You're going for certain?"

"I accepted this morning. And I got an application for you, too."

I hadn't realized how much I'd missed seeing Zayed's sly grin.

"They have a fine graduate program in modern Middle Eastern and North African studies. There is a very large Muslim youth population there. People to whom you can teach those valuable lessons you've learned."

"I knew you were capable of great things, Mars. I knew it from the night of the blackout. Thank you for giving me this chance."

"You're also spending Christmas with us this year. As part of our family, not as a guest."

Zayed smiled. "Am I dreaming?"

"You'll wish you were once you see the demands I have of you."

"*Why* are you giving me this chance?"

"You said before you believed we were meant to be together, that you are here only to serve me. I need you to prove that to me over and over again."

"I will never stop proving it to you. I will prove it to you every day for the rest of your life." He hadn't stopped grinning. "Don't you see? My brother and your father have conspired to bring you back to me. I will never let you go again."

"No, you won't. That's part of accepting the proposal. You will never lie to me again. Ever."

"I accept your proposal on all conditions. I swear to never leave your side again. I am dedicated to you for the rest of this life and the next."

"Don't make promises you can't keep," I said sternly.

"Watch me keep it." Zayed's voice was suddenly much lower. Husky. So sexy. "I will do anything for you, Mars."

Zayed and I had both risen from the scattered ashes of war, scarred from painful pasts but still here. Some mystical force had made sure our lives from across continents and worlds had met and become entwined.

Now it was up to us to make sure they stayed that way.

Done talking, Zayed pulled me into him and brought his lips—finally—down on mine.

It was well worth waiting for.

Don't miss Dona Sarkar's
exciting new novel:
Three Sides to the Story
Available from your favorite etailer
Spring 2017!
Turn the page for a preview!

CHAPTER 1

Quinn

Why did he have to ruin everything by proposing marriage?
Quinn Montgomery shook her head, wishing the previous night had been some sort of bad dream. The velvet box, exactly the size of an engagement ring, weighed heavily in the hidden pocket of her sixties-style shift dress. Everything had been going incredibly well. Why not let a good thing be?

Quinn should have known something was up when Shalin had insisted on a weeknight dinner at one of the nicest restaurants in the college town in Ann Arbor, Michigan. Chop House was definitely a "special occasion" place, mainly for long-time faculty and students' parents. Right after the server had cleared away their dinner plates, Shalin had taken both her hands in his.

The first time, I was forced to marry against my will. Eventually I grew to love her, and when she died, I thought my life was over. Then I met you. Shalin had turned his focus from the candlelight to Quinn's face.

Quinn, will you do me the honor of spending the rest of your life with me?

"Hey, you listening?" A voice with an edge of impatience snapped Quinn out of her memory.

"Wha—?" Quinn Montgomery spun her chair around. Kashmira. The last person she wanted to see right now. Quinn forced herself to smile for her mentee's benefit. "Kash. Sorry. I, ah . . ."

Quinn stuttered as she noticed the knowing look on Kashmira's face. *You're keeping something from me,* it practically blared. However, this was definitely not the time to tell Kashmira about the very sudden and unexpected marriage proposal. She definitely would not handle it well.

Kashmira had a tendency to lock herself into a shell of gloom and immediately make everything about her own unhappiness. Quinn couldn't deal with that now and suddenly make everything about Kashmira. Not on top of everything else. Like Shalin's whisper lingering in her ear.

"You've been acting weird since this morning." Kashmira tucked a silky strand of raven hair behind her ear and raised an eyebrow. "What's going on?"

I'm in love with a completely amazing man and now he wants to take our relationship public. Goddamn.

"I'm late," Quinn said instead as she glanced around the minuscule Teaching Assistant's office she and another graduate student shared. She grabbed two textbooks off her overflowing desk and stuffed them into her bag. "Your dad'll be *pissed* if I miss his lecture today. He's expecting the students to come trickling in here with questions during office hours. The joys of ghazal poetry."

Kashmira's poker face gave no indication of whether she believed Quinn's lie.

Quinn shouldered her red top-handle crocodile tote, one of her favorite vintage scouring finds, as she closed the door of the office behind her.

"I'll walk with you. I'm here to listen." Though Kashmira fell into step alongside Quinn without another word, her tone begged Quinn to confide what was really on her mind.

Quinn chose diversion over confession. "You went home this weekend, right? How was that?"

"Tiara-centered, as usual," Kashmira said in an exasperated tone. "Her boyfriend, her friends, and the White Party. And how my life is so pathetic and boring."

"The White Party?" Quinn barely heard Kashmira's words. This speech was nothing new. When complaining about her fun-loving younger sister, Kashmira could find faults forever, though everyone knew Kashmira was Tiara's biggest fan and supporter and would happily give up her sanity for her sister.

"Tiara's getting her own apartment next year. Just so her boyfriend can come over whenever he wants. And my dad actually agreed. I mean . . ."

Too sluggish to climb even the two flights of stairs on the muggy Monday, Quinn pressed the UP button on the elevator as Kashmira continued to revisit every detail of her last trip home to see her father.

Late spring in Michigan was usually cool and dry, rather than the sudden heat and humidity that hugged the city that week. Today the heat in the ancient, non-air-conditioned building was almost unbearable. Sunshine streamed into the dim classrooms and offices through smudged windows. Not exactly ideal studying weather. Stale dust tickled Quinn's nostrils as she tried to focus her attention on what Kashmira was saying.

Despite Quinn's diminished attention span, the hint of jealously in Kashmira's voice didn't go unnoticed as she continued to talk about her younger sister. Kashmira made sure—again—to point out that because Tiara had inherited all the looks in the family, she had a dedicated boyfriend at the ripe old age of nineteen.

Quinn gave Kashmira, not so old at twenty-two, a sidelong glance. Kashmira's eyebrows were knitted together and her lips moved in words that Quinn didn't care much about at this moment. When Kashmira smiled, her face absolutely lit up. She was a beauty. Even more so than her sister. However she hadn't figured that out yet, and a dour expression was her standard.

Poor clueless Kash. If she knew what was really going on, Tiara would be the last thing on her mind, Quinn thought.

Quinn changed the subject—again. "Did you finish the first draft of that Overseas English Literacy paper?"

"Barely," Kashmira said, and traces of worry lined her eyes. "I'm out of ideas at only fifteen pages. I don't know how I'm going to stretch it to a full thirty."

"What are you going to do about it?"

Quinn cringed as the elevator shrieked before making a struggling ascent to the fourth floor. She definitely did not want a repeat of last month when the elevator had stalled with her inside. Especially with Kashmira in this mood. She was relieved when the doors opened on the right floor for a change.

"I don't know. Double-space?" Kashmira acted like she was kidding, but Quinn was fully aware that she was not.

Both women stepped aside to let a swarm of students gallop by, excited to enjoy one of the best things about Ann Arbor—sunny days on the Diag. "You need to do more research, Kash. Wasn't this paper going to be the basis of your master's research?"

Kashmira looked distraught. "That's what I thought. But I better find something else."

"It's up to you, of course," Quinn replied, on autopilot. This might be the thirtieth time she and Kashmira had had this discussion. "I think you should pick a topic and stick to it."

"Yeah well," Kashmira muttered. "I don't know what I'm going to do."

You and me both, champ.

Everyone had their own problems, but Quinn couldn't help but feel hers was exceptionally worrisome.

What the hell was she going to tell Shalin? How could she refuse him after everything they'd shared? She hated the idea of marriage; he *knew* that. She's sworn she'd never be *legally bound* to someone ever again. She loved their relationship and had no doubt that he was the love of her life. But being financially and forever tied up with someone again? That was when people stopped trying to be their best, started taking each other for granted, and eventually ended it with ugliness and hate. She didn't want that for their beautiful relationship. *No thank you.*

Quinn pressed a thumb and forefinger to her temple as they made their way past the empty classrooms to the main lecture hall. She felt as if a rubber band was encircling her brain.

She needed to talk some sense into Shalin. Convince him that there were several more steps they needed to take together before even discussing marriage. Like actually meeting each other's families in the right context.

Not that Quinn was in any rush to do that at the moment. The age difference. The cultural difference. The everything difference.

Sharp footsteps from Quinn's ankle boots and cushioned ones from Kashmira's black loafers echoed in the deserted hallway as the women walked in silence.

"Here we are." Quinn gratefully saw the lecture hall up ahead. As she pulled the door open, she felt a twinge of guilt for not having been honest with Kashmira. Unfortunately, there was no way to tell her the truth now. Kashmira would never understand. She would assume Quinn was deserting her for a man, or worse yet, that Quinn had used her.

Quinn's guilt got the best of her, finally. Damn conscience. "How about this? Come over tonight, and I'll take a look at your paper."

"Oh, that sounds great. Thanks." Kashmira smiled, looking unsurprised. This was not the first time Quinn had bailed her out on a problematic assignment. "I'll see you tonight. Say hi to Dad for me, okay?"

"Sure." Quinn glanced quickly behind her shoulder to see if Dr. Roy was giving her a displeased look for being late.

He was.

Excellent.

"See ya," Quinn whispered and quickly scurried into the back of the auditorium. Mortifying. She was sure nothing looked more ridiculous than for the TA to be late for class.

"As I was saying, last week we discussed the poems of Rumi. This week we're going to a new area, the ghazal. This is a lyrical poem with a set number of rhyming couplets and a repeated refrain." Dr. Roy continued his lecture.

Quinn opened her fat spiral notebook and tried to take notes. Instead she found herself doodling pictures of diamond rings with giant X marks over them.

After two years of seeing Shalin every day and dating him for the past year, he had proposed. And he was adamant, either she marry him or they end the relationship. He wanted everything, he said. He wanted to wake up with her on Sunday mornings and walk to the farmer's market and have dinner with other couples. He wanted a real family with her.

She was almost thirty years old; old enough to know that he meant it. She knew she loved him. He was someone she could actually trust. He would never betray her. Not like—

A tiny voice inside her head whispered, *What about his family? All that baggage?* Did she really want to deal with family and society drama? Wasn't getting away from all that bullshit part of the reason she'd moved to Ann Arbor in the first place?

"Ms. Montgomery?" Dr. Roy thundered, staring at her.

Quinn blushed again. "Yes, Professor?"

"I was requesting that the class attend the *mushaira* on Saturday. You will be at the recital, am I right." He phrased it as a statement, not a question.

Quinn nodded dutifully. "Of course."

"Brilliant." He turned his attention back to the class. "As you see, both Ms. Montgomery and I will be there, so please feel free to come. Now, who wants to recite a ghazal for the class? Anyone?"

The class full of juniors and seniors squirmed. At forty-one, Dr. Roy was the head of the Asian Studies department, though many people guessed his age to be ten years younger from the sparsely distributed flecks of gray in his black hair and the very slight laugh lines in the outer corners of his light brown eyes. His storytelling skills, beautifully clipped British accent, broad shoulders, and perfectly pressed suit jackets attracted throngs of admiring students every quarter. Especially the women.

His Poetry of Asia lecture was by far the most popular class in the department and while the Professor was well-liked for his engrossing lectures and exotic field trips, he was a tough person to please and expected complete dedication from his students. Quinn had come to know this from being his Teaching Assistant for the past four semesters. The students were learning it now as they shuffled their feet and avoided eye contact so they wouldn't be called on.

"Ms. Montgomery?"

Quinn glanced up warily. Why was he picking on her today? She was the TA, for God's sake. Didn't that give her the license to daydream in class without being disturbed?

"Could you recite a quick ghazal for us? Something short, even two stanzas will do."

Now it was Quinn's turn to squirm. He was getting revenge, she was sure of it. She pulled her buttery blond waves into a knot at the base of her neck and stood as tall as possible, not too difficult at her five foot eight inches. She raised an eyebrow at him. *Dude, seriously?*

"Ahem." She cleared her throat and thought. She spoke clearly, her voice resonating through the lecture hall.

"Seek and you shall find happiness, they say,
I am very sure that is not the way.

"Oh Quinn, you must explain to me today,"
Why does the teacher torture me this way?"

The entire class burst into laughter. Even Dr. Roy looked mildly amused.

"Okay class, settle down. Amazing. Ms. Montgomery illustrates a very good point. Note that she used the same number of syllables in every line. Well done."

Relief. Finally, she had done something right. She half-listened to the rest of the lecture, making a note on the corner of her notebook: *mushaira. Saturday. WTF.*

But her thoughts soon went back to the previous night.

Marry me.

It would be so easy to finally let him in. Stop holding him at arm's length the way she knew she had been. But that meant being in *his* life completely. And she still wasn't ready for that level of scrutiny from everybody in Ann Arbor. What was wrong with a secret love story anyway? Why make anything official when they were so good together without anyone knowing?

You're my true love. The voice insisted. *Why does it matter what everyone else thinks?*

What if this changed everything? Could she take such a risk?

"Ms. Montgomery, may I see you for a moment?" Dr. Roy's voice broke through Quinn's thoughts as the students slammed their textbooks shut and clattered to their feet.

Quinn nodded and gathered up her notes. His tone told her she was in for it now.

Dr. Roy turned to make sure the last student had left the room before murmuring,

"Please answer this question from above,
Why Shalin, are you a fool in love?"

"Jerk!" Quinn half-heartedly punched him in the shoulder. "Do you really have to embarrass me in class?"

Shalin Roy smiled. "I love watching you fidget. You seem distracted today. Are you all right?" He looked closely at her. "Thinking about last night?"

Quinn sighed. For such an abnormally intuitive man, Shalin could be a moron sometimes. "How could I not? You broke the rule!"

"*Your* rule. And a stupid one at that. Who swears off marriage forever? I wanted to marry you last year." Shalin shoved his laptop inside his briefcase, perfectly matched to his dark grey jacket, his legs encased in distressed denim jeans. He was among the most distinguished and well-dressed members of the faculty at the University of Michigan. He was a tan Indiana Jones, minus the hat.

"And I said hell no to marriage back then. Specifically because it brings *these* kinds of issues into my life."

"You need to relax," Shalin closed his briefcase and turned his attention to Quinn. "This is supposed to be fun."

"Easy for you to say." He'd given her an impossible choice. Stay with him and face certain disaster, or lose him forever.

Quinn's heart sped up and her breath quickened as Shalin grabbed her wrists and pulled her to him. "I've wanted to marry you since I first laid eyes on you." Shalin brushed her hair off her neck to give himself easy access to her throat. "But you wanted to finish grad school. So, here we are." His fingertips traveled up the back on her head as his lips came down on hers. "You graduate in two weeks. We'll be married this summer. Anywhere you want. Hawaii. Paris. In a forest. At the mall. Here. You decide. Our ethically touchy teacher-student liaison can come to an end. And our lives can begin."

Quinn felt herself curling, from her toes all the way up to the roots of her hair. As usual, Shalin had gotten to her. But she had to stay focused. She couldn't lose herself to him like she had so many times before. Like last night.

She pulled away from the kiss. "Kash and Tiara won't accept this. They're going to be furious. You know how they are. And God, we've kept this from them for so long!"

"They'll have to accept it. They're adults with their own lives. It's time for me to have my own too. If word had gotten out, we both could have lost our jobs, and the girls would have been out on the street. They'll be surprised but will eventually accept it. Trust me."

Yes, trust him. As if he knew the minds of temperamental young women.

"Do we really have to get married? What's wrong with status quo? We're doing just fine. A secret relationship . . . it's so much more romantic this way."

"I want to walk in the park with you. I want to hold your hand when we eat in restaurants. More than anything, I want you to wear my ring. I want you to be mine." Shalin cradled Quinn into his arms as she craned her neck to look at all six feet two inches of him. "My whole life I've been doing what other people expect of me. I married the woman my mother chose for me when I was nineteen years old. I had children because Vidya wanted them less than a year after we were married. It's my turn to live now. My life is finally in my hands. And I want to share the rest of it with you. And no one is going to stop us."

Quinn sighed, trying not be influenced by his inviting words or the strong arms and tender kiss.

Why make it all pubic and risk everything now?

Dona Sarkar wishes she'd been born as a cat, so she could have had nine lives. Since that didn't work out, she decided to live nine lives in this one. She spends her days making holograms at Microsoft, celebrates diversity in STEM fields as a fashion blogger at Fibonacci Sequins, and is launching her first fashion line, called Prima Dona Style, this year. She is also the published author of three novels and one nonfiction title. She lives in Seattle with her really patient husband and her muse, a very bossy tabby cat named Ash. You can reach Dona on her website, www.donasarkar.com, on Twitter @donasarkar, or on Facebook at www.facebook.com/donasarkarbooks.

www.ingramcontent.com/pod-product-compliance
Lightning Source LLC
Chambersburg PA
CBHW020804250626
47155CB00003B/1204